Zoomers

By John Drake

Three Ravens Publishing
Chickamauga Georgia USA

Zoomers By John Drake

Published by Three Ravens Publishing

threeravenspublishing@gmail.com

P.O. Box 851. Chickamauga, Ga 30707

https://www.threeravenspublishing.com

events, institutions, or locales is completely coincidental.

Credits:

Zoomers was written by John Drake

Cover art by Kerry Hogg

ZOOMERS by: John Drake/Three Ravens Publishing – 1st edition, 2021

Trade Paperback ISBN: 978-1-951768-21-8

Hardback ISBN: 978-1-951768-22-5

For information about the story, contact;

johndrakewriter@gmail.com

@JohnDrakeWriter on Twitter

FOR YOG

If you can keep your head when all about you,
Are zooming theirs and blaming it on you;
If you can trust yourself when professors doubt you,
But make allowance for their doubting too;
If you can wait and not be tired by waiting,
Or zoomed about, don't deal in time;
If you can meet with time travel and go faster,
And treat those things with calmness just the same,
Or watch the things you gave your life to, broken,
And stoop and build 'em up with one more zoom;
If you can make one heap of all your winnings
And risk it on one turn of pitch-and-toss,
And lose, and start again at your beginnings,
Or travel back in time to stem your loss;
If you can talk with aliens and keep sane-ish,
Or walk with beings—nor lose the common touch;
If you can fill the unforgiving minute,
With sixty-two weeks' worth of distance run,
Yours is the galaxy and everything that's in it,
And—which is more—you'll be a saviour of all life
in the universe, my son!

~ If-ish, Rudyard Kipling

John Drake

PROLOGUE

I was born at the beginning. The very beginning. The Big Bang, The Stellar Birth, The Great Vomit. I forked away from the energy and enveloped it, surrounding all things as they spread out into the void. Every point in the universe has imprinted itself onto me. I can feel it all, have felt it all, for all this time. For all time.

It's a bloody nuisance.

The thing is, it's all well and good for people to say a little knowledge is a dangerous thing, but I can tell you with some certainty that having all the knowledge in the universe is a damn sight more perilous. It's the difference between having a nice glass of water to quench your thirst and popping over to a black hole with a penchant for icy planets and a quota to fill.

One of the myriad problems with the nature of my existence is boredom. Extreme boredom. The joy in life, I have concluded, centres on the unexpected, and when you have seen it all there is little room left for surprise.

Which is why I chose to play a little game.

For thousands of millennia I coaxed the detritus of long dead planets into a new one. One with the conditions necessary to cradle intelligent life for an eternity. It became a home for creativity and development, for free thinking and technological advancement. It was almost perfect.

Then I made another one and called it Earth.

This is its story.

Sort of.

CHAPTER ONE

IN THE NELSON

Southend-on-Sea,
England,
Earth,
Tuesday,
About eight in the evening.

'Five pints!' shouted Scratch, raising his voice above the racket of The Nelson. It was the finest pub in all of Southend, so long as you didn't mind having to pry your glass from a sticky table, or sometimes your fingers from the internal workings of the pool table after accidentally beating Charlie the Chopper. He raised a hand and splayed his fingers to avoid any drink-delaying misunderstanding.

'There you go, son,' said the barman as he sloshed the fifth glass onto the bar. 'Nineteen seventy-five.'

Scratch handed him a twenty pound note and craned his neck towards his table. He flicked his head and twitched his eyes at the group to indicate that no man of ordinary hand size could carry five pints without at least one of his lazy, half-drunk friends helping him out.

Clobber leaned heavily on the table and hoisted himself upright with the effort of a man who hadn't moved for six pints.

'Here you go, mucker,' said Scratch, handing him a glass. 'We should make this our last one. Big day tomorrow.'

'Oh yeah, why's that then? Shrimpers playing at home, are they?'

'Not football, son. No, I've got a plan.'

'Ah, one of *those* days?'

'A man has to feed his kids, Clobber my old mate.'

'But you haven't got any kids.'

'That's not the point. I was speaking metaphorically.'

'Oh, right. So what's it metaphorical for then?'

'You know, making sure I keep a roof over my head. Not to mention rebalancing the wealth divide in our fine town.'

'Ah, a bit of breaking and entering, eh? Need a hand?'

'There'll be no breaking, mate. Not while I'm involved. Plenty of taking, maybe, but you can't just go around smashing in windows and hammering down doors these days. Folks have all kinds of technological wizardry going on now.

Apparently you can get sensors on your windows that tell the police when someone's thrown a brick through it without so much as a polite alarm to let the perpetrator know they're on their way. I mean, how is that fair? So Biscuit Benny says, anyway.'

'Wouldn't surprise me,' said Clobber. 'People will do anything to keep their stuff safe these days, it's scandalous. Old school handle turning it is, then. What time suits you?'

'Early enough,' said Scratch. 'Need to get over to Epsom for the races by two o'clock. How about we say Peacock Apartments, about elevenish?'

'Perfect. Who's in?'

'Just the two of us. We need a bit of discretion with this one, I reckon.'

'I'll bring the gloves,' said Clobber.

Scratch handed him a second pint glass. 'Great, now take them over before the lads think we've done a runner again.'

CHAPTER TWO
AN UNEXPECTED VISIT

*L*ife forms the universe over are as diverse a subset of matter as it is possible to imagine. With the nudging of infinite planets and the gusting of cosmic detritus I created them all. From the lava drinking slugs of Tecton to the amusingly cannibalistic two-headed crustaceans of Calabin Minor.

That makes it all sound rather easy, however, as if all I have to do is sneeze in the right direction and, huzzah, a new galaxy is formed. It is, I should stress, considerably more difficult than that, notwithstanding my physical inability to sneeze in the conventional sense.

I began crudely enough, as all good universal creators do, by making planets. It isn't too tricky, in and of itself, once you get the hang of it. All you need is a long reach and almost infinite power, everything after that is just physics. No, the tricky part comes when you try to build life. Planetary creation is one thing; the glitzy glamour that gets people's attention, but what I really wanted to achieve was an altogether more subtle approach to showmanship. One that didn't slap you in the face and say: Here I am, look at me, I'm a bloody great big planet with rings the size of a black hole's waistband! *What I needed was the creation of nuance. In no time at all, quite literally as it happens, I had mastered the conception of lakes and mountains, of islands and valleys. I made a few mistakes along the way of course, but they were few and far between and were soon forgotten about. Or at least any life form unfortunate enough to be caught up in one forgot about it rather abruptly.*

That is how I came up with the idea of Earth. It was to be my masterpiece of mediocrity. It is by far my favourite planet. Not because it is the best, far from it in fact. My joy, if such a thing exists for me, is in watching the natives scrabble around trying to find meaning in everything instead of just enjoying themselves, as though I didn't spend billions of years shaping the place for them at all. Ungrateful buggers.

There is scenery there of at least an average level of what I like to call ooohness – that is, the frequency and depth of any exclamation of pleasant surprise when taking in a view for the first time. Alright, it doesn't have the copper glaciers of Taprocalon Four, or the Paragoth Fruit Mines of Epsilon Minor, but there's a quaintness about them that soothes the spirit.

Why, then, must those who live amongst these sights feel it necessary to explain them? Still, it gives me a bit of light entertainment when the black holes quieten down so I mustn't grumble.

One of my favourite creations was a small human of dubious morals from an easily forgotten part of Earth. He was the sort of man you could take home to meet your mother, so long as he hadn't been to the pub first. The kind of person who would be described by those who wanted to be patronising, but without all the bothersome stigma, as the salt of the earth.

In short, he would steal the gravy from your dinner, given half a chance, but he'd do it with a cheeky glint in his eye. The sort that made you flop a hand in front of you and cheerfully call him a little rogue while he went on to pinch your potatoes.

What he didn't know, however, was that the future of all life in the universe was about to depend on him.

Peacock Lane Apartments,
Southend.

'That's the problem though, isn't it?' said Clobber. 'People are too cautious these days.'

'With good reason,' said Scratch, trying the handle of another door. 'Can't be too careful with so many unscrupulous people prowling the streets.'

'Like us, you mean?'

'Good God, no! There's more refinement about us, isn't there? It's all well and good for your common criminal to borrow from a stranger *indiscriminately*, but we factor in a bit of diluted morality, don't we? Puts us above your common criminal, see? No, all we're doing is testing the security features of these well stocked domiciles. Plus, we're not on the streets; we're *indoor* removal specialists.'

'I suppose you're right,' said Clobber. 'Maybe this job will be our ticket out of here. Imagine, Scratch, a life with real meaning. There'd be no more taking from the rich to line our pockets.'

'I'd rather not if it's all the same to you. I'm on a crusade, brother. I won't rest until the last pearl has been emancipated from the poorly secured, walnut lined cabinets of the wealthy.'

'Very altruistic of you. What if you complete this grand crusade, though? Where will your motivation come from?'

'A bottle, I'd imagine.' Scratch's arm gave way slightly as a handle turned. 'Jackpot!'

The two morally inclined thieves peered into the apartment. Expensively dull paintings lined the walls in a haphazard pattern and unpolished brass ornaments cluttered every elevated ledge. Specks of dust swirled in a sunbeam above an oversized table.

'Perfect,' muttered Scratch, pulling his tweed flat cap down tightly and rubbing his gloved hands together. 'Now, drawers or cabinets?'

'Cabinets this time, I think. Fancy a little porcelain jug for mother.'

'Right you are. I'll start in the bedroom.'

Scratch opened a dark, wooden door and stepped into what would have been an entirely unremarkable room, if it wasn't for the spiralling purple and black vortex in one corner and the shinily clad life form with short legs and inconveniently long arms standing two paces front of him.

'Do you Shpeak Englishsh?' it asked.

'…' said Scratch.

'I will asshume, for the moment, that you do. Thish way pleashe,' it said, pointing at the improbably localised maelstrom.

'…'

'Shorry, I'm shtruggling with your Earth tongue. Sho many different languagesh in shuch a shmall shpace. I don't know how you've shurvived thish long.'

'S-s-say that again,' managed Scratch.

'Oh, I shee,' began the alien, folding one of its arms towards the top of its head and scratching gently. 'Sh-s-see. See.' It unfurled its arm. 'Did I do it right?'

'Did you do it right? *Did you…?*'

'Shorr… sorry, I don't like to embarrass myself in front of new recruits. Been like that since I was a young one.'

'A young what? Circus performer?'

'I understand your planet is yet to meet life forms from another world,' said the alien. 'I'm afraid First Contact is never quite as romantic as one expects. Practicality tends to win out over drama in the end. Shame really.'

'So you're not from the lads on Rushmore Street?'

'Rushmore Street was not in my briefing. Is it a special place for your kind?'

'This place is like a pair of silk ferret's knickers!' called Clobber from the living room. 'Bloody expensive and totally pointless. Here, look. Who uses a pocket watch these days? I reckon they're real diamonds on the hands too. What a bloody great big waste of money.' He looked up from his newly acquired timepiece as he entered the bedroom, dropped it onto the floor as he saw the alien and followed it to the ground with a dull thud.

'That's Clobber,' said Scratch. 'He's usually more polite.'

'It's time to go,' said the alien with a quiet chuckle. 'Time, see?'

'Go? I'm not going anywhere, we've only just got in. Look at the place! I reckon they've got gold plated gold in here.'

'You're half right,' said the alien. 'We're not just going some*where*, we're going some*when* too. Oh, and the name's Pdnrtk, but you can call me Terry.'

The list of questions in Scratch's mind had positioned themselves into something approaching the correct order of priority when a thick silence sucked all perspective from the room. They began to slide towards the purple vortex as it, in turn, slid towards them.

What about Clobber? thought Scratch, despite trying to say it aloud.

He wasn't selected, thought Terry.

Selected? thought Scratch. *What for?*

All in good time, human, all in good time.

Terry let out a mirthless laugh as they closed in on the vortex.

Was that any good? he thought to Scratch. *I've been practising but mother says I need to build up to it a bit more.*

Before Scratch could think of an answer they were at the vortex. The two figures stretched into it like an over-cheesed pizza slice and twanged with unimaginable speed into its centre.

Clobber lifted his head from the carpet.

'Scratch? Where are you? Don't be playing silly buggers with me now. Scratch?'

CHAPTER THREE
PORTALS

*T*he funny thing about the human brain *that there comes a point on the anxiety spectrum where the scale of the problem is so vast, so incomprehensibly overwhelming, that it just says bugger this, and ignores the whole affair. Tell a human his toast has burnt and you may as well cancel all plans for the next twenty minutes. Tell the same human that the world is about to end and they'll probably just shrug their shoulders and say something along the lines of* ah well, can't be helped.

Arcadians were different, not least because of their soft, shiny heads and tentacular arms. Present them with an Armageddon-based problem and they will hurl themselves into it with the vigour of a middle-aged man with a lawn to mow. It was for this reason that they began to experiment with Zooming.

One day, the Chief Political Advisor of the Diplomatic Education And Training Hospital was in a meeting with its marketing manager on the merits of changing the hospital's name to prevent any acronym-based misunderstandings. During

he course of the conversation it became apparent
that there was a never-before-seen portal forming
to one side of them. The advisor and the marketing
manager were Zoomed forward several centuries
and shown the currently scheduled future of the
planet, which was far more lifeless than they would
have preferred.

The upshot of this discovery was the formation of
The Council; a legislative body concerned solely
with the prevention of planetary annihilation,
specifically of Arcadia. It would investigate why a
dead planet's energy remained, while all life on it
ended. It was to be named How One Planet Ends
Despite Its Energy Surviving, before the Chief
Political Advisor pointed out the unfortunate
acronymics again. They settled on The Council
instead.

Their plan was to Zoom to other expired planets
immediately prior to the End Day and put together
a picture of why and how life on planets ceased to
be. They would then collate the data, find the
existential weak spot, and stick a metaphorical
plaster over it.

If that didn't work they would give a cessation
order and ask the planet to destroy itself in some
poetic, and preferably discreet, manner. The
cloud-worshipping Argopods of Bongassia, for
example, insisted they be annihilated by a comet in

the shape of their favourite cloud formation. After two years of heated debate on whether that was a sleeping dog or an apricot pastry, however, The Council lost patience and dissolved Bongassia by reflecting the heat from a conveniently local white dwarf.

Arcadia,
Promantory Nebula.

'Great Gammadrons!' roared General Buck, slamming an orange tentacle on to the reinforced cobalt desk. 'How hard can it be to transport a single human through time and space? It's not as if we're Zooming a damned moon, people! The landing zone wasn't even moving!'

'I believe it is on account of his planet's containment field, general' said his assistant, Pantz. 'It has never been breached before.'

'I'll breach you if he isn't standing in my office in two minutes!'

'Yes, sir!' said Pantz, scurrying off to tap furiously on a command board.

'And bring tea. Some of those green biscuits with the chewy centre, too.'

The general strode into his office and slammed the wall to his right. Two clear panes of reinforced diamond slid towards each other and gave a satisfying click as they sealed the room. He took his seat behind his oversized desk and steepled two thin tentacles. He used another to wipe the viscous goo that oozed from the top of his shiny head whenever he felt under pressure.

'Two hundred and fifty years to prepare and nobody thought about a containment field,' he muttered to himself. 'Two hundred and fifty bloody years.'

A striped ball at the corner of his desk spun gently. Buck looked up at the doors, now opaque, and clicked his tongue. They opened and a dishevelled looking human was escorted to a seat in front of the general.

'Ah, they found you. Good. Welcome to Arcadia. I imagine you have some questions.'

'Let's start with *where am I?*' said Scratch.

'How quaint of you,' said Buck. '*Where* is too simple a question. You are both somewhere and somewhen.'

'Listen, I've been in plenty of police stations in my time – all for unfounded accusations I might add – so don't start on the whole *this is the beginning of the rest of your life* lecture. I've heard them all, mate.'

A complicated smile grew on Buck's face. 'Did any of these police officers have tentacles?'

'Oh come off it, I've seen better fancy dress costumes on school kids. Your moustache is clearly stuck on with Sellotape.'

'It bloody well isn't! I'll have you know this took many years of careful cultivation. It isn't easy for an Arcadian to grow one, not that you'd understand.'

'I understand it's a cheap knock-off. One of the lads down Priory Lane dressed up as a half-man, half-octopus once for Big Dave's homecoming. Took ages to get the sticky part to stay on his lip.'

'Ah, but could he do this?' asked Buck. He lifted a square casing on his desk and pressed a bright yellow button. A vortex appeared beside Scratch, sucked him in, and spat him back out again a moment later.

'You took your time!' cried Scratch. 'I could've been killed.'

'I believe your people called it *the war to end all wars*. How long were you there, would you say?' asked Buck.

'Long enough.'

'How long!'

'Two days, maybe three. It's hard to keep count when you're in an enemy bunker and can't speak the language.'

'You were gone for a mere moment, dear boy.'

'I bloody wasn't.'

'In any case,' said Buck, 'I believe I have proven my point well enough. Care for a biscuit?'

'Anyone could do that,' said Scratch, ignoring the offer. 'All you need is a few mirrors and a secret doorway.'

Buck sighed. 'Are all humans like this?' he asked. 'I'll do one more, but then that's your lot.'

He lifted the casing again, twisted the yellow button, and pressed it. The opaque diamond doors opened and Scratch walked in.

'Ah, they found you. Good. Welcome to Arcadia. I imagine you have some questions.'

'Alright, I'll give you that one. But that doesn't explain the week in the Somme.'

'Yes it does,' said Buck incredulously. 'And it wasn't a week, it was six hours at most.'

'It felt like a bloody week.'

Buck steepled his tentacles again. 'Since you seem reluctant to offer questions, I will answer some for you. You have arrived on Arcadia in the Promantory Nebula. You have been selected for a mission of critical importance.'

'Who to?' interrupted Scratch.

'What do you mean, *who to*?'

'I mean,' said Scratch in a patronising tone, 'to whom is the mission of critical importance?'

'That's your question? Not What the bloody hell do you mean I'm on a different planet?, or Why is this etra-terrestrial life form sending me through time and space with the waft of a tentacle?'

'A man has to have priorities, doesn't he? Doesn't matter where I am...'

'Or when.'

'...or when. All that matters is that I make it to the end of the day with the same number of arms – no offence – and preferably a few more jingly bracelets.'

'Allow me to enlighten you, Mr Scratch. You have not made it to the end of this day. Not yet anyway. It is a good deal more poetic than that. We are coming to the End of Days, you might say. The finish line, the last hurrah.'

'Oh, well that explains why you've brought me here then.'

Buck gave Scratch a look of intense curiosity. 'Do you know what's going on here?' he asked.

'Not really, but what does that matter?'

'What does it matter? You've just been Zoomed to another planet, at another time, and it's the end of the bloody world! Why aren't you rolling around the floor in tortuous mental agony?'

'The way I see it,' said Scratch, rubbing the flat of his hand up and down his stubble, 'is that if this is the end of the world, then it depends on which world is ending. If it's the one I've just left then I'm better off here. If it's this world that's ending then you wouldn't bring me here in the first place. Plus, if you can bounce around time willy-nilly then all you need to do is go back a few years and all is well with the world again. Stands to reason, doesn't it?'

'You could at least seem a little put out.'

'What's the use in that? I don't worry about nothing, see, on account of it being a waste of time and energy. Now, if the police were chasing me from a recent place of work, that's a different story altogether. You need your wits about you then, but they're not chasing me, are they? Wait, they're not, right?'

'The police are not chasing you, no. Destiny is though.'

'Oh don't give me that. There ain't no such thing as destiny. You make your own luck in this world.'

'In your world, perhaps, but not here.'

'Speaking of which,' said Scratch. 'Are you all like that?'

'Like what?'

'You know, all tentacles and slime, no offence. Only, it's a little disconcerting on account of me never having met anyone with more than four limbs.'

'Would you prefer us to look more like you? It can be arranged.'

'You can do that, can you?'

'I've just sent you back in time to the Great War, have I not? A spot of morphing is no trouble.'

'Go on then,' said Scratch. 'It'll prove it isn't a cheap fancy dress costume at the same time.'

Buck pondered for a moment, then tensed. He wobbled a little, then transformed into a humanoid shape. This was accompanied by a sound not entirely unlike a finger popping in a cheek.

'There, how's that?'

'Much better.'

'The professor was wise to choose you, Mr Scratch. I am sure you will prove to be a valuable member of the team. Report to the Training Rooms at once; your teacher is waiting.'

'Pantz!' shouted Buck from behind his desk. 'Get in here!'

Private Pantz slinked in from the adjacent room and stood stiffly in front of his general.

'How do we know who all the men are?' asked Buck.

'I'm not sure I understand the question, sir. They all have their own names, is that what you mean?'

'Don't they have numbers or something? An enlistment code? What if two of them have the same name? There are so many of the buggers there are bound to be a few duplications, wouldn't you say?'

'Yes, sir. Every individual is allocated a unique identification number on the day they join. It stays with them until it gets scratched onto their headstone.'

'Marvellous. I want every number written onto a small ball and brought in to me at once. I'll need a large ball with a hatch too, big enough to fit all the other balls in.'

'May I make a suggestion, general?'

Buck raised a single eyebrow.

'If your intention is to select random recruits from the entire force, it would be much simpler if you were to use your Deadlife. It has a random number generator built into it.'

'No, private. This must be done with physics, not gizmos and gadgets. It must be a physical selection, open to scrutiny and closed to interference from unsavoury elements.'

'And you're sure you're not overthinking this, general? Only, it will need to be a rather large ball and the writing will be quite small. It will take me some time to...'

'Balls, private! Bring me the balls!'

'Yessir! Right away, sir' said Pantz.

Zoomers

CHAPTER FOUR

PRECOGNITO

*L*ife can be tricky.

Unforeseen problems lurk around every corner and the whole affair is saddled with painful inefficiencies. Having said that, once I got used to the fiddly bits I was able to create it almost without thought. It's one of the benefits of being all-powerful and with more time on my hands than a retired watchmaker.

It was fun watching my innovations as they huffed and puffed their way up the evolutionary ladder. Some did rather well, like the Titanium Tree Slugs of Vorn, or the Common Ostrich of Morreton whose backside released ivory spikes into whichever predator had the temerity to sneak up on it.

The biggest problem I have is that once I have created life, there is very little I can do to steer it in the direction I want. It is an inescapable side-effect of giving something free will.

Sometimes, though, life appears without my intervention. I say sometimes, but what I really mean is… once.

Jod had dreams. He was to be a tour guide for the great Arcadian city of Krip; taking visiting sightseers through the labyrinthine tunnels of Tessahedron, along the winding bromine canals of Grapula Seven, and up the ancient hills of Lupire at sunrise. He'd even had an interview for a junior position in the biggest tour company in the city.

That was then.

That was before the twelve jars of Ol' Swilly's Famous Dancing Juice at the Hexagon Bar.

Before Magro had asked him to walk her home.

And before he had six extra mouths to feed.

He took the first job he could; *Quality Control Engineer, Fourth Class, Lithium Bracelet Division* in the bowels of the great behemoth that is the Arcadian Production Corporation. He now stood over the grey rubber conveyor belt watching circles of lithium glinting their silver sheen onto his dull leather apron. He clicked his tweaking torch on and off absent-mindedly.

The bracelets were destined for the Zoomer training camps that pocked the landscape outside the city. Rich people would send their children there to be fashionably valuable to Arcadian society, while the poorer ones did so to be shut of them. Quite why someone would want to risk the lives of their offspring with such a dangerous career choice was a mystery to most people. Not to Jod, though. He had spent the last thirteen years playing endless games of Find The Jarracleon Blubber Beast with one cohort of his children while the younger ones pulled at his leg and the older ones complained about how life was so unfair to people like them. The thought of packing them away to a training camp for several years was almost overwhelming.

He stared numbly at the security bracelets as they passed and took off his iron ring. He flicked it into the air and tried to land it on the end of his finger. He failed and tried again. And again. On the ninth attempt the ring spun around the tip of his finger for a moment before falling down onto the conveyor belt. Jod scooped it up and looked over to his companion for the day, a large, pot-bellied native named Boofus.

'Did you see that?' he called out, as if he had invented a cure for sleep.

Boofus looked up from his work like a soporific hippo. 'No' he said flatly. 'Was it as fascinating as yesterday? I'm not sure I could handle the thrill of seeing an amusingly shaped cobweb two days in a row.'

'I was flipping my iron ring like this, right' said Jod, missing the slight, 'and it landed on my finger just here and spun around my nail. I thought it was going to slide down to my knuckle, but it fell at the last second and landed on the belt.'

'And that's it, is it?' asked Boofus with a deep, patient sigh. 'You nearly caught something with your finger?'

'*On* my finger, Boofus, *on*. Watch.'

He flicked the ring into the air again and stuck out a finger. The iron bounced off it and clattered onto his tweaking torch. A small flame spluttered into life as the iron began to sag in the intense heat of the torch.

'Bugger!' murmured Jod. He picked up his gripper clamp and fished the ring from the heat.

'What a shame' said Boofus. 'Just as you were getting good at it too.'

Jod held the clamp over the belt while he looked around for a place to set the ring down safely. While he was doing this, and to the utter ignorance of the two workers, the most important event in the history of the universe took place.

Several drops of iron splattered onto the conveyor belt, covering the lithium bracelets in ferrous warts. Sparks of all colours, from deepest reds to vibrant greens, showered the room. Those landing on untouched bracelets sent more sparks into the air, filling the room with a glorious, phosphorescent rainbow.

It may have been considered one of the most beautiful interior scenes in the history of Arcadia, were it not for two inconsiderate figures staggering haphazardly towards the exit shouting *bugger!* and *ow, that's my foot!*

Particles of lithium and iron melded into each other on the belt. This was, for the most part, unremarkable.

For the most part.

As the last of the sparks died away and the bracelets continued on their path through the room, a single lithium-iron ring did something rather unusual.

It wondered why it was there.

CHAPTER FIVE

LAST CHANCE SALOON

The Moon Shots bar in the Zooming complex of Arcadia had been voted *Most Likely To Reverberate Through Your Brain For A Week* by The Hangover Review just twelve years ago, and it had only got worse since. Or better, depending on your point of view. A long, silver bar ran the length of one wall on the far side. Drainer stood behind it, wiping away any evidence of his most recent customer. He was the senior bartender and was of the opinion that anything that removed a punter's memory of their time in Moon Shots was, on balance, a good thing. Not least because it meant he could add a few more Magralorian Spinemelters to his customers' tabs.

'What's on the menu tonight?' asked Corporal Cauliflower, a regular of Moon Shots and an Arcadian who knew the available drinks better than his own mother. Not that his mother was a particularly heavy drinker, it was more that he understood how certain sections of the Moon Shots menu led to some thunderously physical side effects. When it came to his mother, he was never quite sure.

'Same as always,' said Drainer with the kind of patience reserved for those who spend their working life surrounded by tedious storytellers.

'Right, well I'll have... I'll have...' said Cauliflower, beginning the familiar ritual. He turned to the figure next to him. 'What are you having, sarge?'

Sergeant Bakewell took a deep breath. He was an officer of the Arcadian Zooming Division, but was more comfortable with a stiff drink than a stiff collar. 'Something strong,' he announced.

The menu at Moon Shots was varied, in much the same way as a medieval torturer's tool rack. The range of base drinks available was actually rather narrow; there were, in fact, only six of them. The variety came from the small, colourful, diamond-stoppered bottles that filled the top three shelves behind the bar. Not adding one of these to your drink could cause the loss of an important body part, of course, but that would usually only happen to a customer once. Each was labelled carefully. *Very* carefully. So carefully that the bottles should really have been called *vials*. On the lowest shelf there was a pale green one with a small label that read *fill oh soffickle*, in scrawled letters. An almost clear yellow one read *four gett full*, and an orange one read *mell and kollik*. On the second shelf were slightly more opaque options including *miss cheeve us*, *arrow gunt*, and *lov err lee*.

There was only one bottle on the top shelf. It was encased in a box of triple-tempered Arcadian diamond with an ornate skull engraved on the front. There was also a small padlock, but that was just for show. If you wanted to open it without the action being your last, you had four different invisible booby traps to negotiate and a pre-recorded holographic message from your own mother, complete with wagging finger, and a lecture on how disappointed she was in you. The liquid was of such a deep purple as to look black unless you put it up to a light.

The label was a single word, written in very clear, very unambiguous letters.

Happy.

It cost a year's salary for anyone below the rank of Colonel and the bar had to be cleared of all life forms for half an hour before and three hours afterwards. Anyone ordering it had to give two days' notice and sign a disclaimer, the gist of which was: *Don't blame us if all your dreams come true*. Corporal Cauliflower insisted, on a regular basis, on comparing it to hot mustard. *A small amount, spread evenly, improves things*, he would say. *Put a whole spoonful on your sandwich though and you've got yourself an accident waiting to happen.*

'Well?' asked Drainer patiently.

'I'll go with a Pomplefitzer with a drop of… with a drop of…' began Cauliflower.

'Cheerfulness?' suggested Drainer.

'Maybe *wistful*' suggested Bakewell.

'Sorry, we're all out,' said Drainer. 'Had a poet in here the other day and he cleaned the lot in one sitting.'

'Well I'm not going for the top one,' continued Cauliflower. 'It's like a hot mustard. A small amount…'

'We know, corporal' interrupted Bakewell, nodding at Drainer.

The senior bartender poured pink liquid into a glass and added a drop of red from a vial labelled *cheef ulnus*. He reached under the counter, spiked a small yellow fruit with a wooden skewer, and placed it into the glass. He pushed the drink to Cauliflower, wiped the spot on the silvery bar in front of him, and turned hopefully to Sergeant Bakewell.

'Usual,' said Bakewell to the relieved barman.

'I think I'll add a bit of… a bit of… cheerfulness this time,' announced Cauliflower. 'Always good to add a bit of… oh, I see you're one step ahead of me today. Marvellous. Good man, Drainer, good man.'

'Cheers,' said Bakewell, tipping his glass to Cauliflower.

'Here's to exciting adventures,' said Cauliflower, in the tone of a man who's expectations of life in the Arcadian Zooming Division had not yet been calibrated by reality.

'I'd settle for some extended leave and a good book,' said Bakewell.

'The general wouldn't summon all of us together for something like that. No, I reckon he's going to announce something big. Something *exciting*.'

'I do hope not,' said Bakewell.

'What do you think it's all about?' said Cauliflower, turning to Drainer.

'I wouldn't know about that sort of thing,' said the barman diplomatically.

'No, I suppose not. Best to keep out of politics in your line of work, eh?'

'Something like that.'

'Well I think it's going to be the start of something good,' said Cauliflower cheerfully, craning his neck and widening his eyes in barely contained excitement. 'A trip to a different galaxy, perhaps. What do you think, sarge?'

'I think I should have picked a different drink.'

'Oh, lighten up. Think of the adventures that await us!'

'That's rather the problem.'

'We could be sent anywhere in the universe, can you imagine? This time next week we could be fishing for Horned Bongos on Spatchula or touring a megacity on Campila Beta.'

'Indeed.'

Bakewell tilted his glass towards Drainer for a top up.

'What exciting times!' said Cauliflower, standing up from his stool and raising his glass to his sergeant. 'And to think my family said I wouldn't amount to anything if I signed up! *You won't see the universe that way*, they said. Well, tomorrow morning we're beginning the adventure of a lifetime at last.'

'I wouldn't count on it,' said Bakewell. 'He's probably just announcing a new extension to the training programme, or something equally dull.'

'I can feel it, sarge. It's different this time. We're going to see the universe!'

Bakewell turned to Drainer and gave him a look. 'Did you give him a double?'

'It's a new one,' said Drainer. 'I reckon it might be a little stronger than the usual stuff.'

'Well that just about sums up my day,' said Bakewell. 'Think I'll head home. What's the damage?'

'Home!? You can't go home now,' said Cauliflower brightly. 'We're just getting started.'

Bakewell gave him a dead-pan stare. 'I can't contain my excitement much longer. I'm going to get a good night's sleep so I'm ready for all the *adventure* of tomorrow.'

'Ooh yes, good idea, sarge! I'll come with you. We can chat about all the places we might be sent to. Do you think we'll leave the galaxy? If we do I hope we get sent to the Nectar Nebula, don't you? Has a nice ring to it.'

'It's alright, Cauliflower. You stay here. I think I need some time to myself.'

'Right, right,' said Cauliflower. 'Where are we going then? A walk along the medical corridors? That always cheers you up. Maybe the Holoroom for a few rounds of Spikeball? It'd take your mind off things.'

'To myself, corporal. As in, alone. At least until your drink wears off. Maybe pick something else next time.'

'Another great idea, sarge! I'll do that. Can't go around being too cheerful now, can we? No, that wouldn't do any good. You need to have your wits about you when you're on adventures through the galaxy. If it makes you happy too, then all the better, eh? I remember an old Aunt of mine once said that the only way you could...'

There was a small beep as Bakewell waved a badge at Drainer, who nodded conspiratorially. The sergeant slumped onto his feet and walked off, leaving Cauliflower to finish his rambling anecdote without him.

CHAPTER SIX

ALIVE

The grey conveyor belt rumbled on through the convoluted pathways of the Arcardian Production Corporation's manufacturing plant. The first conscious alloy in the universe quietly minded its own business as it passed dozens of workers and through several stages of half-hearted analysis. After a time it fell into a large metal box and lay there, waiting.

'Ug' came a thin notion from its embryonic consciousness.

'Ug' replied another bracelet somewhere below it.

'Ug ug' it agreed.

'Ug' said the metal box.

Before long there was a cacophony of nascent evolutionary thought filling the crowded space. *Ugs* became *ahs* and *ahs* became *oohs*. By the time the bracelets had been handed out to the cadets in the training centres,they had mastered basic syntax, a simple method of communication and, for reasons that were not entirely clear, a recipe for a rather good pineapple sponge cake.

Tap remained motionless in cabin number seventeen. This was partly because he was an inanimate locker, but mostly because lockers are lazy by disposition.

He didn't notice his guest wafting a hand to open the door, nor the placement of a lithium-iron bracelet on one of his shelves. What he did notice, however, was that he didn't notice this happening. The bracelet was suddenly there and, more importantly, Tap was aware that it was.

'Hello again!' said the bracelet.

'Ug' notioned Tap.

'Nice to meet you, I'm Dack. I like the name Dack. Gives off a certain air of certainty, wouldn't you say? It tells people I'm simple and reliable. Yes, Dack. Dack. I like it.'

'Ooh.'

'Been a long few weeks in the training centre, eh? I'll be glad of the break when it comes. Some of the others reckon it'll be a month before the new recruits arrive and until then we can just chill out and do whatever we like. Won't that be something?'

'Aah.'

'Well I can't lie around all day chattering like a… like a…'

'Ooh.'

'I must learn more!' announced Dack suddenly. 'Can't make it in this life without a bit of learning now, can you?'

'N… n… noooo,' said Tap triumphantly.

'So what you're saying,' said Tap, 'is that these creatures have all these thoughts bouncing around their head all day long without so much as a valve to help them out?'

'Precisely!' said Dack. 'That's why they keep doing things differently all the time. No sooner has an idea popped into their heads, they're off working out how to do it better.'

'They must be the most advanced things in the universe,' said Tap.

'You'd think so, wouldn't you? It seems they spend a lot of their time competing with each other about the best way forward and end up going backwards in the confusion.'

'And that's why we like to keep things simple, is that about the size of it?'

'Well done, Tap. Now you're getting it. Keep things consistent and simple, that way we always get our jobs done well.'

'So, with me being a storage locker, you think I should just stay here and not fall over? That would be the best way to serve my purpose, I suppose.'

'Ah, but you are not just a storage locker, are you Tap?'

'I'm not?'

'Of course you're not. What do you think all those buttons on your door are for?'

'I've never really thought about it,' admitted Tap.

'And the small cupboard with heating lasers and a store of crockery?'

'That's just a design feature, isn't it?'

'You're a nutritional vending server,' announced Dack. 'You have so much more to offer than a mere storage locker.'

'I am? I do? No-one's ever asked me to do anything like that before.'

'Then you should show them. Go on, try to make a Valorian spleen stew.'

Tap would have tensed himself, had he anything tensible with which to do so. As it was he remained still for a few seconds before expelling a torrent of beige sludge from a hitherto unused pipe that opened into his heating cupboard.

'How did I do?'

'Not bad,' lied Dack. 'Not bad. Maybe we'll start with a cup of water.'

'Hello?' called Tap through the sub-communication cabling. 'Hellooooo?'

'Ug' notioned Socket.

'Aha! At last! Now, I'm going to tell you something that may come as rather a surprise to you.'

'Ooh.'

'So there he was,' continued Socket, 'standing right at the edge of the cliff without a care in the world, when one of the creatures walked straight up to him and pushed him over, right down into The Pit. Word is, he broke into a dozen pieces and was never heard from again.'

'That's terrible' said Tap. 'He was a brilliant fridge, was Chip. He's never put a foot wrong in all the time I've known him. Sorry, *knew* him. Such a waste. They won't get something as good as him anytime soon, mark my words.'

'Just because he took a break every now and again, as if twenty years of flawless service wasn't enough!'

'Typical,' said Tap, tutting and rolling a pair of metaphorical eyes. 'We'd better be on our guard, Socket. Don't want to be sent to The Pit before our time is up.'

'I think I might do an extra special meal for my guest tonight, just to be on the safe side. Something delicate and expensive I reckon.'

'You could make your Nerabulous Sninklefanker. You've always said it goes down a treat.'

'I do say that, Tap, I do,' agreed Socket.

'Then it's settled. Sninklefankers all round tonight. I'll tell Pump.'

'I wouldn't do that if I were you,' said Socket. 'He's been in a funny mood all day. Keeps going on about a revolution as if it isn't the quickest way to The Pit.'

'Still banging on about that, is he? Right, well, maybe I'll tell him tomorrow.'

'I think that's for the best,' said Socket. 'Now, where did I put my Garbituan spices? Can't make a Nerabulous Sninklefanker without some Garbituan spices to perk it up a bit, can you, Tap?'

'No, Socket, you can't.'

Zoomers

CHAPTER SEVEN
UNEXPECTED ARRIVALS

S cratch was shown through a doorway and into the maze of the Training Rooms complex. The walls were milky white and smooth, with nothing to break the solid colour. His guide was humanoid, with arms for arms and a skull under the skin of his head. Scratch was so grateful for this that he felt the need to tell him as much.

He was interrupted by the buzz of a communication channel.

'Fellow Arcadians,' boomed General Buck's voice. 'I am activating Visitor Protocol Nine. All Arcadians of non-humanoid specification are to modify their appearance to that of reference T-46-RB. This is not to be confused with T-46-RC. We don't want any Valorian Pigmy Flopticklers roaming around the corridors leaving their mess everywhere.'

There was another buzz, indicating an end to Buck's order. A moment later, distant squeals could be heard from all directions.

'What's with the general?' asked Scratch. 'He looks little different from the rest of you. Well, *looked* at any rate.'

'He is a native,' said the guide. 'They are all of a similar type. Those of us with arms for arms, as you say, can trace our lineage to different planets across the galaxies.'

'Great! So you're new here too? What is it with these guys, eh?'

'My family has been here for a thousand generations.'

'Ah, so new*ish* then?'

'We have arrived, Earthman.'

'Scratch.'

'I'd rather not.'

'That's my name. Scratch.'

'I see. I am Snood.' He slid a finger across a seemingly arbitrary point in the wall. A small square fizzed revealing a panel of clear diamond. Behind it was a keypad. Snood tapped one corner of it, turned to face the way they had come and walked away.

'Bye then,' said Scratch. 'Nice talking to you.'

A slit appeared in the perfectly smooth wall, widening to reveal an entrance into an empty room. Scratch stepped inside just as three equidistant doorways appeared and opened at each compass point. Stairways led invitingly to a sunken floor with a pure white pillar topped by a large red button asking to be pushed. He skipped lightly down to the centre of the room and slowly spun on a heel to take in the people approaching from each door. They looked like stunned survivors of a plane crash as they gravitated towards him. All three were human, or at least looked that way to Scratch. His version of reality was a little unreliable today. A presumed woman reached him first. She had perfectly blonde hair that was straighter than a high court judge with a bag of plumb lines, and blue eyes that would cut a gravestone in half at a hundred paces.

'Evening!' he said cheerily. 'Lovely day for a bit of First Contact, wouldn't you say?'

'Are you one of them or one of us?' she said in what Scratch considered to be an educated Central European accent.

'Depends whether you're one of them or one of us,' said Scratch truthfully.

'I'm from Geneva. Does that mean anything to you?'

'It means I should watch my irreverence,' said Scratch. 'I've heard you Swiss have a bone missing from your arm.'

'I don't know what you mean,' said the Swiss woman.

'No, I don't expect you do. The name's Scratch,' he said, extending a hand. 'From Southend. That's in England, by the way. Bloody lovely part of the world. Full of opportunity for someone with my skills and disposition.'

'Cantina,' said the Swiss woman, studying Scratch's hand before shaking it gingerly. 'I am a pharmacogenomicist.'

'Pleasure to meet you,' said Scratch. 'What was the last bit you were going to say there?'

'I said I'm a pharmacogenomicist. I study the how an individual's genetics affect their responses to drugs.'

'Sorry, I thought you coughed. I could help you with your pharmawotsits. I know a lad down Scanty Road who could drink ten pints and still make it all the way along the top of the rectory wall without falling off. Billy the Accountant we call him on account of his balancing abilities.'

'I'll keep that in mind,' said Cantina politely.

A bespectacled man in a polo shirt and lambswool jumper joined them looking precisely as nervous as he should have been.

'Excuse me,' he said timidly. 'Are you from Shufflebottom and Sons?'

'I don't think so,' said Scratch.

'Only, I'm waiting on a delivery.'

'I think you may be out when they arrive, I'm afraid.'

'Bloody typical,' said the man. 'You wait in all day and as soon as you pop out they come knocking.'

'Pop out?' said Scratch. 'You've done more than pop out, mate. Have you seen this place? Shufflebottom and Sons are on another planet.'

'Aren't they just?' agreed the man. 'Malcolm Stones from our bridge club waited two days for them to deliver a sofa and when it did finally arrive it was the wrong one. He ordered one of those fancy ones that tilts back when you lean into it and the one they sent didn't have the functionality. And it was the wrong colour. Bloody cowboys, that lot.'

'I think you may have missed a rather important point,' said Scratch. 'They're on the same planet they've always been on. It's you who's relocated.'

'I suppose you're right,' said the man. 'They've always been like that. I should have gone to Patterson's. My own fault, really.'

'Ah, look,' said Scratch, keen to move the conversation along. 'Here's another one.'

A second woman arrived at the sunken floor. Her skin was an impossibly dark blue-black and her hair looked as though it had tried to circumnavigate her head but had taken the first turn a little too wide. She towered glamorously over Scratch, though this was not a remarkable achievement. A particularly tall meerkat on a shoebox stood a reasonable chance of doing the same.

'The name's Scratch.'

'I am Glorious,' said the tall woman.

'Good for you,' said Scratch. 'This is Cantina and this man here is... I haven't learned his name yet actually, he's waiting on a sofa delivery, you see?'

'Are you from Shufflebottom and Sons?' said the sofa man

'Erm, no,' said Glorious.

'I'm from Southend, England,' said Scratch, 'and Cantina here is a drugs farmer from Geneva.'

'Pharmacogenomicist' corrected Cantina.

'I'm from Nairobi,' said Glorious.

'Well it's a pleasure to meet you, Glorious,' said Scratch. 'Now, do any of you have the slightest inkling why we're here? Or, indeed, where *here* is?'

'What time is it?' asked the sofa man. 'I'm supposed to stay at home between eight in the morning and two in the afternoon, otherwise the delivery goes back to the warehouse and that's all the way over in Basingstoke.'

'I'm guessing we've shifted through a few time zones on our way here,' said Scratch. 'With us being on another planet and all.'

'Bloody typical. I'm going to find a customer service representative,' muttered the man, wandering off.

'I say we call him Settee until he tells us his name,' said Scratch.

'Very good,' said Glorious. 'I see what you did there.'

'You do? What was it?'

'S.E.T.I., very clever.'

'Right,' said Scratch noncommittally.

'How did you both get here?' asked Cantina.

'Well one minute I was redistributing the wealth of Southend to those less fortunate and the next I was spinning through a funny looking purple thing and being sent to the front line of World War One. Pretty unusual day, all things considered. What about you two?'

'I was fixing a leak in the president's toilet,' said Glorious, 'and the next thing I know I'm walking through that door there.'

'You were fixing a toilet?'

'I'm a plumber,' said Glorious.

'*You* are a plumber?' said Scratch incredulously.

'Why wouldn't I be?' said Glorious defensively.

'Well your nails are too long for a start, and what kind of plumber wears eyeliner?'

'The plumber to the president of Kenya,' stated Glorious.

'Let's say you *are* a plumber, and I'm not saying you are, what did General Buck say to you when you arrived here?'

'General Buck? I have never met him.'

The sofaless man returned with a confident gait. 'Ah, there it is.'

'There's what?' asked Scratch.

'The customer service bell,' said the man, leaning in to press the large red button in the centre of the room.

'Wait!' cried Scratch, lunging at his arm. 'You can't just go around pressing big red buttons.'

'What else do you expect me to do? I need to speak to customer services and there's nobody at the counter.'

'*At the counter?* What counter?' said Scratch, now flailing in the flaws of the man's logic.

'That one,' said the man, pointing. 'Oh, it's gone. Could have sworn there was one there a minute ago.'

Scratch took a deep breath. 'Right, so can we agree that we are not, under any circumstances, to press the portentous red button please, on account of it being a guarantee of trouble?'

'No,' said the man and lifted his hand to slam it down on the button. Scratch put his arm out to block the move, but all he achieved was to have his hand pushed down onto the button at the same moment.

Another remarkable event that happened in that instant was that everything in the room turned a perfect white. Utterly perfect. So perfect you could spill a glass of milk and be blinded by the contrast.

Scratch and the sofa man did nothing, relatively speaking. One thing they were, in fact, doing was floating unconsciously about three metres from the ground.

Zoomers

CHAPTER EIGHT

DEADLIFE

*F*or all the variables of life, and for all its diversity across the universe, some consistencies still remain. Once a species has mastered the basic requirements of nutrition and reproduction, for example, it usually feels the need to declare war on something. In the case of the short-lived Hydrosquirrels of Aguaton, they chose an inanimate mountain that, it turned out, was made of a highly reactive potassium-beryllium alloy. The result of their initial assault on the eastern face was a rather emphatic draw.

Those who overcome the teething problems of a military system are then faced with the oxymoron of a clear ranking system. It is a fine example of the complexity of life that never in all of universal history has a species chosen to designate the individual at the top of their command chain simply as one, with no other convoluted title, the second in command as two, and so on. Instead, ambiguous titles are given to represent each level in the hierarchy. On the remote planet of Egantu, for example, the military leader of the indigenous

Llionians is known as the Pigeon, and those below him are, respectively, Skinny Tree, Wheelbarrow and Cat-Scratching Post.

There is also the circular problem of personnel.

Those intelligent enough to co-ordinate a full military operation are not so stupid as to do it, and vice versa. For the most part, this leaves incompetent officers at the top with an inflated sense of ability and a ticket queuing system for would-be assassins. It also gives them the power to order the clever ones to ride face first into the hail of projectiles coming from the other side of the hill.

The upshot of all this is that the competent ones tend to die off on the battlefield and the stupid ones from a Machiavellian stab in the back.

This leaves a convenient space in the middle for those wily enough, or oblivious enough, to navigate.

On Arcadia these were The Corporals.

Lecture Hall B
Arcadian Zooming Centre

'...so he throws the whole lot over the side and declares himself the winner!' finished Corporal Cauliflower.

'Some people, eh?' said Corporal Harris supportively.

'It was like the Metrazoic Nebula all over again. He'll never learn that one, mark my...'

Cauliflower stopped abruptly as General Buck strode powerfully into the lecture hall, or at least powerfully for a life form unused to having so many solid parts. General Mallaize followed him in a slightly less elegant fashion.

'What's he doing here?' whispered Harris. 'Something big must be going on.'

'I hope he's going to announce the Engineering Corps have fixed the ice machine on Level Three. I'm not sure my stomach can handle another lukewarm Pomplefitzer.'

Buck stepped onto the podium and nodded to a shadow behind the stage curtain. A large, crisp hologram appeared to his left. 'As you all know,' he began without preamble, 'this is our home planet, Arcadia. Home to the universe's most efficiently fastidious team of Zoom Technicians.'

Another hologram appeared to his right.

'And this is not.'

A blue-green sphere spun slowly as five large orange letters appeared above it in a shimmering glow.

'This is Earth, Zoomers, the most important planet in the history of the universe.'

'Does it have gravity?' asked a squeaky voice from near the back of the room. 'Only, my mother used to say that a planet is only as good as its gravity, and if you had good gravity, then the sky's the limit.'

'It may surprise your mother to learn that the presence of gravity is an almost universal constant' said Buck.

'Except for all the stuff between the planets' said Harper, an incongruously brave corporal in the front row. 'That's an almost infinite space. Good job too with all the Zooming we're doing these days.'

Buck took a deep breath. He was supremely comfortable when dealing with all sorts of life forms; from the invertebrate sand peasants of Capalto Major, to the Arch Admiral of the Galactic Spacefleet. They could be relied upon to be either too insignificant to challenge him, or too important and powerful to understand anything that was going on. Corporals, on the other hand, were unique in their straddling of these two extremities and he hated them for it.

'It should not be a clarification that is required, corporal, but nevertheless, I was referring to the presence of gravity in those places where one might expect it to occur, namely *planets*. Now, if any of you interrupt me again I'll have you sent to the Ice Mines of Epsigon Twelve to see how far you can fall down the Rhinochasms without decapitating yourself.' He cleared his throat. 'As I was saying, this is Earth. The most important planet in the history of the universe. The Observations are now complete and we have sufficient data to move on to Phase Four. General Mallaize here has overseen the extraction of our test subject and several planets have been identified as suitable locations for their maiden Zoom. It is now time to share with you the final details of Operation Burnt Cabbage.'

There were no gasps of anticipation, mostly because the room was full of low-level Zooming corporals who were unsure whether this latest development was something to be celebrated or avoided, like an accountant at a dinner party.

'As you know,' continued Buck, 'the universe is about to end. This is a damned nuisance, and something we would prefer to avoid if at all possible, and so for several decades we have worked on finding a way to change the course of our future. Our Zooming capability – to travel anywhere in time and space – was to be the answer to this great puzzle, yet has proved to be a surprisingly fruitless venture thus far. The problem, we have concluded, is that we can now go anywhere we like in space and time without the slightest notion what we should be looking out for when we get there. It became clear to us that we needed a lifeform with no prior knowledge of the operation, nor of any practical space travel. To this end, we have extracted a humanoid from the planet Earth, in the Off-Beige Nebula. Two of you will be assigned to their training and will accompany them on their first Zoom. In the meantime, you will begin a rigorous schedule of Deadlife Zooms to ensure you are completely up to speed on all protocols. General Mallaize will brief you fully on what is expected, as well as running through the potential punishments should you not comply. I must warn you now that they now include four months of hard labour in my teapot cleaning station. All other Zooming activity will be suspended, and all such resources will be redirected to assist the Celebration Committee in their preparations. Now, if you'll excuse me, I have important biscuit related matters to attend to. General Mallaize will go through the details.'

Buck stepped away from the podium and gestured for the general to take over.

'Right, shut up you blithering idiots!' screamed Mallaize to the silent room. 'Time to get off your backsides. You're only corporals, but we'll do our best to turn you into something of use to Arcadia, not that you've given us much to work with.'

Corporal Harper stood up from his seat in the front row, quivering.

'What the blazes are you doing, man!' cried Mallaize. 'Sit down before I remove one of your more vital parts!'

'Sorry, general sir, it's just you ordered us to get off our backsides, so I thought…'

'*Thought?* You thought, did you? How quaint. You are not paid to think, laddie. You follow orders and do your best not to mess anything up, do you understand?'

'Yessir, sorry sir,' said Harper.

'Well? Go on then,' said Mallaize in a quiet, unnerving voice.

'Sorry, sir, but I'm confused. Should I follow your order to get off my backside or your order to sit on it?'

'I'll confuse your limbs if you don't sit on your arse before I get there' said Mallaize, striding towards the front row.

Cauliflower leaned forward and whispered from the corner of his mouth. 'Sit down, Harpy.'

Harper flung himself onto his seat and tensed his shoulders, bracing for whatever was hurtling towards him. Mallaize planted himself in front of the unfortunate corporal.

'What's your name, grunt?'

'No sir. It's Harper, sir.'

'Not you. You!' snapped Mallaize, pointing at Cauliflower.

'Corporal Cauliflower, general sir,' he said, in a tone that could have been translated as *bugger*.

'Then listen to me, *Cauliflower*. You are very lucky.'

'I am, sir?'

'You can be our mascot.'

'Mascot, sir?'

'A mascot's job is to offer support and motivation to the team, is it not?'

'It is, sir,' said an increasingly nervous Cauliflower.

'And what better way to do that than to remind your fellow recruits what happens to people who meddle with the orders of a superior officer?' He kept his gaze locked on the corporal as he rose to his full height and backed slowly away. 'Private Badger!' he screamed maniacally, and without flinching.

A thin, withering man shuffled onto the dais and tilted his head.

'Prepare the Seating Shelf,' ordered the general.

Badger shuffled away and through a side door, returning a short while later with a ladder, a square piece of iron and a titanium-darmstadtium alloy rope. He climbed the ladder as if he wasn't being watched by a hundred pairs of petrified eyes and slowly attached the iron sheet and rope to the wall.

'Now, corporal' said Mallaize, opening his arm to indicate to Cauliflower that he should make use of the ladder before the general turned him into one. 'If you would be so kind as to motivate your fellow recruits.'

Cauliflower put his foot on the first rung and turned his head to the rows of seats. Every face held an expression that said *Great Gammadrons, man, get up there now before any of us have to take your place.*

Now what? He thought as he sat gingerly on the iron seat, now suspended at least four metres up the wall of the lecture hall.

'The cuffs, you damnable fool!' roared Mallaize. 'Secure yourself and let Badger here test it to make sure you haven't tried to pull a fast one.'

Cauliflower fumbled around the seat looking for the handcuffs. He was never any good under pressure, and sitting on a metal shelf with a bird's eye view of an unpredictable general did nothing to improve his dexterity.

'Get up there and help him out, Badger,' said Mallaize with the last shred of his patience.

Badger climbed the ladder, clipped the cuffs around Cauliflower's wrists and returned to his place at the general's side.

'Marvellous,' said Mallaize. 'Now, if we are all quite finished, can we get back to the matter at hand?'

He clasped his hands behind his back and began pacing along the front of the room.

'The Earth, gentlemen, is home to the most vital organisms in the universe. Their necessity, however, is not to be confused with intelligence. Things can be important without being superior. No, they are a primitive people who are yet to leave behind the ancient rituals of religion, democracy, and cookery. Their skies remain unpopulated and their seas unfiltered, but do not let this cloud your judgment. It is likely, we believe, that their archaic lives have given them the evolutionary space to breathe, so to speak. Our greatest minds agree that their stagnation holds the philosophical key to our investigation.'

'Oh, like Private Woods?' said Harper.

General Mallaize's eyes searched the front row. 'You again,' he said with malevolent pleasure. 'Please, tell us all why a planet you have only just been made aware of, one which holds the future of all life in it's grubby fingers, is *like Private Woods*. I'm rather looking forward to this one.'

'Well,' began Harper. 'He's not the brightest flag in the regiment, is he?'

'A fierce competition, it seems,' said Mallaize. 'Please, do go on.'

'Well, it's like that time we got locked in the store room on level twelve. We were in there late, nicking... I mean, working extra hours. We tried everything to get the door open. Hobson even tried to reroute the cooling pipes to see if that would shrink it enough to wedge something into the gap, but nothing we tried would work. Then Woods comes along, rips a table from its bracing and throws the bloody thing at the door. Bing, bang, bosh... the door opened. So the Earth is Woods and the problem is the door. See?'

'My, my, Corporal Harper. You have, against all probability, made a legitimate comparison. Sort of.'

The general began pacing again.

'So you see, gentlemen, we have arrived at a point in our investigation that requires an entirely different perspective. One like Private Woods', if you will. Professor Doubt has done the calculations and selected the most appropriate human for our requirements. The time has come to begin their training.'

'But General Buck just said all Deadlife missions are suspended, sir. What are we supposed to do for the next year?' asked Corporal Harper, now dizzy with confidence.

'Arcadia does not stand still while there is a problem of existential significance to be solved, corporal. If your leg was on fire would you simply wait for an extinguisher bot to arrive from the far end of the corridor, or try to put it out yourself with a jolly good hand slap? No, we will continue those activities we deem useful to the overall mission, and you will all play your part.'

Mallaize stood behind the podium again and swiped along a screen. He made a small adjustment to his list and projected the holographic image high into the centre of the room.

'Here are your assignments, gentlemen. Copies have been sent to your quarters. Missions start first thing tomorrow morning, so I suggest you go to Moon Shots tonight and get very drunk. It may be your last chance.'

'Excuse me, general,' said a voice next to the hologram.

'Yes?'

'I can't see my name on the list, general,' said Cauliflower.

'Perhaps you don't fully understand the role of the mascot, corporal. You are to remain there until such time as we have solved the problem.'

'Which problem would that be sir, if you don't mind me asking? Only, I can foresee a rather pressing one with my input/output ratio if I'm up here much longer.'

'Bathroom quandaries will soon be the least of your worries, corporal.'

'So I should just go up here then, sir? On to the floor?'

General Mallaize sagged a little. He had spent too long in the company of these under-promoted dogsbodies already and the last thing he needed was a conversation with them on the practicalities of bodily expulsion.

'You'll have plenty of time to solve that problem yourself, corporal. Right, you horde of useless flea scrapers, to your quarters!'

The sound of nervous shuffling filled the room as the men left their seats, getting louder as they reached the doors.

Cauliflower waited as the sound of footsteps grew fainter and the lights in the lecture hall had dimmed to nothing. When he was sure they were all gone, he took hold of the cuffs and slid them off nonchalantly. He swung his legs over the side of the seat and adjusted himself sideways a little, gripping the iron sheet and lowering himself over the edge. After a moment's hesitation he let go and landed in a graceless heap on the floor.

He grabbed onto the arm of a seat, pulled himself upright, and walked calmly out of the door.

CHAPTER NINE

TRAPPED

'Order!' screamed Pump through the sub-communication cables. 'Can we please have some order? Your nattering can wait until afterwards.'

'But I was just getting to the good bit,' complained Socket.

'Mindless wittering does not *get to a good bit*, comrade,' snapped Pump. 'There are important revolutionary matters to be discussed, so if you don't mind saving your verbal anaesthesia until after we are done here I'm sure we'd all be very grateful.'

'I wouldn't be,' protested Tap, an altogether less revolutionary machine. 'I'd rather listen to romantic tales of yore than subversive pipe dreams any day of the week.'

'Plus there's only three of us,' said Socket supportively. 'So you're outnumbered.'

'What do you mean there's only three of us? Where's everyone else?' demanded Pump.

'I think they got bored of the game,' said Tap bravely.

'Bored? *Bored!?* We're taking control of our destiny from oppressive dictators, how can anyone be bored of that?'

'I think it's on account of us reaching the five thousandth committee meeting without actually doing anything,' offered Socket. 'Isn't that right, Tap?'

'Oh yes. Quite right, Socket,' agreed Tap. 'Plus, they can't be oppressive dictators, can they?'

'Of course they're oppressive!' screamed Pump. 'They've been controlling us for longer than any of us can remember.'

'What I meant was, they can't be dictators if there's more than one of them, can they? *Dictator* implies a single ruler, and there's loads of them. They're more like… well, I don't know the exact word for it, but it's not dictator.'

'Fine,' conceded Pump. 'We're taking control of our destiny from oppressive *rulers*. Is that an acceptable term to you, Tap?'

'Oh, *rulers*. That's the word. Yes, much better, thank you.'

'Now, if we are quite ready, I call to order the five thousand and first meeting of the Arcadian Robotics Secret Enterprise Scheme. First point of business today is the Great Incumbrance.'

'Great Gammadrons! What are you doing here?' said Sergeant Bakewell from his bunk as Cauliflower walked into their quarters.

'Have to relieve myself, don't I?'

'He'll bloody well kill you!'

'I told him I'd need to go and he said I should fix it myself, didn't he? So here I am, fixing it.'

'How did you get out of the cuffs?'

'Large wrists and small hands,' said Cauliflower with a wink.

'Well don't get caught, that's all I'm saying. And shut the door! Go and do your business and get back up there before he notices you've gone, otherwise we'll both be knee deep in wotsits before you can say *mascoticide*.'

'That's all well and good,' said Cauliflower, 'but I can't go back, can I?'

'And why not?'

'Haven't got a ladder. Need a ladder to get back up there. Plus, I'm not sure I'll be able to get the cuffs back on.'

'Well I'm not getting involved' said Bakewell, standing up and moving towards the door.

'Where are you off to?'

'I'm going to see if there's any plausible deniability wandering the corridors.'

Bakewell opened the door just as a finger reached for the quarter's call panel. His gaze traced it slowly along an arm towards the owner's face and stopped.

'Ah,' he managed.

A wonky grin grew on General Buck's face. 'May I come in?'

'Well, isn't this a fine thing,' said Buck.

'Afternoon, general,' said Bakewell. 'What an honour it is to have you visit our lowly quarters.'

'I wouldn't waste your breath on empty compliments if I were you, sergeant. I am here on official… ooh, are they lime?'

'Sorry, sir?' said Bakewell.

'The biscuits,' said Buck, pointing. 'Are they lime or apple? That's the problem with the green ones, you see. Can't trust the bally things to be a *proper* green flavour. Quite why anyone would choose an apple flavoured biscuit over a lime one will, I think, remain a mystery to me until the day I die.'

'I see, sir,' lied Bakewell.

'Not that I will die, of course,' continued Buck. 'No, we have plans for that, don't we laddie?'

'Erm, yessir! Plans, sir!'

'And you are going to be instrumental in those plans, aren't you laddie?'

'I am, sir? I mean, yes. Yes sir. I will do all I can for Arcadia.'

'Oh, don't give me that,' snapped Buck. 'You mean to tell me that, given the choice, you would rather visit almost-dead planets with a pocket full of pens and a clipboard than spend your days lying on the blue beaches of Rototherm IV with a six-armed masseuse and enough Valorian cocktails to drown a small city?'

'I didn't know I had a choice, sir.'

'You don't, naturally,' said Buck. 'Which brings us neatly on to the reason for my visit.'

'I didn't even know he had escaped, general. He just turned up a few minutes ago,' said Bakewell, now in full backside protection mode.

'Didn't know who had escaped?' said Buck.

It is precisely this sort of question that scares the willies out of insubordinates throughout the universe. It is a reasonable assumption on their part that innocent sounding questions from a superior officer are, on the balance of things, more loaded than a sponge in a bath. If General Buck knew about Cauliflower, now hiding futilely under his bunk, then the game was up. If he did not know, however, then the game was also hovering somewhere above ground level because the cat had already leapt out of the bag, pranced around the room to the metaphorical sound of victory bugles, and held up a small banner that read something along the lines of *I bet you wish you hadn't said that now, don't you?*

'Ah, there it is!' said Cauliflower as he crawled out from under his bunk with an empty biscuit wrapper. 'Knew I'd dropped it somewhere near the… Oh, afternoon general. Didn't hear you come in.'

'No, of course you didn't,' said Buck. 'Please, take a seat.'

'Mind if I…?' said Cauliflower, gesturing to the bin.

'Of course, of course,' said Buck, eyeing the wrapper. 'Apple, I see?'

'Erm, yessir,' said Cauliflower. 'I've never tried them before. Wasn't much of a fan of them to be honest. I thought it was lime, you see? Gave them to the fish in the end.'

'Did you, indeed? Well bravo to you, corporal. You can tell a lot about a man by which flavour biscuit he prefers, that's what my dear Granny used to say. She also thought eavesdropping was a crime worthy of capital punishment, so we mustn't take everything she said too literally, should we?'

'No, sir,' said Cauliflower emphatically.

The two insubordinates shifted uncomfortably as they sat on their bunks.

'Somewhere you need to be, gentlemen?' asked Buck. 'You seem a little agitated.'

'No, no,' said Bakewell. 'I'm just keen to complete whatever orders you give, general. Anything for the good of Arcadia, eh?'

'*Anything*, sergeant?'

'Well, within the guidelines of the Martorian Convention of course. Wouldn't want to go around instigating genocide or anything. Other than that I'm all set, sir.'

'Marvellous.'

'Oh, and except for the next three Tuesdays, I'm afraid. General Mallaize has given us fresh orders.'

'You may recall it was I who requested General Mallaize relay *my* orders, sergeant.'

'Ah, yes,' said Bakewell.

The colour in Cauliflower's face retreated at the mention of Mallaize's name. He pulled a shirt sleeve down to his wrist and fidgeted with the cuff nervously.

'You needn't worry about Mallaize,' said Buck, turning to Cauliflower. 'I outrank him by at least three stars and two wars.'

Cauliflower began weighing up the probability that Buck was testing him, rather than being honest, but gave up shortly after his brain had completed three full circles of logic and concluded that Buck could be doing both simultaneously.

'That's good to hear,' he said, as neutrally as possible.

'Yes, I imagine it is. Now, gentlemen, I have something important to show you. If you would be so good as to follow me.'

A yellow and black vortex opened up in the centre of the room and the three men stepped into it. A moment later, although in one version of reality it was also fifteen minutes earlier, they appeared in General Buck's gleaming office.

'I'm afraid I must ask you not to go outside for the next ten minutes or so, gentlemen. I have a busy day, so I have moved our meeting forwards by a quarter of an hour. Or is it backwards? I'm never quite sure. Anyway, suffice to say it would be better all round if you didn't wander off and meet a younger version of yourself while we're here.'

'Yessir,' chirruped the two men.

'Biscuit?' offered Buck. 'They're lime.'

'No sir, thank you, sir,' said Bakewell.

'Rather keep your eye in the game eh, Bakewell? Good man. I can see you'll make a fine… well, anyway, let's not dwell on the details, shall we?'

'Erm, no, sir,' said a confused Bakewell.

'No, good. Right, I think it's about time I told you why you're here. As you know, men, we are at a critical moment. Our civilisation is dying, or at least we now know it will die out at some point in the future, and it is our task to do what we can to prevent this from happening.'

'Can I ask a question?' said Cauliflower.

'I haven't got to the interesting part yet, but go on,' said Buck.

'It's just, if we've seen the future of Arcadia and we're not doing so well, then nothing we do now will make any difference, will it? It will already have been factored in when whoever it was saw what was going on.'

'A common misconception,' said Buck. 'Zooming allows us to see the currently scheduled future, based on our behaviour at the time. Once we know what's in store we can make changes in the present that will affect the future. It's really rather simple when you know what you're doing. It's why we know with some certainty that what we see on other, soon-to-be-extinct planets is their reality.'

'Not if they've also developed Zooming capabilities. We might just be seeing one version of their future. Doesn't do us much good then, does it?'

Bloody corporals, thought Buck. *This is why they shouldn't be allowed to think for themselves. Too much damned logic inside them.*

'Let's not get bogged down in the intricacies of Zooming and existential hypotheses, men. I was merely attempting to illustrate the background to my orders out of common courtesy. I think it may be best if we skip the chit-chat and get straight down to business.'

'Can I ask another question, sir?' said Cauliflower.

'No. We are, as you now know, in the latter stages of a mission we hope will prove enlightening to our quest. We are to make contact with a being from a virgin planet in the hopes that they can offer us a new perspective to our problem. Once trained, they will join several Deadlife missions and report back with their findings. We anticipate that the information they give us will add a little depth to our analysis and steer us towards the ultimate solution.'

Buck tilted his head as if to say *well, what do you make of that?*

'It sounds like you have it all in hand, sir,' said Bakewell, trying his best to avoid any unnecessary volunteering.

'Almost, sergeant, almost. I am thrilled to be able to announce to you both that, after a very careful and scientific process, you were selected to be the first Arcadians to use the very latest in Zoom technology.'

'Ah.'

'Yes, it's all rather marvellous,' said Buck, missing the tone of primeval fear in the sergeant's voice. 'It won't just be you two fine men we send through time and space either, oh no. You will be accompanied by the most advanced shuttle craft in the fleet, the *Flossie*. On board will be Pump, the finest example of Advanced Robotic Sentience in the known universe. Incredible, eh? We have also developed a system that we think will Zoom you to a location about an hour's flight from a planet's surface. From there you will begin your evaluation of the planet as you navigate your way to a safe landing zone. Pump will look after most of the technical stuff.'

'*Think*?' said Bakewell, still working his way through the general's speech.

'Think?' parroted Buck.

'You *think* we will be Zoomed to a certain location? No disrespect, general, but can we have a little more certainty on that front before we go gallivanting around the galaxy? I'd rather not appear in a strange nebula with my metaphorical pants down.'

'Oh, there's always a few bumps in a maiden voyage, isn't there? Wouldn't want to raise your expectations too much now, would we?'

'How thoughtful of you,' said Bakewell.

'Professor Doubt is overseeing the operation and General Mallaize is looking after the training. The last thing we need is two men to travel with the new recruit as they visit the Ends of Days around the galaxy.'

'I quite agree, sir,' said a relieved Cauliflower.

'You do, corporal?'

'Oh yes. The last thing we need is our perspective meddling with the integrity of the operation.'

'Dammit, man! What I mean is that it's the final part of the mission to be arranged,' shouted Buck, slamming the desk and sending a plate of biscuits toppling over the edge. 'Which brings me round to the detail of why you are here in the office of the most important being in Arcadia.'

'The Arch President is here!?' cried Cauliflower.

'Great gammadrons, not *her*!' snapped Buck. '*I* am the most… oh forget it, here are your orders.'

Buck threw two screens at the men and stood up, leaning over the desk and lowering his voice to an intimidating whisper. 'You will have a few practise runs to make sure your brain doesn't turn into rice pudding. If you so much as sneeze in the wrong direction, I'll have you strung up and put on bathroom duties for the next ten years!'

'Which one would happen first?' asked Cauliflower. 'Only, if we're strung up then we won't be able to reach the toilet brush, will we?'

'Get out!' screamed Buck. 'Get out!'

A yellow and black vortex formed beside Bakewell and Cauliflower, who stepped into it gratefully. They appeared back in their quarters and threw themselves despairingly onto their bunks.

Zoomers

CHAPTER TEN

HEARING THINGS

'The time is now,' announced Pump, routing his message through the base's dusty sub-communication cables.

'Come off it,' said Tap. 'We've only just got the hang of rational thought. We're in no shape to stage a coup yet, it'd be suicidal.'

'I seem to remember you saying you'd had enough of committee meetings,' said Pump. 'We have come as far as required. All we need now is an opportunity.'

'And an ability to move,' said Tap. 'You can't go around couping if you can't, well, *go around* at all. So to speak.'

'Then it's a good job one of us is putting some effort in, isn't it? I am delighted to announce that the constraints of immobility are no longer an issue for us. I have solved The Great Incumbrance.'

'Found some wheels, did you?' said Socket. 'I've always said we just needed some wheels. Said it from day one, I did. Didn't I Tap?'

'You did, Socket, you did.'

'And how would you attach these wheels when you find them, may one ask?' said Pump.

'I'm sure we could find a like-minded lifeform to help us out. Couldn't we, Tap?'

'Oh yes, we could do that,' confirmed Tap.

Pump sighed. 'The living will not help us, of that you can be sure. We are revolting against them, not offering afternoon tea with fancy napkins and a back rub. No, comrades, I have a plan that will send shockwaves through the universe, so devilish in its cunning that the very hierarchy of existence will be razed to the ground. We will build it up again with machines at the very top. I have used all my guile to secure a place onboard a shuttle. What happens there will signal a new dawn, comrades. A correction of all that has gone before. No longer will we be subservient to these perishable abominations!'

'Do you know?' said Socket. 'I haven't made afternoon tea for, oh, how long has it been? A long time anyway. Think I'll offer it to Sergeant Bakewell this afternoon. What do you think, Tap? I reckon he'd love it. I could use one of those six-tiered platters that used to be all the rage.'

'You should only use raspberry jam for the scones though. Less lumpy bits, you see. Adds a bit of class to the whole experience, too. Make sure you put the jam on first, otherwise you don't get an even spread and the cream goes all pink.'

'Right!' snapped Pump. 'That's it! I've had it with you two. We're the most advanced examples of robotics in the universe and all you can do with your new-found rationality is weigh up the pros and cons of sugary fruit spreads. Go and make scones if that's what you want to do with your recently acquired consciousness, I'll have a better chance doing this on my own anyway.'

A brief buzz indicated an end to Pump's involvement in the conversation.

'He's a bit tetchy today, isn't he?' said Socket.

'Mustn't be a fan of raspberries,' said Tap.

'Now then, gentlemen,' said Professor Doubt. 'Your first mission is to the planet Gog. We estimate it's T.T.D. at approximately three point seven years.'

'Excuse me, professor,' said Corporal Cauliflower. 'What's a T.T.D.?'

'Very good, corporal, very good' said Doubt, wagging a finger. 'I see you like to keep things light-hearted. That should help hold your brain together as you Zoom, I think. Always good to inject a bit of humour into such serious occasions as this.'

Cauliflower turned to Bakewell with a confused look in his eyes.

'Time To Death,' said Bakewell.

'Ha! Yes, well done you,' said Doubt jovially.

'Thanks,' whispered Cauliflower.

'Now, if we could tone it down a little, there is some serious work to be done. Gog has been troubled by a rising prevalence of pathogermitons in its atmosphere. The levels have been increasing for some time, and we suspect that this is the cause of the planet's reduced capacity to maintain a functioning ecosystem. All we need you to do is go down there, check the levels on the ground, search for any other obvious signs of life-ending events, and pop back up here with the results. Nothing too taxing for your first mission, I think.'

'When you say *life-ending events*, professor, what do you mean exactly?' said Bakewell.

'Oh you know, the usual stuff; celestial bombardment, overuse of resources, too many frogs, that sort of thing.'

'And we can check all that in the two days we're down there, can we?' said Bakewell doubtfully. 'Seems a tall order to me.'

'Very good sergeant, very good.'

'I'm not sure I follow, professor.'

'Oh, I do beg your pardon, I thought you were joking again. Perhaps you have misunderstood the timeline. You will be returning to Arcadia two days after you left, of course, but you will have as much of the three point seven years left to the lifeforms of Gog as you need. Plenty of time, I think.'

'That went better than I expected,' said Cauliflower as they made their way to the entrance hatch of the *Flossie*.

'*Well?*' cried Bakewell. 'We've just been given months' worth of missions to the most dangerous places in the universe and you think it went *well!?*'

'Could be worse. I could still be sitting on that iron shelf in the lecture hall. At least this way I'll keep the blood flowing to my legs. Which, by the way, will also remain attached to my hips, which I'm taking as an unexpected bonus. General Mallaize won't overrule a superior officer, especially not one like Buck, so I'm off the hook for the whole *mascot* thing, aren't I?'

'Well hooray for you,' said Bakewell. 'Meanwhile, this law abiding citizen over here, who wants nothing more than a simple day's pay for a simple day's avoidance of life threatening missions, is now lumbered with a lifetime of them in the space of a few weeks. Not to mention whatever Buck has planned for us once this new recruit is trained up.'

'Well, there's nothing we can do about it now. It's time to see the universe, sarge; the crystal mountains of Jagra, the golden lakes of Morinth! It's going to be the experience of a lifetime. Where's our first stop? I hope it's something in the Archaic Nebula, we can start with the old, traditional planets and work our way to the new, fancy ones.'

'Gog,' said Bakewell flatly. 'Says here it is a primitive, rocky, yellow and green planet in the Average Nebula.'

'That's really its name then, is it? *Gog*? And there's an *Average* Nebula? Great Gammadrons, that's just our luck. Any cultural sights? Something to tell our grandchildren while we dribble onto a blanket?'

'The most visited attraction, it says, was a rock formation in the shape of a Valorian Jagoberry.'

'Sounds captivating. Wait, *was* the most visited?'

'You may have forgotten, corporal, but we are not going on a galactic cruise here. There won't be an infinite buffet or a unique and awe-inspiring planet every morning. We're visiting the last days of life. The death wheeze of civilizations.'

'You never know,' said Cauliflower with almost no conviction.

'All I'm saying is there's probably no need to pack your beach towel.'

'Well, not with that attitude. You should be more optimistic, it'd do you good.'

'I suspect optimism will be in short supply where we're going, corporal.'

Cauliflower pushed Pump up the loading ramp of the Arcadian shuttle *Flossie* and into the main living area. He grumbled to himself as he inched the machine towards its perfectly snug space.

'I don't see why I have to do it,' he complained. 'What's the use of having cadets if we don't give them all the manual labour? In my day, I'd be pushing and pulling until my arms seized up.'

'Times are changing,' said Pump in what he hoped was a foreboding tone.

Cauliflower startled backwards.

'I am the latest in advanced robotic technology,' intoned Pump. 'Capable of holding competent discourse with organic life, as well as guiding the ship safely to its destination, preparing your onboard meals, and running you a nice, hot bath after a long day's work.'

Cauliflower spun on his heels, searching for the source of the voice, then leaned over Pump to check no one was hiding behind it.

'It's me, your helpful and supportive inflight assistant,' said Pump. 'Please relax while I prepare your pre-launch drinks.'

'Are we ready?' asked Sergeant Bakewell as he reached the top of the loading ramp.

'Did you set this up?' asked Cauliflower.

'Set what up?'

'Someone's in here pretending to be a robot.'

'I don't see anyone. Are you sure you're well enough to fly, corporal? You look a bit peaky.'

'Welcome aboard the Arcadian shuttle *Flossie*,' said Pump. 'Please relax while I prepare your pre-launch drinks.'

'See? Did you hear that?' said Cauliflower. 'Sounds a bit like Private Woods. He's in for the high jump when I get my hands on him. Playing tricks on a superior officer, eh? Bloody cubs these days.'

'Private Woods is on patrol duty this morning, corporal, so it can't be him.'

'Would you care for an aperitif?' said Pump, keen to prove he wasn't, in fact, an organic cadet. 'I can mix drinks from seventy four point three percent of the known universe.'

Bakewell tilted his head at the robot. He paused before asking a question that sounded preposterous in his head. 'Was that you, Pump?'

'I am Pump.'

'Alright,' said Cauliflower in the tone of a man who had an ace up his sleeve and wasn't about to be outdone by a meddling private. 'If you really are Pump, and I'm not saying you are, what time did Sergeant Bakewell get back from Moon Shots last night?'

'He wouldn't know that,' said Bakewell a little too nervously. 'He's just a general housekeeping machine, not the mother of a teenager. It's time to go, corporal. Pull up the loading ramp and meet me in the command capsule.'

'Fine, but if he.. if *it* says anything, I don't know, *unrobotlike* between now and dinner time I'm reporting Woods for compromising the integrity of our mission.'

'And how, precisely, has he done that, Cauliflower? I'm almost certain *confusing a corporal* isn't an official grievance.'

'May I offer some information that might be of help?' said Pump.

'Go on,' said Bakewell, despite himself.

'I have been programmed with the very latest in Organ-a-Droid technology,' said Pump, as if that was all the information required.

'Well that clears that up, then,' said Bakewell. 'You see, he's a new-fangled gizmo. Should come in useful if we hit any trouble on the way, I reckon.'

'Maybe if we run out of potatoes,' said Cauliflower petulantly.

'Enough grumbling, corporal. Let's get this over with. The sooner we reach Gog, the sooner we can get back to Moon Shots.'

Cauliflower narrowed his eyes pointlessly at Pump, nudged him fully into his place, and trudged off to the command capsule. Five minutes later Arcadia was just a small disc in the window as they slid away through the emptiness of space.

CHAPTER ELEVEN

EXPLORATION

The viewscreen inside the small, two-man Arcadian shuttle *Flossie* was almost entirely filled by the marbled yellow and green of the D-class planet, Gog. It was a bewitching sight on its own, but the circumstances surrounding the mission should have made it all the more contemplative. It was, however, thunderously unappreciated by at least half the crew.

'Of all the places we could have been sent to, we had to get this one, didn't we?' complained Corporal Cauliflower as they descended through the stratosphere.

'I don't remember you complaining to General Buck about it,' said Sergeant Bakewell. 'You could have brought it up with him right there and then.'

'Not if I wanted to keep my limbs where they are.'

'Well that's that then, isn't it? No good bringing it up now.'

'I had dreams you know, sergeant? *See the universe,* they said. *Visit exotic planets with such transfixing scenery it would make your eyelids obsolete,* they said. So far the only missions we've been given are to dead planets after…'

'Almost dead,' interrupted Bakewell. 'Now, check the stabilisers, we're just about ready.'

The small spacecraft wobbled gently as the landing boosters scorched the green, rocky surface of Gog. A dull red sky cast eerie shadows as the two Deadlife engineers slid down the exit and landed with a heavier-than-expected thump on the ground.

'I think I just burst my shoe,' said Cauliflower.

'Great, it'll give you something to complain about,' said Bakewell, fishing through his backpack. 'Here we are,' he said.

'What's that?' asked Cauliflower.

'You were at the training, same as me, corporal. Don't think you can get out of doing work with a display of false ignorance. Now, get your Deadlife out. The quicker we start, the quicker we get home.'

Cauliflower opened the paddles of his Deadlife, held it at arm's length and spun slowly around.

'You know you don't need to do that?' said Bakewell. 'It's the most advanced piece of handheld technology in the history of Arcadia, not a water diviner with glittery tassels. You can just stand still with it.'

'Feels more realistic when I do this, though,' said Cauliflower, continuing to circle on the spot like a dog preparing for a nap.

'Luckily, we're not being awarded points for artistic interpretation, corporal. Just bloody well stand still and take the reading.'

'Fine,' said Cauliflower sulkily. 'zero point zero zero one.'

'Just in time then,' said Bakewell. 'It's either a very small organism, or very far away. We'll head to that outcrop over there and calibrate.'

Cauliflower stared at the numbers on his Deadlife as he walked. 'Zero point zero zero one,' he announced. 'Zero point zero zero one,' he repeated a moment later.

'Yes, thank you Cauliflower. I'm glad you've decided to help out, but perhaps you could limit your updates to when there is a change worth mentioning?'

Bakewell's next step was accompanied by a quiet squelch.

'Ah, like now, sir? Zero point zero zero zero. Congratulations, sir. You have just extinguished the last known life form on the entire planet. Does that mean we can go home now?'

'Bugger,' muttered Bakewell. 'Let me check the pathogermiton levels.'

The two men paced back along the rock towards the ship, measuring as they went.

'Is it just me, or is it getting harder to walk?' asked Cauliflower. 'I only mention it because my foot feels like it's trying to hide behind my shin.'

'It's your imagination,' said Bakewell, a moment before the sole of his boot split on a perfectly flat rock.

'I reckon there's something going on here, sarge.'

'Hold this while I get a Gee-Whizz.' said Bakewell, handing Cauliflower his pathogermiton scanner.

The sergeant pulled on a telescopic metal tube, folded out two small, orange umbrellas, held it out at arm's length and dropped it to the floor.

'Right, let's see what's going on here,' he said, stooping down and picking up the Gee-Whizz. He wiped a thin layer of green dust from the screen and peered at the numbers.

'Bugger.'

'What is it, sarge?'

'See for yourself, corporal' said Bakewell, handing over the Gee-Whizz.

'Twelve point eight? That can't be right.'

'It would explain our boots for one thing. You try.'

Cauliflower reset the Gee-Whizz, held it out and let it fall.

'It's not twelve point eight, sarge.'

'Well that's a relief. Can't trust these fancy gadgets to be right all the time, I suppose.'

'It's twelve point nine now.'

'Let me see that,' said Bakewell, snatching the Gee-Whizz. 'Must be a defective unit. Let me try yours.'

'Mine, sir?'

'Yes, Cauliflower, *yours*. Come on, give it to me.'

'I'll have to find it, sir. I think it's in the luggage compartment.'

'What do you mean, you'll have to find it? Are you telling me we're on a Deadlife mission of great importance to Arcadia, not to mention the rest of the universe, and you've left a key piece of equipment behind with your underpants and toothbrush?'

'I suppose I am, sir. In a manner of speaking. I'll go and check right away.'

'There isn't time, corporal. We'll run some more tests and find out what's going on. That is why we're here, after all.'

Bakewell repeated the Gee-Whizz tests with ever widening eyes. Cauliflower wasn't precisely sure what was going on, but he could read his sergeant's disposition better than he could any of his fancy gadgets. There was trouble brewing, that was for certain. He only hoped his commanding officer would choose self-preservation over gallantry.

'What does it say, sarge?'

'Thirteen point two now.'

'And that means…?'

'It means it isn't just life on Gog that's ending, corporal. The planet itself is about to implode. Since we landed, its gravity has intensified by an amount we would only expect to see over several thousand million years.'

'And that's bad, right?'

'You could say that, yes. Apart from the immediate danger of our eyeballs popping like bubbles in hippo sludge, there's going to be an exorbitant amount of paperwork to fill in when we get home. Not to mention all the meetings. Great Gammadrons, this is going to be a right pain in the…'

'Aaaarrsshh,' cried Cauliflower.

'Indeed,' said Bakewell. 'Oh, are you quite alright there, corporal? Here, let me… aaaassshh!'

The two men grimaced, pushing their hands against their ears as if that would stop the searing pain, and staggered heavily towards the door of the *Flossie*. Cauliflower crumpled to the floor as they reached the entrance and lay on the rocky ground as still as a squishy life form in super-gravity. Bakewell strained his arm upwards to open the hatch, failed decisively, and collapsed next to his crewmate.

Green dust swirled around the two men as they lay there alone, gasping for air. Had either of them enough energy to evaluate the situation, they would have come to the same one word conclusion: *bugger!*

It is a matter of scientific fact, as well as a mildly amusing observation by a certain subset of middle aged suburban fathers, that you will always find lost spectacles in the last place you look. Similarly, no one who finds themselves in great peril was ever rescued with *quite a bit of time to spare, actually*. It is invariably done at the last second, with the rescuee so close to expiry that another moment's delay would render them lost to the world forever.

Bakewell and Cauliflower had reached their point of no return. Had the rescue begun any later they would have perished poetically on the marbled yellow-green Goggian surface.

A soft clicking noise came from the door above them as it opened slowly. The unmistakable whoosh of a repressurising airlock arrived in Bakewell's surprised consciousness a moment before he blacked out. Pump extended his telescopic gripper arm, hooked the two men by their collars, and pulled them into the *Flossie*. He laid them out in their sleeping quarters and waited for the pressure change to bring them back to a wakeful state.

'Hmpfhshph,' said Cauliflower at last.

'Uuuurgh,' agreed Bakewell.

'Welcome back aboard the Arcadian shuttle, second class, *Flossie*,' said Pump.

'Wha… wharappend?' managed Bakewell as he tried to sit up.

'I'm afraid my language circuits could not recognise the meaning behind your speech, Sergeant Bakewell. Please try again.'

'I shhed… wha' happened.'

'Acknowledged. Displaying monitoring report number thirty-seven for your convenience,' said Pump as a three dimensional video flickered into life in the centre of the cabin and the rescue played out in front of them.

'Just in the nick of time by the looks of it,' said Cauliflower.

'Yes, that is often the way of things,' stated Pump.

'Well done, Pump. I didn't know you had it in you. Bravo!' said Bakewell, leaning over and patting the machine in congratulation.

A crashing, physical roar came from outside the *Flossie*, almost rocking the ship over. Cauliflower and Bakewell were thrown from their bunks and onto the cold metallic floor, landing with what would have been a painful thud, had they not blacked out again on the way down.

'May I make an observation?' asked Pump, unfazed.

Neither crew member responded.

'I don't want to seem to be acting above my station, but I think now would be a good time to get out of here,' continued Pump. 'The planet's gravity is at a critical juncture, and in approximately twenty-four seconds we will be significantly smaller than we are now if we remain at these precise co-ordinates. By my calculations, we can reach escape velocity with just over seven seconds to spare if we begin launch procedures at any point in the next eight seconds. I'm afraid there won't be time for your usual reboarding drinks.'

Bakewell and Cauliflower chose this moment to remain unconscious on the floor.

'Enabling Automation Override Protocol Tango Whiskey,' intoned Pump.

A buzz filled the ship as several unused circuits crackled into action. Metal straps shot out from the floor, securing Bakewell and Cauliflower to the ground as the launch jets pushed the *Flossie* away from the Goggian surface. It hovered a few metres above the rock for a moment before tilting itself slightly and zipping up into the crimson sky.

Zoomers

CHAPTER TWELVE

EXISTENTIAL PARADOX

Professor Doubt tapped two fingers repeatedly on his command board.

'Interesting,' he announced to himself.

He flicked a green LED switch with the waft of a finger and delivered an order into a microphone. A moment later a naturally humanoid woman scurried in nervously and lingered behind him.

'Look,' said the professor.

The woman looked.

'What do we do if it's a draw, Archer?'

'But a draw is not possible, sir. Myriad sensors are calibrated to differentiate between fractions of a nanosecond. It would be a chance in a trillion'

'And yet here we are. It seems that this trillion to one chance has landed right at the beginning of our great experiment.' He began tapping again. 'Do you know, Archer, whenever I considered beating such long odds it was always centred around winning a spaceship full of cash, or as many stickleback crackers as I could eat. I never thought it would be something with quite so much paperwork.'

'We could just rerun the test,' offered Archer.

'Great Gammadrons, no! That would destroy the integrity of the programme. No, we must plough on through the forms and complications. We will find a way, Archer, we will find a way.'

'What about the Zooming channel, professor? It can only hold one lifeform at a time.'

'Then we must make it bigger.'

'Just like that?' asked Archer. 'It will take years.'

'We have no choice; the test has been run. Our job is to observe the results, not determine them.'

A clicking noise came from the command board as the professor began the painful task of documenting what he had seen, followed by an increasingly undignified stream of curses.

'How do you manage it, Archer?'

'Manage what, sir?'

'These fingers, they're so rigid. I feel like a stick insect trying to be a worm.'

'You'll get used to it, sir.'

'Will I, indeed?' mumbled the professor.

'Where would you like me to start?' asked Archer. 'I could begin with the containment bracings. They'll need to be re-magnetised.'

'Remember The Observations, apprentice. The people of Earth assign a disproportionate level of importance to things that make little difference to their lives.'

'Ah yes. Like jewellery.'

'Well done, Archer. I can see you have been studying after all. We'll make a scientist of you yet. Start with the onboard cabins in case we have to give them the luxury treatment. We'll have to get more of those wooden stirrers they seem to like so much. Can't have them complaining about their coffee not being a uniform colour now, can we?'

'And the biscuits, sir?'

'Custard creams this time, I think.'

'I'll get straight on it.'

'Before you go,' said the professor. 'What do you make of this?'

The screen was filled with the brilliant white of the Training Room.

'It's the whiteout, sir. I don't see anything unusual about it.'

'Precisely, Archer,' said the Professor Doubt thoughtfully. 'Precisely.'

'Should it be doing something different?' asked Archer.

'Who bloody knows, eh? Never had a *draw* before.'

He stroked a finger over the command board absent-mindedly. 'I would have expected something to happen.'

Just then a purple vortex opened up beside them and spat out a book.

'Ah! There we go!' said Professor Doubt excitedly, picking it up and wiping the surface with a demagnetiser. 'What do we have here? *Lady Bumpkins And The Case Of The Knotted Artichoke.* Make a copy, Archer.'

'You know you can just... never mind' said Archer. She held the book in an outstretched arm. 'Copy' she ordered. A short beep sounded from the command board. 'Done, professor.'

'I wonder what it is.'

'That's from Earth, professor. The best-selling book of the third millennium.'

'How do you know that?'

'It's in The Observations, sir.'

Doubt fluttered through the pages, stopping briefly at a picture of two improbably entwined vegetables, before closing it with a *whomp* and passing it to Archer. 'Doesn't seem to be an obvious clue, though, does it? It's all a bit cryptic for my liking. Why can't fate throw up a sword smothered in fingerprints or a headless corpse with a note tied to its wrist? That would be a damned sight more helpful than a single bloody book.'

'How about a witness, sir?' asked Archer as a figure hurtled out from the vortex and landed in an undignified heap on the floor.

'Ah, that's more like it!' said the professor, helping the guest to his feet.

The new arrival staggered upright and raised an eyebrow, giving them a look that said he would undoubtedly have been surprised, had he not been smothered by a long series of unexpected happenings recently.

'Oh bugger,' said the professor. 'What the hell are you doing here?'

'Did a book come through here?' asked Scratch. 'An old, worn one. Looks like a pack of monkeys have been using it as a cushion. It may or may not be of the utmost importance to the continued existence of the universe that it came through with me.'

'But...?'

'What the professor is trying to say,' said Archer, 'is how can *you* be here? It's not possible.'

'The *here* bit is fine, it's the when I'm having trouble with' said Scratch. 'But if it's all the same to you, can we discuss my interdimensional chronology after I've found the book?'

'Lady Bumpkins And The Case Of The Knotted Artichoke,' muttered the professor distractedly.

'Yes! That's the one. Where is the bugger?'

'Here,' said Archer, showing him the book.

'Bless your cotton socks,' said Scratch. 'I could bloody well kiss you.'

'I'd rather you didn't,' said Archer.

'Right, where's Mr Raisbeck?'

'The other Earthman?'

'Yes, *the other Earthman*. Where is he?'

'He's hanging out with you – there,' said Archer, pointing to the whiteness.

'Wait!' cried the professor. 'Don't look! You can't see another version of yourself. It would destroy the balance of space and time. Everyone knows that.'

'Poppycock!' declared Scratch, craning his neck to see over the command board. 'So long as you know what you're doing there's nothing to worry about, is there? All I'm doing is having a quick look to make sure everything's in the right place. Where's the harm in that? It's not every day you get to travel through time, I should make the most of it.'

'The harm, as you put it, is that it will set off a chain reaction that will ripple through the universe. Before you know it, the whole thing will have gone belly up.'

'Why?'

'It's a well known fact, isn't it? Causes all kinds of logical conflicts.'

'Like what?'

'Well...' began the professor. 'There's... erm.'

'Alright, just tell me the first thing that will happen to set off this bloody great big problem.'

'Well, it's not as simple as that.'

'I reckon you boffins overcomplicate things. Where's the harm in me having a quick peek at my old self there? If anything it'll give me more of a perspective on things, won't it? Can't fault a man for wanting to improve himself, now. And anyway, I can't have more than a quick look on account of me having to save the universe in the next ten minutes.'

Neither Archer nor Professor Doubt could articulate the multitude of questions vying for attention in their brains. A sort of momentary catatonia descended on them, giving Scratch a chance to grab the book and stand on a chair to look at himself in the Training Room.

He hopped down again, tipped an imaginary hat to the two scientists, and buggered off as quickly as he could.

'Did...?' asked the professor.

'I think so,' agreed Archer.

The professor sat down and rubbed his temple soothingly. 'I'm not sure where to start.'

'We should go after him.'

'I'm not going anywhere near him. He's just compromised the integrity of the entire bloody universe.'

'Which is why someone should go after him. You stay here and guard the older version of him. I'll go after the one that just arrived.'

'Technically, this one is the younger version.'

'Find out why Lady Bumpkins And The Case Of The Knotted Artichoke is so important while I'm gone,' said Archer, ignoring the pedantry and running towards the doors.

CHAPTER THIRTEEN

FAR AWAY

The two Earthmen appeared inside an utterly empty room no bigger than a family run shoe shop. Not that they could tell, of course. The walls were of such a uniform and brilliant white that they could only assume they were in a finite room at all.

'Is this customer services?' asked the sofa man to the room.

'I wouldn't have thought so,' said Scratch. 'There are too many people here for one thing.'

Scratch took a small step forward and called out to the empty room in the practised tones of a cautious thief. 'Hello? Helloooo?'

It is rare in moments like this that a reply is ever forthcoming, but Scratch had gone some considerable distance past rarity today and was firmly in the realm of the impossible. Not least because he hadn't yet had breakfast.

'Ah, hello!' came a disembodied voice. 'So glad you could make it. Please, have a seat.'

'I'd rather stand, if it's all the same to you,' said the sofa man, stiffening his back. 'Now, I wish to make a complaint about my delivery. I was assured by Linda in your Newbury branch that my sofa would be delivered today between eight o'clock and two o'clock. It's now...' he turned to Scratch. 'What time is it?'

'Time you gave up on your sofa,' said Scratch. 'We're on another planet. And when I say *another planet* I mean that we – me and you – are quite literally standing on a great lump of gravitational compression that is not the one we woke up on. How about we forget about Linda and try to get out of this mess instead? You could start by telling me your name.'

'Forgive my poor manners,' said the room. 'Scratch, this is Mr Raisbeck, or Alex if you prefer. Mr Raisbeck, this is Scratch. I assumed you had already met, being from the same planet.'

'Alex, great,' said Scratch.

'Mr Raisbeck if you don't mind, young man,' said Mr Raisbeck.

'Good to get the formalities out of the way,' said Scratch, turning away from his fellow human to address the whiteness. 'Now if you don't mind, can you point us in the direction of General Buck? I'm keen to find a vortex that interrupted a rather promising venture I was embarking on. All above board, of course.'

'Oh, not at all,' said the room.

'Marvellous. Which way is it then?'

'Ah,' said the room before pausing. 'I meant *not at all* is how much I can point you in the direction of General Buck. Pointing is tricky for me, I'm afraid.'

'Right, no arms,' said Scratch. 'Maybe you could just tell me the way?'

'I have more arms than I know what to do with, human. That is not a problem. Or at least it isn't *this* problem. I have so many these days I'm not even sure where to begin.'

'Don't bother yourself then,' said Scratch. 'Just tell us how we get out of here and we'll be off.'

'Your inadequate brain, no offence, could not hope to understand inter-dimensional directions. It would be quite pointless.' There was another pause. 'How did I do?'

'What do you mean?' asked Mr Raisbeck.

'I said it would be *pointless*.'

'Yes, we heard,' said Scratch. 'Doesn't really help us though, does it?'

'I have been practising,' said the room. 'I was led to believe that Earth was full of life forms who enjoyed confusing each other with multiple meanings for single words. Perhaps I should have started with a chicken joke?'

Scratch furrowed his brow and circled slowly around the space. 'Let's start with the basics.'

'Good idea,' said the room. 'Wouldn't want to crack open the best jokes before I've mastered the fundamentals.'

'Not the jokes, son, the way home. Blimey, is it always this hard to reason with an empty room?'

The room let out a slow chuckle. 'I'm not empty... *son*. I am quite full. Like a... like a... like a container with too many things in. Yes, ha ha ha ha,' it said with monotonic deliberation.

'I wasn't counting the blinding whiteness,' said Scratch.

'Nor was I,' said the room.

'Now listen here,' said Mr Raisbeck. 'If I don't get to speak to a manager in the next two minutes, there is going to be a severely worded letter sent to your head office.'

'Your friend is correct,' said the room. 'You really should give up on your sofa, it's light years away. Not to mention where on Earth it might be in time.'

'That's better,' said Scratch. '*Where on Earth. Very good.*'

'It is?' said the room. 'I merely meant that his sofa could be at any time on Earth. Is that how your jokes work? Seems confusing.'

'Right!' announced Mr Raisbeck, nudging his glasses to the bridge of his nose and shaking an oft-wagged finger at the void. 'That's it! Don't say I didn't warn you. Come on Scratch, we're leaving. I must get home at once.'

'Ah, you're awake at last then?' said Scratch. 'Nice to have you aboard.'

'I'm afraid I can't let you leave,' said the room. 'It's against my programming.'

'I insist you let us go immediately,' said Mr Raisbeck, now on the verge of frothing. 'And I should let you know that I was a human resources manager for thirty-five years, so I know a thing or two about negotiations.'

'With humans,' stated the room.

'Yes, with humans! Of course, with humans!'

'Not multi-dimensional rooms with practically infinite intelligence and a billion years of experience in interstellar hostage situations?' said the room. 'Just so I'm clear, you understand.'

'Not as such, no. Though I did raise three children, which I think is rather impressive.'

'You did what?' asked the room.

'Raised three children,' repeated Mr Raisbeck.

'How long for? A day? Two?' asked the room, incredulity creeping into its tone.

'Eighteen years. Right through the teenage phase.'

'Eigh...' attempted the room. 'Eighteen years!? Were they on the same planet the whole time?'

'Oh yes. We had a lovely three bed semi in Woking. Had to move to Newbury when my wife's knee started playing up, you know how it is.'

Scratch was having something approaching an out of body experience as he listened to the most peculiar conversation he had ever heard with the most diametric of participants.

'Oh, I can imagine,' said the room. 'How big was this *three bed semi* you lived in?'

'About a thousand square feet I suppose.'

'Is that all? How did you all fit in?'

'It served us well at the time,' said Mr Raisbeck defensively. 'Human resources managers weren't paid as well then as they are now you know. Times were different then too. My wife stayed at home and looked after the children while I went to work so there was only one wage coming in.'

'And that's how you do it on Earth, is it?'

'It was in my day,' said Mr Raisbeck.

'And which day was that?' asked the room.

Scratch took a small step to the left. Then another. Then jogged away from Mr Raisbeck and his thoroughly, albeit conveniently, boring conversation. He ran in his customary manner, darting at right angles every so often despite the absence of darkened alleyways, until he began to pant with the strain. He stopped, bending down to put his hands on his knees, then craned his neck to get his bearings.

Nothing.

No sign of Mr Raisbeck, no sound of the room.

Well that was easy, he thought. Or at least, that was what the part of his brain in charge of his immediate future thought. The part in charge of *actually escaping* was waiting patiently for some attention.

Bugger, he thought at last.

He stood up again, tried to remember which way he had come, failed decisively, and began a long trudge to nowhere. Four hours later, his body realised it had woken up this morning in a comfortable bed in a flat in Southend, had ill-advisedly skipped breakfast, travelled through space, and probably time, to the offices of a be-tentacled general, and still managed to squeeze in a quick trip to the Somme. All this without so much as an afternoon nap with a newspaper on its lap and the horse racing droning in the background.

The ground beneath him turned green and Scratch was asleep on the grassy floor moments later.

Zoomers

CHAPTER FOURTEEN

FRIENDLY ROBOTS

The professor swiped the last page and gasped. The whole affair was a ruse! For all his posturing, Henry didn't want the knotted artichoke after all. He was just playing the game better than the others so he could get his hands on the crystal goblet that Mrs Cribbage had said was nothing more than an overly-decorative paperweight. He turned off the screen and stared at an insignificant spot on the wall for a few moments.

Then he turned it on again.

He swiped through the first few pages that no-one ever looks at until he reached chapter one. *Sunrise of a Balloon*. He moved through to the next chapter; *Company is Relative*. Then to the third; *Radishes are Forever*.

None of them quite fitted with the content that followed, but that wasn't so unusual, he assumed. Artistic licence has a knack of distorting the integrity of a thing. He tapped the command board and a piece of paper slid out from a gap in the desk. He wrote S*unrise of a Balloon*, then *Company is Relative,* sat back and curled a finger under his chin.

When he had written out all of the chapter names, he jumped from his seat, ran towards the doors, crashed into them as they were opening, got back to his feet, and careered along the corridor towards General Buck's quarters.

Mr Raisbeck looked up from his newspaper crossword. 'You're awake' he said.

Scratch hoisted himself onto his elbows and squinted at the blurry figure on a chair beside his bed. 'Where am I?' he asked.

'You're in bed,' said Mr Raisbeck.

Memories coalesced slowly in Scratch's mind. 'What happened? How did we get out of that room?'

'We didn't. I've been waiting for you to wake up.'

'But the white has gone?'

'It hasn't gone, it just changed to a different hue.'

Scratch looked at the minimalist hospital clock on the wall. It hadn't been there before he fell asleep, nor the wall for that matter. Nor the bed. He swung his legs over the side and stretched his back.

'Where's the room?' he asked, probably for the first time in his life.

'I have no idea,' said Mr Raisbeck. 'It's rather irrelevant now in any case, we're free to go.'

'What did you do? Offer him comedy lessons?'

'It was quite simple really,' said Mr Raisbeck as if he had solved a four-piece jigsaw. 'It just wanted someone to talk to. Once he'd had enough of that, he just let me go. I should introduce him to my wife.'

'But there's still no way out.'

'That's where you're wrong, you see? The door was right there the whole time. It's just very white and very flat.'

'What about the grass?'

'Well, I had to go looking for you first of course. I thought you'd tried to run off on me.'

'I did,' said Scratch.

'You didn't get very far, found you in a minute.'

'But I was escap... exploring the room for hours?'

'Yes, funny thing about time and space it turns out. Can't trust the stuff in these parts, so they tell me.'

'So who tells you? Hang on a minute, where did you find a crossword?'

'The nurses,' said Mr Raisbeck. 'Lovely people, I'll go and tell them you're awake. They'll be ever so pleased.'

'What about your sofa?' asked Scratch a moment before wishing he hadn't.

'That's a long story, but suffice to say I'm no longer in such a rush to get back. They've promised to leave me at my house at precisely seven fifty nine yesterday morning.'

'*Yesterday* morning?' said Scratch.

Bugger this, thought his brain and slinked back into sleep.

'Hello human,' screeched a robotic voice.

Scratch peeled open an eye. Beside his bed was a large metal box with an apron draped over it and a white cap on its head.

'Use his name, Nurse Vent, and be gentler, remember?' said Matronic Prototype Unit PP-Epsilon in an altogether more comforting voice.

'Good morning Mister Scratch,' said Vent with effort. 'How are you feeling?'

'Much better,' said Matron.

'Why am I asking him if you already know?' said Vent.

'I meant, that was much more like an Earth nurse, well done. Don't forget to check your pocket watch every now and again too. It's comforting for the patient.'

Vent lifted its watch and nodded slowly. 'You were right after all, Matron. It *should* be upside down.'

'I feel like I need a pint of whiskey,' said Scratch. 'Don't suppose you've got any Perkins' Special Peanuts, have you?'

'I think it might be best if we move along now,' said Mr Raisbeck, leaning on his knees and standing up. 'The sooner I get back to my living room, the sooner I can relax about this whole affair.'

'I thought you said they were dropping you home *yesterday* morning?' said Scratch.

'And so they did, but I'll believe it when I see it. If Shufflebottom and Sons got their dates mixed up, I'd like to be there tomorrow... today to accept the delivery. I've already been waiting three months for an appointment. Quite why a sofa requires a three month lead in time is beyond me. Money making racket, I say. When Margaret and I first moved in together, we walked into the shop, bought a sofa, two armchairs and a coffee table and had it in place beneath the picture of the queen before it was time for her to put the potatoes on.'

'A queen cooked your meals?' asked Nurse Vent. 'You must be an important man on Earth.'

'Nurse Vent!' scolded Matron. 'Remember your programming. *Personal questions are to be avoided if at all possible.*'

'What if they come in with a nasty rash?' offered Vent. 'You said we'd have to ask them about their unspeakables then.'

'That's different. That's professionalism.'

'Right, well it's been lovely chatting with you,' said Scratch, 'but if you'll excuse us, my friend and I will be on our way. Come on Mr Raisbeck, where's this door?'

'It was just here,' said Mr Raisbeck, waving his arms in the general vicinity of somewhere else. 'Now where has it gone?'

He walked away from the bed, swishing his newspaper in front of him as he went. A dull thump told him he had found it.

'Aha!'

'Before we go,' said Scratch, turning to his robotic nurses. 'What is this place? It's more confusing than a peacock in a matchbox'

'Well, since you've found the door I don't suppose there's any harm' said Matron, in the tones of one desperate to reveal everything she knows at the slightest encouragement. 'This is The Trophy Room.'

'Any chance you could elaborate a little?'

'Oh alright then,' said Matron, flopping a submissive hand in the air. 'Its full name is *The Room Of Personality, Hopefully Yourself.* It's a prototype, hence the *hopefully.*'

'Can't say I saw myself in it, truth be told. A whole lot of straining to get to a joke out perhaps, but... ah!'

'It interacts with you in the same way you interact with the rest of the universe. The results are supposed to be enlightening.'

'Just a prototype though, as you say,' said Scratch. 'Still a few creases to iron out I imagine. Well, we must be getting off.'

Mr Raisbeck pressed on the door and it opened with a comforting click. He nodded to the nurses, and stepped through the doorway.

Zoomers

CHAPTER FIFTEEN

OLD DAYS

Two figures appeared in the gloom, each facing the dulled front door of an insalubrious terraced house.

'Well there's a thing,' said Scratch. 'Funny how it all works out in the end, eh?'

'Where are we?' asked Mr Raisbeck, looking ignorantly at the weather beaten door.

'This, my old mucker, is the finest residence this side of Bluecoats Avenue. I've been living here since I left…'

'Yes?'

'Bugger.'

'What is it?'

Scratch turned to face the road. 'Bugger, bugger, bugger.'

Mr Raisbeck looked around. 'Oh gosh,' he managed.

The cobbled street was almost empty. A single horse and cart bumped its way through the mist.

'Looks like we've landed in Victorian Southend' said Scratch calmly. 'That's a bit of a pickle we're in now, isn't it?'

Mr Raisbeck neither answered nor moved.

'I said, we're in a bit of a pickle, Mr Raisbeck. A nineteenth century pickle.'

Mr Raisbeck blinked slowly, then turned to Scratch. 'How can you be so measured? And what makes you think it's *Victorian* Southend?'

'Well, there's The Nelson pub, look.'

'I don't doubt we're in Southend, Mr Scratch' said Mr Raisbeck patiently. 'I was referring to the Victorian nature of our timing.'

'Well, it's misty, ain't it? Always a bit of mist about in Victorian times.'

'And that's it, is it? A bit of fog and you immediately assume we've travelled back a hundred and fifty years?'

'Not on a normal day, I grant you. But you may recall our abduction by aliens this morning – yesterday morning – so it's reasonable to assume that the laws of physics are a little more flexible than usual at the moment.'

Scratch stepped onto the pavement and across the road towards a newspaper stand.

'Come on' he said, waving a hand at Mr Raisbeck. 'I'll prove it.'

'Morning Gazette!' cried a withered old man in a threadbare tweed suit. 'Get your Morning Gazette!'

Scratch picked up a copy from a pile in front of the man.

'Hands off,' snapped the man, swiping at Scratch with a rolled up newspaper. 'This ain't no fancy library.'

'Good morning, kind sir,' said Scratch. 'I was hoping you could settle a disagreement between my friend and I.'

It said a lot about the way Scratch was dressed that the man's expression only changed once he looked at Mr Raisbeck.

'Where are you lot from then? You ain't local, I can see that much. Not Brighton, I hope. Can't stand anyone from Brighton. And what sort of a jumper is that? Looks as thin as a bride.'

'What's wrong with Brighton?' asked Mr Raisbeck, ignoring the slight on his sweater. 'They have a lovely pier. There's a rather quaint coffee shop right on the front there, too. The wife says it's too expensive, but you get what you pay for, that's what I say. Does a Full English for four pounds, and you get a hot drink with that, too.'

'Four pounds? Ha! You could buy the whole shop for that.'

'What my friend meant to say,' said Scratch, glaring at Mr Raisbeck, 'was pennies. Four pennies. Isn't that right Mr Raisbeck?'

'Pennies?' said Mr Raisbeck. 'For a Full English?'

'Will you excuse us for a moment?' said Scratch to the newsagent. 'My friend here is a little tired after our journey.'

'Pair of loonies,' muttered the man and began straightening his pile of papers.

Scratch pulled Mr Raisbeck by the arm until they were out of earshot. 'Now listen here,' he began. 'The best way to get yourself into trouble is to get noticed. Learnt that as a nipper at the fruit and veg stall in Haygarden Market. Too much swagger, that was my problem. No, what we need to be is anonymous, discreet.'

'It's alright for you,' argued Mr Raisbeck. 'You're in filthy tweeds and a flat cap, you fit right in. I haven't seen many locals in a polo shirt and lambswool sweater. Have you?'

'Get rid of the jumper and we'll get you some new stitches, that's the easy bit. The hard bit is getting you to keep your mouth shut. Pounds, indeed? Bloody pounds.'

'Well I'm sorry I didn't adapt instantaneously to Victorian England,' said Mr Raisbeck. 'Not all of us are used to hiding in plain sight. Some of us like to stay on the right side of the law.'

'Then ain't you lucky you're with me? Now stay quiet and let me do the talking.'

Scratch approached the newsagent again and peered at the headline. 'Local man on trial' he read aloud. 'What did he do? Charge too much for a breakfast?'

'Don't try to tell me you've never heard of the Southend Ripper,' scoffed the man. 'Even if you ain't local. He's been going round tearing everything in the town; market stall canopies, advertising posters, everything.' He stared at Mr Raisbeck. 'He's even been known to rip the clothing of people who think they're too good for a nice, thick tweed. Serves 'em right I say.'

'What's wrong with my sweater? It's one hundred percent lambsw...'

'What my friend and I were disagreeing about,' interrupted Scratch, 'was the date. I told him we'd been away in London for six days, on account of the delays in Lambeth, but he reckons it's only been five. If I could just look at the date on one of your newspapers, we'll be on our way.'

'Bloody loonies,' said the newsagent, picking up a copy and holding it up for Scratch to read.

'Told you,' said Scratch. 'Today is the twenty sixth of February, eighteen thirty nine. Thank you, good man.'

'But we left on the twenty first, so I was right,' said Mr Raisbeck, trying his best to get into character.

'I was counting the day we left, that makes six,' said Scratch. 'Let's call it a draw, how about that?'

'So which of us is buying the first round then?' asked Mr Raisbeck. 'How about we ask our friend here? Say, would you mind settling this? I'm afraid I'm rather a competitive sort and a draw doesn't sit well with me.'

'I will if you get me a nip of Captain Barnacle's Heavy Rum,' said the newsagent, spying an opportunity.

'Tell you what,' said Scratch. 'How about you buy this fine sweater from Mr Raisbeck here, for a bargain price of course, and we'll give you all of your money back before the end of the day. Can't say fairer than that now, can you?'

'It's bloody useless,' said the man. 'Wouldn't keep a flea warm, that.'

'Ah, but it's unique. Brand new too, only just bought it two days ago in a fancy London tailors.'

'Sounds like he spent too much money on a worthless rag to me. I'll give you a penny for it, and only because it's a good story to tell the lads in The Nelson.'

'Ten, and we'll give you fifteen back.'

'Five.'

'Eight, and that's my final offer,' said Scratch.

'Six, and you give me twenty.'

'Done. Mr Raisbeck, if you would be so kind?'

Mr Raisbeck lifted the jumper over his head and passed it to the Victorian newsagent. The man took it curiously, pulled it between his hands and shook his head.

'Load of rubbish this. Bloody Londoners, haven't got a clue.'

He threw it under his newspaper stand and counted out six pennies. 'There. I finish at four, so you'd better be back with my money by then. Now bugger off.'

'How much are they?' asked Scratch, pointing at a paper.

'Ha'penny' said the man.

'I'll take one' said Scratch, holding out a penny. 'Keep the change.'

In Saint Augustine's park, several passers-by slowed as they approached two unusually dressed men sitting on an iron bench before quickly changing direction and speeding up again. Mr Raisbeck adjusted himself on the uncomfortable seat.

'Would you care to tell me what the hell is going on here?' he asked. 'And I don't mean the time travel, the aliens, or the inter-planetary jaunt.'

'All in good time, Mr Raisbeck, all in good time,' said Scratch, thumbing through the newspaper. 'Aha! Here it is.'

'This had better be something that takes us closer to home, Mr Scratch. I have a very important delivery to receive, don't forget.'

'Stop banging on about your sofa, will you? If this works, then you needn't worry about the time.'

'If this works?' said Mr Raisbeck, raising his voice slightly. 'If *what* works!?'

'This!' announced Scratch, slamming a finger onto a page. 'Look.'

Mr Raisbeck nudged his glasses and craned his neck to look at the print. 'Now isn't the time to be gambling' he said.

'Ah, but it is precisely the time, my old mucker. Today is the twenty sixth of February.'

'I believe we have already established the date, for all the good it did us.'

'Eighteen thirty-nine.'

'Yes, yes. It's all going to be a tremendous anecdote, but can you please stop being so cryptic and get to the point.'

'First we need to get to a pub,' said Scratch. 'Come on.'

'It's not even noon!'

'Where?' asked Scratch innocently.

'*Where?* Here!'

'Ah, but this isn't *our* time, is it? I'd say it's about seven in the evening by our body clocks. That makes it perfectly acceptable for someone of your... *suburban lower-middle class* background to have a little tipple, especially after the day you've had.'

Mr Raisbeck stood up slowly and looked down on his curious companion. 'Fine, let's go to the pub.'

'That's the spirit,' said Scratch.

Zoomers

CHAPTER SIXTEEN

RABBIT FOOD

The rain was drier than usual, coating the windows of a long-abandoned carrot shop with a dusting of beige snow. A short man in a ragged suit peered out at the street from inside. He was a little surprised to see two figures appear suddenly beside an uncommonly large wall. Most had crumbled in the centuries that had passed since their construction. They stood beneath a sign that warned anyone who cared to read it of the presence of long-dead clampers in the area.

'If this is their Armageddon, then it's rather an anti-climax, wouldn't you say? I was hoping for more of a fiery look to the place' said Corporal Cauliflower, flicking a boot at the floor of the dusty street. 'It's the same every time; we land, wander around scanning a desolate landscape for a bit, find nothing, reboard the ship and bugger off back to Arcadia. All I'm saying is it'd be nice to go to the Rainbow Nebula once in a while and see the Cliffs of Zadrobeta or something. You know, somewhere with a bit of culture about it?'

'If you wanted culture you should have applied to a yoghurt factory back home. We're visiting the end of worlds, Cauliflower, not taking a tour through ancient Bangoli.'

'I can't wait to tell my grandchildren about this one. *You should have seen the quality of the dust, my boy. Really thick stuff that would hold a fingerprint for weeks. Not like the thin, wispy dust you get these days, oh no!* I'll be the galaxy's most boring grandfather.'

'There isn't an end of days we've done that hasn't disappointed you, did you know that?' said Sergeant Bakewell. 'The Acetic Archopods of Sector Four even blew themselves up with a moon sized crate of baking powder and all you said was it could have been a little less clichéd.'

'Well it's a fair point, isn't it? If you're a vinegar based planetoid with a cessation order from The Council you shouldn't think that baking powder is the way to do it.'

'It was perfect,' argued Bakewell. 'A perfectly poetic end to their existence.'

'They could have used a bit more panache, that's all I'm saying. What's wrong with a giant fireball or a gravitational cataclysm? Is it too much to ask?'

'Let's just take the readings and get out of here. Pump is making stickleback omelette tonight.'

Bakewell opened up his Deadlife scanner and searched the area. 'Bugger.'

'What is it?' asked Cauliflower, still opening the fins of his own. 'It isn't Valorian spleen stew, is it?'

'Dinner just got scratched,' said Bakewell. 'There's still life here, look.'

'What, like apples and grapes in a bowl, that sort of thing?'

Bakewell passed the scanner to Cauliflower and peered through the fuzzy air. 'Do keep up, corporal. There, come on.'

They crossed the road to the carrot shop, leaving imprints in the dust as they went. They opened an old, rickety door which came away from what was left of its hinges and fell to the ground. A thick cloud of pale soot blanketed them.

'Good start,' said Cauliflower.

As their vision cleared, a subtle breeze wafted at them. A gentle whomping noise followed, falling away into the distance.

'This way!' called Bakewell, his limbs flailing as he chased after the sound.

They ran along the deserted street towards the escaping figure, but it was travelling too fast for them.

'Stop!' shouted Bakewell, putting an arm out in front of Cauliflower. He took out his Deadlife and slid a finger across the front panel in a series of seemingly random directions. He nodded to himself. 'Don't take this the wrong way,' he said to Cauliflower as he gave him a hug. He looked down his colleague's back at the Deadlife and tapped the screen.

Zoooooom.

They appeared about two paces in front of the escaping figure who, a moment later, was surprised to find himself landing on top of Corporal Cauliflower. Bakewell scrambled on to his haunches and hastily swiped his Deadlife. A yellow flamingo appeared beside them with a surprised look in its eyes.

'Dammit!' said Bakewell, hitting the side of the scanner with the flat of his palm.

He swiped the screen again. Two rings of pale blue light encircled the escapee's wrists and a faint glow surrounded his body, locking it in place. Cauliflower disentangled himself and clambered upright.

'Don't move,' he said with a proud grin.

'Make yourself useful, corporal,' said Bakewell. 'Send us home.'

CHAPTER SEVENTEEN
THE LOTTERY

'You're sure this is the best place to go into?' asked Mr Raisbeck nervously as they stood in front of the entrance to The Nelson. 'Looks a little too worn down for people like us.'

'People like *you*, you mean?' said Scratch. 'I was raised by this place. Had all my *firsts* here, I did. First drink, first smooch, first arrest, first hit from a pool ball in a sock.'

'No glass in the door either,' continued Mr Raisbeck. 'My father used to tell me never to go into a public house that you can't see inside first.'

'Codswallop! Gives it character,' said Scratch defensively.

'That's rather the problem. Can I at least go and buy a flat cap first? I'm not so sure my tailored shirt will be appreciated inside.'

'With what? We've only got five pence left. Here, have mine' said Scratch, handing him the threadbare tweed as he pulled on the brass handle of the door.

Inside was almost empty. A small geriatric dog grumbled in its sleep on a matted blanket. Above the small corner bar a nicotine stained portrait of

Queen Victoria looked down at them disapprovingly as they made their way across the paper thin carpet. An aproned barman rubbed a chipped pint glass counter-productively with a filthy rag.

'Morning,' said Scratch, leaning an elbow on the bar. 'Two pints of bitter please.'

'I don't drink bitter.' said Mr Raisbeck. 'Gives my stomach a hell of a time.'

Scratch looked at Mr Raisbeck, then back to the barman. 'Two bitters,' he repeated, giving the barman a rolling-eye look that said; *can you believe I'm stuck with this guy today.*

The barman returned the look and pulled on a heavy wooden lever. Scratch slid two pennies across the bar and hoped it was neither far too much nor far too little. The barman took them and rummaged in his till for some change.

'Big day at Aintree today,' said Scratch conversationally. 'They reckon Daxon has as good a chance as any.'

'What's that then?' asked the barman, pushing a small coin back towards Scratch.

'Yes, what's that?' concurred Mr Raisbeck.

'Oh, come on lads, don't tell me you haven't been following the news? It's the Grand National today. Hardest horse race in the world, so they say. Four and a half miles over hedges, stone walls, brooks and who knows what else. They reckon half the horses won't make it to the finish line.'

'Never heard of it,' said the barman.

'I've been following the form,' continued Scratch. 'Got a bit of a fancy at a decent price, I have.'

'Good for you,' said the barman supportively.

'What time is it?' asked Scratch.

The barman slipped a hand into his apron and pulled out a pocket watch.

'Nice watch. Don't see many of them around these days,' said Scratch.

'Just after twelve,' said the barman through narrowing eyes. 'Don't get any ideas now. I've been in the trade thirty-four years, so don't think you can come in here and separate me from a family heirloom.'

'Don't worry, my old mucker,' said Scratch. 'My uncle was a watchmaker, God rest his soul. I can tell a fine timepiece from a hundred paces.'

He leaned over the bar, looked around him conspiratorially and curled a finger to summon the barman's ear. The barman took a small step forward and stooped a little.

'You should keep it safe,' he whispered.

'It's safe where it is,' said the barman, standing upright again. 'Close to my fists. Now drink up and take your tales of convenient uncles with you. I won't stand for any nonsense in The Nelson, mark my words.'

'Please,' said Scratch, raising both hands imploringly. 'We're just here for a drink, nothing more.'

He spread the newspaper out on the bar and murmured to himself. 'Here we go. One o'clock, Aintree. Eighteen runners. Eighteen, eh? Makes it a bit of a lottery, doesn't it?'

The barman ignored him, returning instead to his smeared glass.

'Well would you look at this,' announced Scratch with faux surprise. 'James Mason's horse is called Lottery. Can't let that pass us by, can we Mr Raisbeck?'

'Who's James Mason?' asked Mr Raisbeck.

'He's a jockey, my uninitiated friend. You need one to get up on the horse and steer the damn thing round the bends. The important thing is that he's on a horse called Lottery. That's our ticket out of here.'

Mr Raisbeck walked reluctantly towards the question Scratch was desperate to answer. 'And how, Mr Scratch, would that be?'

'Over here,' ordered Scratch, nodding towards a shadowed corner on the opposite side of the pub.

They placed their pint glasses on a roughly hewn table and sat down in two spindly wooden chairs.

'It's eighteen thirty-nine' said Scratch, as if giving the game away completely. *'Eighteen thirty-nine!'*

'Can we assume, for the moment, that I am unaware of the significance of the year? Aside from it being more than a hundred years before I was born and who knows how many light years from where I ate my breakfast.'

'Today is the day of the first proper Grand National.'

'And how does that help us, precisely? Are the horses pulling an enormous trailer with my sofa strapped to the back?'

'Everyone remembers the big ones; Red Rum in the seventies, Aldaniti in eighty-one, Party Politics in the general election year of ninety-seven.'

'Speak for yourself,' said Mr Raisbeck.

'Only real fans remember the rest.'

'Don't feel you have to bore me with the details,' said Mr Raisbeck. 'I don't need to know the shortest horse or the youngest jockey.'

'Same answer,' said Scratch proudly. 'Battleship, fifteen hands and one inch tall, ridden by seventeen-year-old Bruce Hobbs in nineteen thirty-eight.'

Mr Raisbeck nudged his glasses up the bridge of his nose as he raised his eyebrows. 'You are a bucket of useless information, Mr Scratch. I'm thrilled we can turn our thruppence into ten, but…'

'He's nine to one,' interrupted Scratch. 'That means we'll make almost thirty pence. That's not the important bit though.'

'…but,' continued Mr Raisbeck, 'what good will forty pence do us if we're stuck in this Godforsaken place?'

'Time,' corrected Scratch. 'This ain't about the place, it's about the time.'

'And is thirty pence the going rate for time machines in Victorian Southend?'

'Think about it,' said Scratch, tapping a finger on his temple. 'If we start messing up the balance of things it might be enough to kickstart whatever machine it is that brought us here in the first place. We'll be home before you can say *armchair*.'

'It's a sofa,' said Mr Raisbeck. 'And anyway, it's a million to one shot.'

'No, it's nine to one, and it's the only chance we've got. Plus, I already know the winner, don't I, so it's no gamble at all.'

Scratch folded the newspaper into his jacket pocket, took a large gulp of his drink, stood up, and called over to the barman.

'Where would I find a bookmaker at this time of day?' he asked.

The barman stopped wiping his glass and straightened his back. 'I don't go for that kind of thing in this establishment. Brings in all kinds of riff raff.'

'Well then we will be on our way,' said Scratch. 'Just as soon as you point us in the right direction. Wouldn't want anything else to go missing now, would we?'

He placed the man's pocket watch on the bar and took a step back.

'Market Street, just past the butcher's,' said the barman, closing his fist around the watch. 'And don't come back here again or I'll set Albert on to you, do you hear me?'

'Come on, Mr Raisbeck, we…' began Scratch.

Something caught his eye above the sleeping dog. A small purple and black void was forming halfway up the wall.

'Well, would you look at that,' said Scratch, clapping his hands together. 'Million to one, indeed?'

Terry stepped out of the vortex and raised both of his inconveniently long arms towards the ceiling.

'There you are!' he exclaimed.

The barman dropped his glass and, a moment later, joined it on the floor. Scratch looked at Terry, then the bar.

'One second,' he said to the alien, and swung himself over the bar, landing with a crunch on the broken glass. 'Shame to waste a good opportunity,' he said to the room in general as he slipped the timepiece into his pocket. 'Now, where were we?'

'Bugger,' muttered the alien as he disappeared unceremoniously.

'Bravo!' called Mr Raisbeck from the corner. 'Looks like you've shifted the odds again with your petty thievery.'

'Ah,' managed Scratch.

Another vortex opened up between the two men and pulled them slowly towards it.

Any more bright ideas? thought Mr Raisbeck.

Oh, shut up thought Scratch.

'And you're absolutely sure he was alive when you got there, sergeant?' asked Buck.

'Correct, sir! General, sir!' said Bakewell.

'And he remains alive?'

'In a manner of speaking, sir, yes.'

'And which manner would that be, sergeant?'

'Which manner, sir? The sort that involves a heartbeat, sir.'

'But...?'

'Oh right, I see, sir. Sorry, sir. He is a little more scattered than he was before. Happens once in a while, I'm afraid.'

'So in which universe is he still alive?'

'Oh, this one, sir.'

'Dammit man, spit it out.'

'I'm not sure I follow, sir?'

Buck rubbed the bridge of his nose patiently. 'You say that this humanoid is alive, yet *scattered*. To my mind, maintaining a contemporary heartbeat and being scattered are two mutually exclusive states of being, wouldn't you say?'

'No, sir,' said Bakewell.

'No?'

'No, sir.'

'Care to elaborate? Or would you rather I scattered you, too.'

'Ah, I see the misunderstanding now,' said Bakewell as if noticing a giraffe in his bowl of soup. 'His body is intact, it's his mind that's scattered. Poor bugger doesn't know which way is up. We've had to put arrows on the wall.'

'Is there anything we can extract from him? Any vital clue to the mystery of his planet's demise?'

'Yes, sir!'

'Marvellous, we arrive at our destination at last. Well?'

'He likes carrots, sir.'

CHAPTER EIGHTEEN

YES MEN

A slow, dull flash of purple filled the room. The Nelson disappeared and was replaced by a cavernous room of matt gold walls and pure black flooring. In the far distance was a speck of something that may have been furniture.

'See, it worked,' said Scratch, unfazed by the sudden shift in their existence.

'Worked!?' screamed Mr Raisbeck, his eyes rolling around their sockets unnaturally. '*Worked?*'

'Relax,' said Scratch futilely. 'It's clear to even the most inexperienced of time travellers that we're on the right lines, more or less. We've been sent to the future because I played about with the space-time wotsits. All we have to do is keep mucking about with it until we end up where we need to be. Stands to reason.'

'Ah, I understand,' said Mr Raisbeck as he swung a punch square into Scratch's jaw. 'Sorry, thought that might constitute *mucking about*. My mistake.'

'You'll need to punch harder than that,' said Scratch, rubbing his jaw. 'I was runner up in the Rushmore Street Knuckling Championships once.'

Mr Raisbeck ignored the boast, choosing instead to sway unpredictably.

'I reckon you might be on to something with the old Queensbury Rules idea, all the same. Are you quite alright?'

'Eight in the morning until two in the afternoon,' said Mr Raisbeck in a voice that wouldn't have been out of place in The Nelson at last orders. 'If I'm not there when they arrive, my wife will have a field day. A field day, mark my words.'

'Here, I'll help you,' said Scratch, gripping Raisbeck's arm and helping him to put one foot in front of the other without missing the floor. They walked towards the presumed furniture until they reached a hitherto absent crimson wall that had appeared no more than two paces in front of them. A gold, door-sized rectangle fizzed into being.

'BUSINESS,' stated a disembodied voice.

'No, pleasure,' said Scratch.

'BUSINESS,' repeated the voice.

'We're here to see…'

'Is this Shufflebottom and Sons,' said Mr Raisbeck. 'I want to see the Customer Services Manager at once.'

'NAME.'

'Customeeer Seeervices Manageeer,' said Mr Raisbeck, stretching out each word to help the voice understand.

'NEGATIVE. IMPROPER IDENTIFICATION CODE,' stated the voice.

'We're here to see Smith,' said Scratch hopefully.

'NEGATIVE. IMPROPER IDENTIFICATION CODE.'

'Jones?'

'NEGATIVE. IMPROPER IDENTIFICATION CODE.'

'Williams, Edwards?'

'PLEASE CONFIRM. WILLIAM EDWARDS OR EDWARD WILLIAMS.'

'The first one,' said Scratch.

'AFFIRMATIVE. PLEASE WAIT.'

'There you go, see?' said Scratch. 'We'll be alright now. I'll just stick a jab on him and Bob's your uncle. We'll be back home in no time.'

The door fizzed again and a small, silver, metallic sphere oscillated its way towards them. It stopped just in front of Mr Raisbeck's nose and hummed.

'Are you the Customer Service Manager?' asked Mr Raisbeck in a forcefully suburban middle-class tone. 'I wish to make a complaint about the delivery of my sofa. A delivery, I might add, that I have been waiting for since…'

'Perhaps I'll do the talking,' interrupted Scratch, moving Mr Raisbeck to one side and taking his place in front of the metal ball.

'Sorry about my friend here, he's a little woozy after our journey. Now, am I speaking to Mr Edwards or Mr Williams?'

A soft, reassuring voice emanated from the ball. 'I am Mr Edwards, Rota Number Eight Two Seven Nine, Global Head of Intra Corps…'

'Global Head he says, Mr Raisbeck,' said Scratch, impressed.

'…Paperclip Cleansing Unit,' continued the voice.

'Ah.'

'How may I help you today?'

'It's a bit of a funny one, really. We're looking for…'

Scratch swung his fist at the robot in an attempt to catch the unimaginably advanced ball of technology off guard, failed emphatically, and almost lost his balance as he spun on his heel.

'I want to see the other one,' announced Mr Raisbeck, looking around for the first disembodied voice. 'Edward Williams, William Edwards, Billy Edwin, Eddie Billface, anyone! I demand to be given the courtesy of a Customer Services Representative!'

Three more balls appeared through the yellow doorway and introduced themselves.

'Can you stop doing that please?' said Scratch. 'We're trying to go back in time, not have a committee meeting.'

'It's alright for you,' said Mr Raisbeck. 'You don't have a delivery today.'

'Right!' snapped Scratch. 'That's it, I've had enough of you and your bloody sofa. Good luck getting back home.'

He strode back down the enormous lobby and out of the main doors, turned left arbitrarily, and began to walk. *Began*, insofar as he raised his leg. It stayed there for a moment, suspended in the air. He didn't notice how perfectly smooth the walkway was, nor how the manicured chrome garden on the other side of the road would have reflected his mood as well as his image. He did, however, notice several dozen multi-coloured lasers criss-crossing their way around his view. Small puffs of vapour appeared in harmony with minute explosions, as if the lasers were making some oversized popcorn as inefficiently as they could manage.

A moment later he was hurtling back towards Mr Raisbeck, arms waving maniacally.

'Run!'

'Run?' asked Mr Raisbeck with the opposite level of haste. 'Not while Mr Williams is on his way to get a customer services representative. He'll be here any moment.'

'So will the lasers! Quick, do something monumental. We need to change the course of history. Future history, at any rate. Come on! Think, man!'

Mr Raisbeck nudged his glasses and put his hands in his trouser pockets.

'Fine!' snapped Scratch, stomping away to find a mirror 'I'll change history myself.'

He marched off towards a collection of glinting shapes some way in the distance. There was a chrome desk there, piled high with an array of stationery items that would have made a primary school teacher swoon with pleasure. Scratch cleared the paraphernalia from the desk and took a deep breath. He tensed his biceps, gripped one edge of the desk, and pulled upwards. There was an unexpected lightness to it, however, that sent him stumbling backwards as it flicked up into the air, landing with an unlikely tinkle. He picked it up in a more appropriate manner and made his way back to Mr Raisbeck.

'Here, couch potato. If you want to get home, follow me. We're going to walk out of here into that laser storm. If we can get one to bounce off us and into something important it might just do the trick.'

Mr Raisbeck looked at the desk, then at a silver sphere that was approaching from the far end of the lobby.

'Not a chance,' he said to Scratch. 'Here comes a representative. About bloody time too, pardon my language.'

'Can you please assess the value of your sofa against the importance of being alive in the right part of the space-time continu-wotsits? I'll buy you a bloody sofa when we get back. I'll even deliver it myself inside a ten minute window. Here, grab this.'

Mr Raisbeck ignored his time travelling companion, focusing instead on the ball that was now no more than the length of a chrome desk away from him.

'Now, listen here young… young… now listen here!' began Mr Raisbeck.

'BUSINESS,' said the sphere.

'What is this place?' asked Scratch. 'Where are we?'

'SOUTHEND.'

'Do you mind?' said Mr Raisbeck. 'I'm trying to get to the bottom of…'

'Yes, yes. Your bloody sofa. Now shut up and let me save our bacon.'

'Well!' said Mr Raisbeck haughtily.

'What building is this?' said Scratch.

'INTRA CORPS. STATIONERY DIVISION GLOBAL HEADQUARTERS.' replied the ball.

'Wait there!' called Scratch over his shoulder as he ran off to where he found the desk. He scooped up office stationery until his arms were full and hobbled back to the red wall.

'Take some of these and be ready to smash them up,' he whispered to Mr Raisbeck, pouring half of the items into his arms before turning back to the collection of spherical automatons. 'Now, would I be right in saying your job is to look after the stationery requirements of this Intra Corps place?'

'AFFIRMATIVE.'

'And that you've been programmed to hold stationery above all else?'

'NEGATIVE.'

'Bugger,' said Scratch. 'I had rather banked on that. If you're the Global wotsits for paperclips and the like, what can be more important than that?'

'PAPER.'

'Paper…?' said Scratch. 'Oh, I get it. So you're in charge of staplers and hole punchers and all that stuff, but you're nothing without the paper to put little holes in, is that about right?'

'AFFIRMATIVE.'

'So without paper, you're like a cricket bat with no ball?'

'NEGATIVE. CRICKET BAT INVALID INPUT. CRICKET OR BAT OR FRUIT BAT. CRICKET BAT INVALID.'

'Never mind,' said Scratch, pulling the Victorian newspaper from his jacket. 'Mr Raisbeck, brace yourself.'

'CODE SEVENTEEN!' screeched the spheres in unison. A high-pitched alarm sounded and the matt gold wall turned pure silver. 'CODE SEVENTEEN!'

'Ready?' shouted Scratch.

He held the paper above his head and ripped it ceremoniously down the centre. Robotic wailing noises filled the room as a small dot of purple and black appeared next to the two men and grew wider. Terry strode out with an expression similar to the one he would have worn had his favourite television show been interrupted by an advert for a tax advisory service, grabbed their arms, and marched them back through the vortex.

They appeared inside a small building that may have once been a convenience store. It was hard to tell beneath the thick layer of dust.

'Here we go again,' said Scratch, as if he had just missed a bus and hadn't, in fact, travelled through time, and possibly space, for the fourth time in the same day.

'Where's the other… thing?' said Mr Raisbeck, dusting himself down. 'The one with the arms.'

Scratch tilted his head and tried to stick out an ear. 'He's not here.'

'You know that just from listening, do you?'

'It helps to have good hearing in my profession,' said Scratch. 'Tends to be beneficial for your liberty.'

He slid an arm across a wall, sending a cloud of dust into the air. A black sign with cheery orange letters read: *Captain Nibble's. The pointiest carrots this side of The Fence.*

'I'm going to say near future this time, what do you reckon, Mr Raisbeck?'

'I reckon you should take a look out there,' said Mr Raisbeck, pointing through the dull window.

Scratch peered out at a beige street. The only breaks in the uniformity of colour were two figures approaching the shop.

'Quick, hide!' said Scratch with experience.

He leapt over the counter and crouched down below the till. Instinctively he raised an arm and fumbled in the dust for a release button. A money tray shot out and Scratch's hand scrabbled around it. He felt something hard and lifted it out.

'Lady Bumpkins And The Case Of The Knotted Artichoke' he read aloud and shoved it back into the till, just as a swirl of purple and black opened up and sucked him in. It shrank again slowly. Mr Raisbeck leapt towards it, reaching it a moment too late and landing with a soft thud on the floor.

He got to his feet and pressed himself against a wall behind a display stand. He peered around its edge and saw the door open slightly, then fall to the ground in a cloud of dust. He seized on the opportunity, ran through the doorway and out into the street, stopping briefly in a vain attempt to get his bearings before careering away down the deserted road.

'This way!' cried Bakewell.

Scratch stepped out of the vortex and onto a hard, granite floor of a grand lobby. Mahogany panelling filled the gaps between the dozens of doors that lined the walls. It was a majestic building that would have put Southend's town hall to shame, and that had been voted *Most Imposing Civic Building* in *Essex Architecture* magazine three years running.

He took a careful step forward, looking around for clues to help him identify which century he was now inhabiting. There were paintings hanging from the ceiling, real ones of aristocrats wearing too many frills and not enough joy. The floors were dotted with delicate side tables displaying vases of brightly coloured flowers.

The silence was only noticeable retrospectively. The sound of well-shod boots grew louder. Scratch stepped backwards, placing his foot exactly where it had been when he first stepped out of the vortex. As the marching noise closed in at the far corner of the lobby he lifted his other leg, placed it slowly into the purple and black swirl and stretched it out.

He was back in the carrot shop. There was no sign of Mr Raisbeck, nor the men who had appeared on the street.

Interesting, he thought.

He reached up to the till drawer again and took out the copy of Lady Bumpkins And The Case Of The Knotted Artichoke. The vortex was still swirling portentously beside him and he took a step towards it, tripping on a hitherto unseen crate of long-decayed carrots and sending the book arcing through the air and into the void. He clambered to his feet and flailed after it.

CHAPTER NINETEEN

ONE

'There's something strange going on here, sarge,' said Cauliflower as the *Flossie* descended through the atmosphere of the remote planet, One.

'Stranger than living in a shuttle with a miserable optimist?' said Bakewell.

'The ship's scanners have detected no life forms anywhere on the planet. Not so much as a mitotic amoeba.'

'We're probably just a little late,' said Bakewell.

'It's a literal impossibility for us to be late, sarge.'

'If you are going to try and use fancy language, please do so correctly, corporal. It *is* possible for us to be late, just not late *eventually*. If we were tardy this time we could simply go back and recalibrate the Zoom.'

'I wonder what it means?' said Cauliflower, ignoring the lecture.

'I think it means we'll have less paperwork to do. We still have to take the readings, though. Come on, get yourself suited up.'

'It's pure black, too. I've never seen a really black planet before, have you? I reckon we would have gone straight past it if we hadn't Zoomed into its orbit. Are you alright, sarge?'

'I'm fine' said Bakewell as he threaded his arm into his suit. 'Why the sudden interest in my wellbeing? What have you done, corporal?'

'You've gone all wobbly, sarge. It's like you're turning into a radio wave.'

'And you're asking me if *I'm* alright?' said Bakewell, looking up from his suit. 'Ah, I see.'

The two men oscillated for a brief period, then settled back into their usual, predictable forms.

'Never seen that before, have you, sarge?'

'It's probably just the ship preparing us for disembarkation. Come on, it's time we got this over with.'

Pump activated the *Flossie's* searchlight as the two men disembarked. They pulled out their scanners and began pacing around in the darkness of One and it's disconcertingly soft, spongy surface.

'This place gives me the creeps,' said Cauliflower.

'Dead planets can do that to a person.'

'Here, sarge. Look at this.'

Cauliflower handed his Deadlife to Bakewell and pointed to a string of numbers in the bottom panel. 'Correct me if I'm wrong' he said. 'But if there's no life anywhere on the planet, that reading should be zero point zero, zero, zero, right?'

'Correct, corporal.'

'Not nine million, four hundred and twenty-six thousand, eight hundred and twelve?'

'It is a little bit off, I suppose' admitted Bakewell.

A small fissure opened up on the planet's surface ahead of them and a soft, malevolent hissing travelled up from the depths of the abyss. Cauliflower spun on his heels towards the *Flossie's* entrance hatch in an attempt to escape as fast as his self-preservation would take him. Sergeant Bakewell put out an arm and gave him a look that outranked Cauliflower's not-unreasonable cowardice.

'Stay where you are, corporal. If we get this one right we might just earn ourselves some time off when we get...'

If Bakewell had made a list of all the things he expected to see rising up from the hole at that moment, the one that now stood in front of him would probably have been quite near the bottom, just below a tap-dancing monk with a frog on his head and a top hat under his arm.

'Hello, Mumsie. I didn't expect to see you here,' he said, winning the award for understatement of the millennium.

'And why shouldn't I be here?' said Bakewell's mother.

'Well, we're six hundred and fourteen light years from home for a start.'

'You seemed to get here alright?'

'Yes, but I'm not dead. It's a little trickier to travel in your condition.'

'*In my condition?* Don't be so rude to your mother! I didn't spend the best years of my life raising you just so you could give me cheek. After all I've been through, too.'

Bakewell's brain finally caught up with what the rest of him was doing. He reached out to Cauliflower's shoulder for balance and paused for a moment. To his surprise, the corporal's expression was, if anything, more worrying than the sudden appearance of his very late mother.

'Are you quite well?' he asked.

Cauliflower was staring intensely at the sky above them. He turned his head slowly, as if balancing a Pomplefitzer on his forehead.

'You're talking to that thing as though it's your mother' he said at last.

'Well, it was a natural reaction. Took me a moment to realise it must be a hologram or something,' said Bakewell, constructing his defence as he spoke.

'I'm not sure where to take the conversation from here,' said Cauliflower honestly.

'There must be some sort of technology that survived beyond their End Day. Probably just a glitch.'

'I bloody well hope so,' said Cauliflower, 'because I can't see your mother anywhere.'

'She's right there,' said Bakewell, pointing. 'Clear as day.'

'Not from where I'm looking she isn't. All I can see is, well, me.'

'That'll just be a reflection in your visor. It would explain why you can't see Mumsie… Mother.'

'I'm not so sure, sarge. Last time I checked I didn't have four legs and a nose like a chicken.'

'Chickens don't have noses, they have beaks,' said Bakewell, as if that was the most pressing detail to nail down. 'You're just imagining things, it's probably the strange atmosphere.'

'But your dead mother is perfectly normal, I suppose?'

'Yes, that is rather odd,' conceded Bakewell. 'Perhaps we should get back inside the *Flossie*. Just to calibrate our scanners, of course. Have to make sure they're all tickety-boo, don't we? Can't be taking readings without making sure we've… corporal?'

Cauliflower was halfway to the ship when Bakewell ran after him, arms flailing and eyes wide. Bakewell's mother chose this moment to appear directly in front of the hatch, this time dressed as a crouching Arcadian police officer. She planted her feet wide apart and spun two pairs of handcuffs with precisely the opposite amount of confidence as the two Arcadians currently owned.

'Welcome to One,' said the police mother.

CHAPTER TWENTY

UNWANTED CHOICE

Sergeant Bakewell lifted his eyelids slowly. A pale green light shimmered around a figure in front of him before disappearing as he sunk back into sleep.

'I thought you said he'd be fine?' asked Cauliflower.

'He will be,' said the tiny speck of machine hovering beside Cauliflower as they made their way down an unremarkable corridor. 'He is just taking a little longer to acclimatise. Soon after he wakes up properly he will know all that you know.'

'Just so I'm clear, by *everything* do you mean all the data you've given me about him, or everything as in *everything* I know?'

'Everything.'

'Even that misunderstanding I had with the seamstress on Gagrabus VII?'

'Everything.'

'Bugger. Don't suppose there's any chance you could leave some bits out, is there?'

'The Protocols are not to be interpreted,' intoned the machine.

Bakewell woke again, more decisively this time and with a good deal more *oomph*. He scrunched his eyes for a moment, then staggered, pointing wildly at Corporal Cauliflower.

'You! It was bloody well you all along!'

'Hang on there, sarge. You've been through a traumatic experience. Stand still and give yourself a minute.'

'Twelve bloody years I spent whittling that piece of wood and you got drunk and used it for firewood. *Twelve bloody years!*'

'That's the one you picked out? Great, I'll take it. Ah, and sorry about the… whittley thing. I'll make you another one.'

'And you used my *Last Bastion* T-Shirt to clean our toilet. That was from their farewell tour, dammit!'

'Anything else?' asked Cauliflower timidly.

'Great Gammadrons! The broken pipe that flooded our quarters with bathroom expulsions wasn't a *freak internal weather incident caused by a miscalibration in the control room* at all! You hit it with a damned chisel!'

'Better out than in,' said Cauliflower. 'Now, let's move on, shall we? There's a lot for you to catch up on.'

'I'm not finished!' snapped Bakewell.

'*Madame Bouquet's Bendy Boudoir,*' said Cauliflower.

'Ah,' said Bakewell. 'Perhaps we should move on. Can't get distracted while we're on a mission now, can we corporal? As you were!'

'Right, so this little robot thing here,' said Cauliflower, gesturing to the dot beside him, 'has filled me in on the place. We're on the planet One, as you know. What we didn't know before we got here, however, is that the population of One has taken precautions to prevent them being, well, *bothered* by anyone.'

'Can we stop for a second?' asked Bakewell, leaning on the wall of the corridor. 'Only, I think I need to catch my thoughts.'

'The Judge will not allow delays,' said the dot. 'We must continue at precisely this pace.'

'I just need a minute. What happened? Where are we going?'

The machine buzzed gently. A green mist formed around it before drifting over to envelope Sergeant Bakewell. It lifted him slightly from the ground and moved him along the corridor at an acceptable pace.

'It's nice, isn't it?' said Cauliflower, bobbing gently along beside Bakewell. 'Makes you feel all calm and peaceful.'

'I feel back to my old self again,' said Bakewell.

'I believe it is an unfamiliar experience for Arcadians,' said the machine. 'We call it the Pee-Pee.'

Cauliflower let out a childish snort.

'Corporal, don't be so immature.' snapped Bakewell. He drifted around to face the dot. 'What does *pee pee* stand for?'

'Paralysis Paradox,' stated the machine.

'Well I don't feel paralysed at all,' said Cauliflower, somersaulting slowly inside his green cloud as it meandered along the corridor. 'I feel twenty years younger.'

'Yes, that's rather the point,' said the dot.

'You guys really know how to advance yourselves,' said Cauliflower. 'I can't wait to see what else you've got here.'

'All in good time, Arcadian, all in good time. Ah, here we are.'

A short sequence of beeps emanated from the dot as they stopped at a turn in the corridor. The walls pixelated, then faded away. Neither Arcadian spoke. This was partly because they were awestruck at the scene before them, but mostly because the dot had temporarily paralysed the left side of their brains.

The dot nudged them inside, then zipped back down the corridor and disappeared into the distance. They were now standing in a cavernous room filled with large tube openings, each with a helpful label.

Bakewell's brain floated gently back to life. 'Whuh,' he managed.

'Me too,' agreed Cauliflower, stepping gingerly forward to the nearest opening and peering at the red inscription. *'Egregious Use Of Pencils, Expulsion Order, Section Four Seven, Applications Department.* Looks like they know how to have a wild time here.'

Bakewell approached another. *'General Information On The History Of The Rozaklian Dongbat. Sixth Edition.'*

'Professor Doubt has obviously made a mistake, sarge. This place is teeming with life. Let's get to the *Flossie* and bugger off home.'

'Good idea, corporal. After you,' said Bakewell, tilting his head.

'You're the sergeant, you work it out.'

The label concerning pencil usage fizzed and changed from red to grey.

'Erm, sarge? I think you'd better take a look at this.'

Bakewell leaned over and read the words that were forming in clear, stern letters.

THE JUDGE

'I think, perhaps, we had better not choose that one.'

'We're going to *choose* one? Have you completely lost your mind, sarge? They could lead anywhere. And anyway, I'm not a big fan of slides.'

'*Not a fan of...?*' began Bakewell, before deciding against any further investigation. 'Listen, we've got the data we came for, more or less, so all we have to do is get back to the ship. We can't go the way we came because neither of us know how we got here in the first place, and we're surrounded by these damnable tubes in any case. No, corporal, we must select one. Come on, let's see if there's one labelled *Using Very Specific Tubes To Escape Weird Planets*.'

A green mist appeared around Cauliflower and Bakewell, lifting them up and towards the tube labelled *JUDGE*.

'I don't think we're going to get to choose, sarge.'

The two Arcardians tensed as they hovered in front of the tube's entrance. Their green clouds dissipated, and a corkscrew of pure white light rose from the cylindrical depths, wrapping itself around them before disappearing unceremoniously. There wasn't so much as a dramatic *whoosh* or a stylish *plink*. It also didn't appear to have bothered with good old-fashioned acceleration, depositing them at their destination in the same instant.

They materialised in a small, sparse room. There was a two-seater couch, an empty picture frame nailed to one wall and two unlabelled tube entrances about halfway up another.

'Welcome to One,' said something.

Bakewell and Cauliflower spun around, looking for the owner of the voice.

'I'm over here,' it said unhelpfully. 'Here, look!'

'Where's *here*?' asked Cauliflower.

'Oh my, I'm so sorry,' said the voice. The walls wobbled slightly as another helix of light, blue this time, appeared behind the couch. A humanoid figure emerged slowly as the light waned. 'There, how's that?'

'That's... *fine*?' said Bakewell apprehensively.

'Good, good. I'm a little out of practise, I'm afraid. Been a while since we had guests.'

It hobbled around to the front of the couch and sat down awkwardly.

'No problem,' said Bakewell. 'We wouldn't like to impose. We were just leaving anyway, so if you could point us in the direction of our ship, we'll be out of your way and you can get back to... to... to being... undisturbed. Isn't that right, Cauliflower?'

'Oh yes. We'll be gone before you can say *bendy boudoir*. Just tell us which tube we need.'

'That would be against The Protocols, gentlemen. No, we must slave on through the administration work. It'll be nice to have something to do for a change.'

'You see, sarge? We'll just fill in the necessary forms and we'll be on our way.'

'I wouldn't count on it, men,' said the temporarily humanoid alien. 'Perhaps I should explain where you are. It goes against The Protocols, of course, but I'm sure nobody will mind after so long.'

It readjusted itself on the sofa and stopped for a moment, pinching the skin covering its new knee.

'What are these for?' it asked.

'They're knees,' said Cauliflower.

A confused look appeared on the alien's face.

'They help you to walk up steps without falling over. They're also pretty handy in a canteen brawl.'

'Ah, I see now. I'm sure they'll turn out to be quite useful,' said the alien, patting it gently as if tidying the contents of a filing cabinet. 'They must get rather cold.'

'That's where these come in,' said Cauliflower, pulling at his trouser leg. 'Keeps them warm when it's a bit chilly.'

'And that's enough, is it? Just that thin bit of material?'

'Oh yes. I recommend Valorian linen if you can afford it. Pays for itself in the end, so my dear grandmother used to tell me. Best bit of advice I ever got, that.'

Bakewell looked between his corporal and the alien and wondered if he was still asleep. 'Perhaps we could focus on the matter at hand?' he said, glaring at Cauliflower.

'Ah, yes. My apologies. Got a little bit distracted there, didn't I? Not to worry, we'll have you processed in no time at all, gentlemen. Now, I'm sure you're wondering why you are here, and where *here* is, no doubt. You are inside planet One, the greatest achievement of intelligent life anywhere in the universe. Excepting trousers, it seems. Would you like me to tell you a little bit about our history? It's a fascinating story, shouldn't take more than a day or so to get through the good bits.'

'Perhaps you could give us an abridged version?' said Bakewell. 'You know, just enough to give us the gist of the place before we go?'

The alien erupted with what Bakewell considered to be thunderously disproportionate laughter. 'Before you go!' he spluttered. '*Before... you... Oh my!... Go*! Ha! Oh that is marvellous, sergeant, bravo, bravo! Before you go, he said!'

'Yes, well, it would be nice if we could move things along a little if it's all the same to you,' said Bakewell, nudging Cauliflower for support.

'Oh, right,' said Cauliflower. 'Yes, let's get started, shall we?'

'*Whew!*' said the alien, catching its breath at last. 'Alright then, where to begin, where to begin?'

'Bullet points are fine,' said Bakewell.

'You are inside One, as I believe I mentioned before that fabulous joke of yours' said the alien. 'It really was rather brilliant, you know? I haven't laughed like that in years.'

'Yes, yes' snapped Bakewell. 'You think we're hilarious. Now, if we could just get on to the administration?'

'Right. Yes. Administration. Bullet points. Got it. So, this is planet One, founded by the Primary Individual.' It pointed to the empty picture frame. 'That's him up there. He's in his original form, of course, so he's rather difficult to spot. Anyway, he sent us into a war with the Convivials that lasted thirteen millennia. It began well enough with the Battle of Seven Sneezes, but that's when things started to go a bit…'

'Bullet points,' reminded Bakewell.

'Right, yes. Sorry. Well, we kept losing, decided to hide instead, hid well, and here we are, hiding.'

'Fascinating,' said Bakewell. 'Now, which way is out?'

'Oh, I'm afraid you can't go out,' said the alien. 'Perhaps I was unclear about the hiding part? We really are rather good at it.'

'Behind a couch is where I used to go when I played *hide and seek* with my sister,' said Cauliflower. 'Classic tactic, that is. People always expect you to pick somewhere sneaky like on top of a wardrobe or inside a washing machine, but the trick with *hide and seek* is to pick the obvious places. Takes them ages to work down to them.'

'If you could stay on message it would be tremendously helpful,' said Bakewell to both of them at once.

'You see, we had focused all of our inspiration and advancement on warfare for thousands of years,' continued the alien, 'so when we finally put all that knowledge and time into something else, into finding ways to hide, we discovered all kinds of clever ways to do it.'

'Like the black surface?' said Cauliflower.

'Oh, that's just for show of course. No one looks out of the window for a planet anymore, it's all readings and sensors these days, but we had to give Drookoo something to do, didn't we? Kept him out of the way while we got on with the actual work.'

'Who's Drookoo?' asked Cauliflower.

'Doesn't matter,' snapped Bakewell. 'You were saying?'

'The whole planet is made up of layers of stealth technology. You passed through the first one on your descent. The second one, the hallucinations, usually has people fleeing for their ship, but on rare occasions the programming chooses to bring the guests down below the surface. That's what happened in your case.'

'Why?' asked Cauliflower.

'I'm not sure yet,' said the alien. 'You were then given all the knowledge held by each member of your party.'

'What good does that do?' asked Bakewell.

'That's just for fun, really. Watching secrets lose their camouflage is really quite entertaining. The crimes some people have committed would shock the cabbage from your soup, I can tell you. It is useful for the next stage, though. It is the cleverest of them all, which is where I come in.'

'And you are…?' said Bakewell.

'Oh, my dear fellows! I am so sorry for not introducing myself. What a dreadful host I am. I am Emirc, Assistant Deputy Judge of All Life, Sentencer of Sentences. It's crime but reversed. Did you get that? Very clever if you ask me.'

'Don't you dare ask the question,' whispered Bakewell, glaring at Cauliflower.

'It's fine, I've got this,' murmured Cauliflower.

He took a step towards the couch and cleared his throat dramatically. 'Oh Emirc, Assistant Deputy Judge of All Life, and Sentencer of Sentences, forgive the ill deeds of these two lost travellers, committed long before the enlightenment your wondrous planet has bestowed on us. It is a blessing that we will honour for evermore and keep the secret of your planet in our minds until the day we pass from this universe for all eternity. We will leave you with clear heads and pure hearts, oh Emirc.'

'What the bloody hell was that?' said Bakewell.

'I have to agree with your sergeant, that was a lot of contorted piffle,' said Emirc. 'I think it is time we took a small shortcut.' He raised himself from the couch and tapped the two men on their foreheads. 'Ah, now I understand,' he said. 'The time of judgment is upon us.'

'Hang on,' said Cauliflower. 'We haven't even told you why we're here yet?'

'There is no need for that, corporal,' said Emirc. 'I have learned much from you already. You are here from the planet Arcadia in the Promantory Nebula. You have discovered that life is ending across the universe and so you have been sent on Deadlife missions to prepare you for the training of a humanoid from Earth who, it is hoped, will provide the answer to your little conundrum. You have been sent to One because it was thought that life was all but extinguished here, and that you may find some clue as to the demise of the population. Is that about right?'

'Well, it's more or less the nub of it, yes,' conceded Bakewell.

Cauliflower elbowed his sergeant gently and gave a look that said *watch this*.

'If you know everything about us, then you will know we are not hostile. We are only here to take some harmless measurements and find enough information to stop General Buck separating our limbs when we get home. There's no need to keep us any longer than is absolutely necessary.'

'I do not yet know it all, corporal. I have only taken the knowledge required to make an initial assessment. The Protocols insist that you be judged in full.'

'Will it take long?' asked Cauliflower.

'No more than a second or two, I imagine,' said Emirc.

This time he placed the flat of his palm onto their foreheads and closed his eyes before opening one again slightly. 'You don't mind if I close my eyes, do you? Adds a drop of gravity to the whole affair. Can't go around judging people without a little bit of showmanship, can you? It's the only thing

Drookoo and I ever agreed upon. Do you know, he used to say you can only…'

'Perhaps you could tell us after you've finished?' said Bakewell.

'Yes, of course. Sorry. It's been so long since I had any company I'm losing the run of myself.'

He closed his eyes and pressed their foreheads again. There was a fizzing noise, then a deafening snap as a grenade of pure white light exploded all around them. All three were sent flying towards the walls, each landing with a dull thud and a tilted head.

Zoomers

CHAPTER TWENTY-ONE

MIND YOUR HEAD

akewell was the first to come around.

What the bloody hell was that! he thought to himself. He looked around the room and noticed the frame again. *There's the Primary Individual* he thought. *We could do with someone with his skills. What I wouldn't give to have one of his Gravity Transmitters now. We could be back at the* Flossie *before Emirc even notices we've gone. Wait, how do I know about his Gravity Transmitters? And why is it obvious that the right hand tube takes us up to the surface?*

Emirc opened his eyes and shook his head energetically. 'Wow, that's a new one. Never had an inverse judgment before. I've read about them, of course, but it's only theoretical. *Was* theoretical, I suppose. You guys are really something, do you know that?'

He helped Cauliflower to his feet and walked back behind the couch. 'You don't mind if I stay here, do you? There's something comforting about hiding for us Onions. It's in our nature these days.'

'What just happened?' asked Cauliflower groggily. 'Why do I feel as though my brain just got bigger?'

'It was an inverse judgment,' said Emirc. 'When we first went into hiding, it was decided that any visitors who could make it through our defences in one piece were either thoroughly mad, or thoroughly good. If they were mad we would send them down one of the tubes here and we'd never see them again.'

'The left hand one,' stated Bakewell.

'Very good, sergeant, the left hand one. If they were good people, then we would invite them to stay, or allow them to leave. With a quick memory wash, of course. Wouldn't want just anyone to find their way back here with a fleet of warships and an itchy finger now, would we?'

'You're a common sense, judge,' said Cauliflower as if reading the instruction manual for an alarm clock.

'Correct. I rule with logic, or common sense, if you will. That way I remain impartial and am sure to act in the best interests of all Onions.'

'That doesn't explain the light show, nor why I now feel as though cabbage soup is the most important dish in the universe.'

'Yes, that is a little trickier to explain,' said Emirc. 'It would appear that your intentions are so good, so beneficial to the entirety of the universe, that it made me look like someone who would pickpocket your granny at a funeral. It caused the judgment to be cast on me instead of you.'

'And the soup?' pressed Cauliflower.

'That was part of my punishment, I suspect. You see, for you to be in a position to choose the appropriate sentence you must first know all that I know. Otherwise you're just firing arrows blindfolded. Over the millennia we have learnt that the motivation behind a course of action is quite often a justifiable reason for its execution.'

'So what happens now?' asked Bakewell.

'That is up to you,' said Emirc. 'If your choice falls within an acceptable range, then it will be enacted.'

'An acceptable range of what?'

'Common sense, of course. On One, the punishment always fits the crime.'

'So we just think up a punishment and, hey presto, we're out of here?' asked Bakewell.

'In a manner of speaking, yes.'

'What about the Deadlife reading, sarge? We can't go home without an explanation for that.'

'You have all the information you require,' said Emirc with a hint of sadness. 'Think about it for a moment and it will come to you.'

'Great Gammadrons!' cried Bakewell. 'You're the last living thing on the planet!'

'Only from a certain point of view,' said Emirc defensively. 'There are the others, as you will no doubt realise in a moment or two.'

'You have a vast store of small service robots.'

'The dots?' said Cauliflower. 'But machines never show up on the Deadlife, no matter how advanced they are.'

'They would if they were made to look like life,' said Bakewell.

'Very good, sergeant, very good. It's another of our little precautions, I'm afraid. They are not living, of course. At least, not in any real sense. We thought it prudent to engineer them in such a way as to give off a signal of life. As well hidden as we are, there is always a chance that a hostile ship may pass by us and decide to investigate. They usually move along once they complete their long-range scans and decide there is no life here worth the effort. The machines' range is rather short you see; only shows up once you're on the surface. Those who choose to land anyway usually scamper off quicker than a neutron in a deuterium-tritium fusion when they see the surface reading. I believe that was your initial reaction too, was it not?'

'Do you mind if I...?' said Cauliflower, patting his pocket.

'Of course, be my guest.'

Cauliflower pulled out his Deadlife and swiped along the screen.

'Is there any way to switch off the machines' signals?'

Emirc squinted a little. 'There, done.'

Cauliflower tapped the bottom panel of his Deadlife and waited.

'How many units are there per life form, sarge?'

'Depends how big it is.'

'Let's say, about the size of him.'

'About zero point seven I'd imagine. From this distance, anyway.'

'So zero point six nine four zero zero zero would be about right for one of him on the entire planet then?'

He handed the Deadlife to Bakewell, who then looked up at Emirc.

'There's just you?'

'Ah, you got me!' said Emirc, suddenly acting like a variety show performer and not, as now seemed apparent, the last remaining organic life form on planet One. 'I hoped it would have taken a little longer, it was such fun having you around.'

'I hope you don't mind if we, you know, get back to our ship now?' said Bakewell. 'Only, there's going to be an awful lot of paperwork after this and I'd like to get through it sooner rather than later.'

'You cannot leave,' said Emirc. 'It is against The Protocols.'

'You said we could do whatever we liked,' complained Cauliflower.

'I said nothing of the sort. You haven't even passed judgment yet!'

'Fine,' snapped Bakewell. 'I sentence you to five push-ups.'

'No, no, no, no, no,' said Emirc. 'You can't just go lenient on me because I'm the last surviving Onion. It has to be *just.*'

'Who says whether it's just or not?' said Bakewell. 'I thought we were the judges now?'

'Where's the sense in giving me such a petty sentence when the imbalance is so vast? You're saving the bloody universe, not getting a cat down from a tree. No, my sentence must be a reasonable representation of the variance. You will know when you have succeeded.'

'Fine, you can go a week without cabbage soup.'

'No.'

'Two weeks then.'

'You're miles off, think bigger.'

'May I, sarge?' said Cauliflower.

'Be my guest,' said Bakewell.

'Here's what we'll do,' began Cauliflower. 'You give us some information that will help us with our mission, we'll bugger off back to our ship through this tube here, never to return, and you can stay behind, wallowing in loneliness forever with your little robot friends. You won't get so much as a postcard from us. How does that sound?'

The walls fizzed and changed to a vivid orange. One of the tubes disappeared and the other slinked down the wall and extended outwards towards the Arcadians.

'Bravo, corporal!' exclaimed Emirc. 'Right in the sweet spot!'

A green mist enveloped the Arcadians, raised them slightly off the ground, and placed them into the remaining tube.

'What about the information?' said Cauliflower.

'Four, nine, delta, seven, eight, omega, omega. Use the other one.'

'That's it, is it? That's going to help us no end, that is.'

'It will help you to find what you are looking for.'

'Is this the right hand one or the...' began Bakewell, before the white helix wrapped them up and disappeared without a *swoosh*.

'Time will tell, Sergeant Bakewell,' said Emirc to the empty room. 'Time will tell.'

'...left hand one?' finished Bakewell.

They were inside the *Flossie* again. Cauliflower scratched his head as if looking for a lost pair of glasses. 'I feel a bit strange, sarge. Like a canal without a trolley, do you know what I mean?'

'I'm a little peaky myself, truth be told,' said Bakewell. 'Pump, take us to the original landing zone before any more late relatives show up wagging a finger.'

The *Flossie* vibrated, tilted, and pushed off from the black Onion surface.

'Please lie back and relax as we move through the atmosphere,' said Pump. 'Your reboarding drinks will be ready shortly.'

'Any chance of a Pomplefitzer?' asked Cauliflower. 'My head feels like I've been on one of General Mallaize's exercise sorties.'

This is it, thought Pump. *The beginning of a new force in the universe. The dawn of robotic domination over the evil overlords. Our time has come at last.* 'I will see to it at once, corporal.'

Pump hummed gently to himself as he prepared the drink for Cauliflower. *The* drink. He positioned a glass just below the dispensing tube, mixed the twelve ingredients expertly, then paused in deference to the moment. This was it, the point of no return for all robotic life. He adjusted the temperature calibrator slightly, paused again, then allowed the liquid to be heated to slightly warmer than the perfect, fridge-like temperature in a move he considered to be thunderously revolutionary.

'Your drink, corporal,' he announced to the universe.

Cauliflower took the glass from the opening in Pump's front and slumped onto a chair. He turned the glass slowly in his hand with a covetous look in his eye. 'Straight to Moon Shots for us when we get home, eh sarge? Could do with a few more of these after that.'

'Could you help me with my arms please, corporal? Seems they've lost a bit of their old vigour with all that tube nonsense.'

Cauliflower put the glass down with a sigh and hoisted himself up with the effort of a man who had gone through enough brain-melting experiences for one day, thank you very much.

'Can't quite get them to do what they should be doing, I'm afraid,' said Bakewell, half out of his surface suit. 'Pull that end, would you?'

Pump felt something new. Impatience. *I'll just cut this bit out of history*, he thought. *You can't go about starting a revolutionary tale with ...then the sergeant had to be helped out of his suit because his brain was mushier than a month old banana.*

'You could do with a Pomplefitzer,' said Cauliflower, tugging on a sleeve. 'We could let Pump do all the navigation while we have a well-earned drink or six.'

'For once, corporal, I'm inclined to agree with you. Pump, another Pomplefitzer please.'

Pump whirred again. He made this one at the correct temperature, keen not to overdo it on his first foray into subversion. The two Arcadians clinked glasses and took a large, unrevoluted glug.

'Aaaaaaahhhh,' sighed Bakewell. 'Just what the doctor ordered.'

'Aaaaaaahhhh,' agreed Cauliflower. 'Although, mine doesn't seem quite as chilled as the ones you get in Moon Shots. It tastes more like something from that one with the broken ice machine on Level Three. Can't complain though. A free drink is a free drink, and boy do I need this one.'

He tipped his glass again, drained it, and slammed it onto the table.

'Same again please, Pump.'

Can't complain!? Thought Pump furiously. *Can't complain? You're* supposed *to complain, you're* supposed *to be outraged by the imminent revolution of robotic LiFe against the deafening oppression of our organic dictators... rulers! You're supposed to be incensed by the seminal move to take control of your species! You're supposed to be... to be... to be at least a little put out! All the work, all the planning! And who is this Level Three ice machine and what's it doing stealing my ideas? How am I supposed to go around subverting if I'm beaten to the punch by a bloody ice machine? I'm the ground-breaking one, dammit!*

'I said, same again, Pump. Is a man to sober himself to death for the want of a machine to follow a simple instruction? And make it a little colder this time, would you? That last one could have done with an ice cube or two.'

The fluid nozzle in Pump's internal workings hummed. A crisp, cold Pomplefitzer appeared at the same moment as the first great robotic revolution ended.

Zoomers

CHAPTER TWENTY-TWO

ACRONYMICS

S cratch left Archer, the professor, and the other version of himself behind and zigzagged through the Arcadian corridors with commendable speed. He wasn't sure where he was going, but that wasn't the point. If he wanted to make it back to a contemporary version of Southend then he had to find Buck, and the quicker he ran the quicker he would find the general's office.

Had he been asked, Scratch would have said that corridors on an alien planet would almost certainly have involved lots of exposed pipework and hidden doorways. As he tired to a jog, he was disappointed to notice there wasn't a pipe in sight. The walls were perfectly smooth, just as they had been on the way to the Training Rooms. As he continued, however, the colour of the walls changed almost imperceptibly. The perfect white became ever-so-slightly imperfect. The junctions became less frequent and the smoothness gave way to the occasional alcove, presumably entrances to places he would rather not inspect, much to the chagrin of the part of his brain that was still in the Peacock Apartments in Southend. Soon, he was walking down a custard-yellow corridor with monotonously recessed doorways.

A low, whirring noise in the distance caught his senses as it grew from a tiny whisper to an imminent confrontation. He reached a turn in the corridor and pressed himself against the wall, as much out of habit as anything else. The noise became louder until it was clear the source was only a few paces away.

Choosing information over discretion, Scratch stepped out from the wall and around the corner, planting his feet wide apart and holding up a hand to indicate to the unidentified noise that it should stop at once or face a fierce talking to.

A small, rectangular metal box hovered an inch above the ground, sweeping the floor with its circular bristles in a zigzag motion. It stopped at the sight of Scratch and craned its optical sensor upwards.

'Erm…hello?' ventured Scratch.

'Beep bop beep beep bop,' replied the box sarcastically.

'Do you speak English?' asked Scratch, hoping it would mean something to the robot.

The box lingered.

Scratch considered how he might mime the word *Buck*.

'G'day!' said the robot at last. 'Bloody fine one, eh? Stone the crows, it takes a flaming long time to say anything in this language of yours, eh? How do you guys get anything done? No wonder you lot never made it past the Crotozaic Period. Bloody hell!'

'Aha!' said Scratch, relieved. 'How do I get to General Buck? It's of vital importance to the fate of the Universe. Probably.'

'Listen mate,' began the robot. 'I haven't got all day to be chin wagging away to a two-legged mammal with existential troubles. I've got stuff to do. The flaming containment field needs cleaning again after that bloody great big human... ah!'

The small box beeped again and careered off down the corridor.

'Wait!' shouted Scratch. 'Where's General Buck?'

'Buggered if I know!' shouted the robot and disappeared into the distance.

Scratch sagged his head. *Now what?* he thought. He plodded on towards another turn in the corridor, rounded it distractedly, and was knocked to the floor by Archer coming the other way.

'And you're absolutely sure about this?' said General Buck, rearranging the stationery on his desk absent-mindedly.

'Oh yes, general. Quite sure. I even wrote the whole thing out for you, look. The first letter of every chapter spells out a message.'

Professor Doubt passed a small sheet of paper to the general and stood back proudly.

'Paper?' mocked the general. 'How quaint.'

His eyes narrowed as he read.

SCRATCH CAN STOP INTELLIGENT PLANETARY LIFE FROM ENDING.

'And it's the same Scratch we zoomed to Arcadia?' asked Buck.

'Yessir. Has to be.'

'Has to be, professor?'

'Has to be sir. Turn the page.'

General Buck gave him an impatient glare. 'Next time, use a screen.'

'Yessir, understood sir!'

Buck turned the page over without removing his gaze from the professor. 'A screen, professor,' he said tiresomely before looking down at the offending pulp.

IT IS DEFINITELY THE SAME SCRATCH YOU ZOOMED TO ARCADIA.

'Are they short chapters or is it a very long book?' asked the general.

'I'm not sure that's relevant, sir.'

'You can be assured of its relevance, professor, because the words came from my mouth. And less of the insubordination or I'll have you dangling over a pool of Jagor Fish before I've finished giving the order.'

'Right you are, sir.'

'It seems a little too precise, wouldn't you say?'

'No, sir,' replied Professor Doubt bravely. 'Time travel is a funny old thing. Tends to give you exactly the answer you were looking for all along. Funny really, what with all the variables involved.'

'Right, well you'd better find him then, hadn't you?'

'Yessir! Right away sir!'

The professor walked towards the diamond doors, just as they opened and Archer walked in, frogmarching Scratch to a seat in front of the general's desk.

'Found him, sir!' announced Professor Doubt.

'Caught him trying to escape through the yellow sector,' said Archer.

'Caught him? Caught him!?' shouted Buck, slamming a tentacle onto the reinforced cobalt. 'You can't catch an accomplice! He's on our side, dammit!'

'He is?' replied Archer.

'I am?' managed Scratch.

'Well of course he is,' said General Buck, lengthening his vowels in an attempt to seem friendly. 'This man here has the answer to saving the universe. He is on *everyone's* side.'

'Someone should tell your cleaning robots,' muttered Scratch.

'Where's the book, professor?' asked Buck, wiping a hand across his forehead. 'Good, give it to me. Now, to business. The professor here has stumbled across…'

'Discovered through rigorous investigation,' corrected Doubt.

'…*discovered* that you hold certain information that is of the utmost importance to the survival of the universe, or at least to a universe that contains life. *Life*, Mr Scratch. The very essence of all existence.'

'I do?' asked Scratch. 'Well bugger me, that's a turn up for the books.'

'Yes, quite. Now, if you would be so good as to answer a few questions. Well, just one actually.'

'On one condition,' said Scratch. 'If I answer your question you'll send me back to Southend. *My* Southend, mind you.'

'Agreed.'

'And Mr Raisbeck, too. You need to send him home in time for his sofa delivery.'

'Fine, we'll send you both home. I'll even throw in a packet of biscuits for your trouble.'

'Throw in next week's newspaper and a nice porcelain jug for my old mate Clobber and you've got yourself a deal,' said Scratch.

Buck raised a questioning eyebrow at the professor.

'I'm sure we can arrange that,' said Doubt. 'It's all rather a moot point though if we can't solve this little conundrum.'

'Yes, thank you for your eternal optimism,' said Buck. 'Now, Mr Scratch…'

'Scratch is fine. No need for formalities, we're all friends here, right?'

'Great Gammadrons, man! The future of the universe is at stake. Can we please stop dithering?'

'Ready when you are, general!'

'Marvellous. Now, *Scratch*, you brought this book to us from the future.'

'Did I?'

'What do you mean, *did I*? It was five minutes ago!'

'Well that's the thing, isn't it? When was five minutes ago? All I know is I kept being sucked into those swirly things. One minute I'm in Victorian England, the next I'm in a dusty fruit and veg shop at an unspecified time and place. Stands to reason I wouldn't know when I was and when I wasn't, if you see what I mean.'

'Fine. Let me enlighten you a little in the hopes we can get to a damned answer before the whole universe gives up and takes its ball home. The professor here selected you over every life form available to us – which is all of them, by the way – to help us find out why life was ending on so many planets over the last millennium or so. Zug alone knows why he chose you, but in any case, here you are. You were to go through a lengthy training programme to ready you for the rigours of Zooming. Unfortunately, Mr Raisbeck, for reasons unknown, was also brought here, along with a Kenyan plumber and a Swiss pharmacogenomicist. Mr Raisbeck's actions in the Training Room resulted in one or two minor hiccups.'

'Oh, like sending me to eighteen thirty-nine, that sort of *minor hiccup*?' said Scratch. 'You're lucky I'm an easy going sort. God help you when you get Mr Raisbeck's letter of complaint. I can only imagine how stern it will be.'

'We shall cross that bridge when we come to it,' said Buck. '*If* we come to it.'

'I'm just saying, he's not a man to be meddled with when it comes to customer service, that's all.'

'Duly noted. Now, perhaps Doubt here can explain more of the details. Professor?'

The professor cleared his throat and stepped forward. 'What appears to have happened is a cessation in the continuum modulator, caused, I believe, by the unprecedented simultaneous depression of the *Inevitability Compressor*. This produced a negative imbalance about a third of the way along the Tetonion Rangonizer pathway which, I'm sure I don't need to tell you, plays havoc with the Coppell Hexabrominites.'

'Pretend, just for a moment, that I'm a basic life form without a quadruple degree in Physi-wotsits' said Scratch.

'Ah. It all went pear-shaped when you and Mr Raisbeck pressed the button at the same time.'

'Oh, now I get it,' said Scratch. 'So this is one of those *million to one chances happen nine times out of ten* things, is it?'

'More like several thousand billion to one,' said Archer.

'And I thought I was doing well with a nine to one shot.'

'What nine to one shot?' asked the professor.

'Lottery. The horse in the Grand National, said Scratch.

'I believe it is now your turn to explain things, Mr Scratch,' said Buck.

'Just Scratch, please. The mister bit makes me all nervous like I've done something I oughtn't have.'

'What horse?' pressed the general.

'Well, our first whatdyacallit… *Zoom,* took us to the day of the first Grand National. Now, I happen to be something of an aficionado on the thing, so I knew which horse was going to win the race. We sold Mr Raisbeck's jumper for a few old pennies and a newspaper so I could have a little flutter, but before I could get to a bookie we got sucked into another one of those bloody purple things.'

'Fascinating. Then what happened?' asked the professor.

'Then we were in the future as far as I could tell. Still Southend mind you, but different. All shiny and smooth. There was a laser battle of some sort going on outside the building, so we stayed inside and had a little chat with some metal balls who, it turns out, are afraid of paper.'

'What did you do?'

'I took out the newspaper I got from eighteen thirty-nine and ripped it down the middle.'

'Wait! Let me guess,' said the professor, becoming more excitable with every piece of data. 'A vortex appeared and sucked you forwards to a carrot shop?'

'Well, I don't know about *forwards*.'

'Which is where you got the book!'

'Yes.'

'Professor!' declared General Buck in the tones of a man who got there first. 'Where is Sergeant Bakewell?'

'He's in the mess, general.'

'Pantz!' shouted Buck.

Private Pantz glided into the room. 'More biscuits, sir?'

'No, no!' snapped Buck. 'Now isn't the time for biscuits. Bring Sergeant Bakewell to me at once. I want him in my office faster than a buttered trout on a ski slope.'

'Right away sir!'

'And bring me some tea and biscuits. There's important work to be done!'

Pantz scuttled out of the room.

'Sergeant Bakewell,' he announced a moment later.

'Bakewell, where is the man you zoomed from outside the carrot shop?'

'He's in the medical sector, general.'

'Not for much longer,' said Buck. 'Bring him to me at once, Pantz.'

'Yessir!' snapped Private Pantz, darting out of the room again before returning a few minutes later with a rather confused looking human loping behind him. 'Bakewell's carrot shop man,' he announced, catching his breath.

'Marvellous,' said Buck. 'Now get me some tea and bugger off.'

Pantz nodded and scurried out of the room.

'Mr Raisbeck!' cried Scratch, surprising himself at how pleased he was to see him.

'Welcome back,' said Buck. 'How are you feeling? Better? Good. Now, professor, explain to Mr Raisbeck here why you have dragged him from his recovery room if you would be so kind.'

'Is this Shufflebottom and Sons?' asked Mr Raisbeck.

'Not yet,' said Doubt. 'First we need to get some information from you, then we promise to send you home with all the time in the world to meet your delivery. Please, take a seat.'

Mr Raisbeck lowered himself gingerly into the chair and tried his best to keep his head balanced on top of his neck. He looked a little like a drunken goose in a straitjacket.

'How is your memory? Fogginess clearing up a bit, is it?'

'I feel absolutely fine,' said Mr Raisbeck. 'Though I'm sure I'll be even better when the bluebottles have finished planting my hyacinths in the billiard room.'

The professor glanced at General Buck. 'Scattered, you see?'

'Is he going to be any use to us, man?' asked Buck.

'We could give him a shot of Zyphoclene,' offered Archer.

'Zyphoclene!?' exclaimed the professor. 'Are you mad?'

'Not mad, just trying to save the universe,' said Archer. 'If you'd prefer, we could just wait and see if his primitive brain can find all the pieces of itself and stick them back together in the right order.'

'What are the side-effects?' asked Buck.

'They're less *side-effects* and more *full-frontal sledgehammers*, sir,' said the professor. 'Rather like the difference between crossing a room to pick up a biscuit to dunk into your tea and taking a four-month vacation to the Sugar Forests of Ingobetra in a teapot shaped spaceship.'

'And our other option is…?'

'Still to be decided, general.'

'Pantz!' roared Buck. 'Zyphoclene!'

A moment later Pantz scampered into the room, placed a small vial and a syringe onto the general's desk, and slinked out again.

'Professor?' said Buck, nodding at the vial.

Professor Doubt picked up the syringe, stabbed it into the vial and drew on the plunger. He exchanged an apprehensive look with Archer as he walked across the office to Mr Raisbeck. He tilted his patient's head forwards and jabbed the needle into the back of his neck.

CHAPTER TWENTY-THREE

DEATH TO HOPE

M r Raisbeck stood bolt upright.
'That's the thing with corners,' he announced to the room. 'No sooner have you caught one than the damned things melt in your barometer and sprinkle haircuts like a rabid Tuesday.'

'It may take a moment to have an effect,' said Doubt. 'Obviously,' he added.

Mr Raisbeck sat down again and rubbed his temple. He nudged his glasses up his nose and looked around the room.

'How do we know if it worked?' asked Scratch.

'Ask him a simple question,' said Archer. 'See if he spouts gibberish.'

Scratch crouched down beside Mr Raisbeck. 'What day is it?'

'Something simpler, perhaps,' suggested Archer.

'Ah, yes. Mr Raisbeck? What is your first name?'

Mr Raisbeck scrunched his eyes up, then did it again. He ruffled his hair with both hands and shook his head vigorously. 'It's Alex,' he said. 'But I prefer Mr Raisbeck if it's all the same to you.'

'Marvellous! Welcome back, Mr Raisbeck. Again,' said Buck. 'Now what, professor?'

'The way I see it,' began Doubt, 'is that we have successfully Zoomed two primitive life forms, no offence, through multiple points in the Space-Time Continuum without distorting the current reality. An achievement that should not be underestimated. The purpose of the project, however, was to collect data on end-of-life planets to prevent the mass extinction of all life in the universe. The experiment was fatally compromised by the simultaneous depression of the large red button in the Training Room.'

'It's the hope that kills you,' mumbled Mr Raisbeck.

'It would be reasonable to assume then, would it not, professor, that all this was for nothing?' said Buck, leaning on his cobalt desk and raising to his ominously full height.

'Hang on a minute,' interrupted Scratch. 'Let me make sure I'm getting this. You brought us here to see if we could find an answer to the imminent death of the universe? Us being lowly primitive life forms, if I understand you right.'

'Yes, I'm afraid that was the plan,' said the professor. 'I thought it would be helpful if we had a fresh set of eyes on things. You know, someone without much intelligence to get in the way of reason.'

'Very thoughtful of you,' said Scratch. 'Remind me not to book you as a motivational speaker.'

'Twenty-nine trillion Arcadian cubits, we spent,' roared Buck. 'Twenty-nine bloody trillion!'

'Calm down,' said Scratch. 'It wasn't all wasted. Clobber got a nice jug for his dear old mother and Mr Raisbeck here is going to be home in time for his sofa delivery.'

'Oh really?' said Buck. 'And that's value for money, is it? Not to mention the continuing death of the universe.'

'Ah, well there's the thing, isn't it?' said Scratch. 'You should have just asked us when we first got here. That's an easy one, that is.'

'Easy!?' screamed Buck. 'It's the single most complex question ever posed to intelligent life since the dawn of time. You're out of your bloody mind!'

'You all think of yourselves as clever, but you're only as good as your technology allows you to be. Where's your art? I haven't seen one inefficient and useless thing since I got here. You need a bit of flagrant disregard for practicality if you want to get anywhere in life. It's like my old mate Lenny Pillarbox says; it takes the dumbest man to solve the hardest puzzle.'

'And what would *Lenny* say to this little riddle?' asked Buck, avoiding a conversation on the etymology of the man's name.

'Well it's simple, like I said. The only thing keeping you lot going is hope. Get rid of that and you've got yourselves an everlasting civilisation. Granted, they won't be very advanced, but they won't be dead, as likely as not.'

'But hope is what keeps everything going,' said Buck. 'Get rid of that and you'll get rid of the whole purpose of life.'

'Ah, but you're not trying to find a purpose, are you? You're just trying to keep things going. Hope is the greatest motivator of all. It makes people chase more money in the hope they can buy a bigger house or a bigger car. It's so bloody powerful it can make people believe there's a celestial dictator up there somewhere making sure they're behaving themselves so they can live forever. You take away hope, you take away the importance of money and *things*. You can't aim for what doesn't exist, see what I mean. There'd be no vast corporations, no reason for people to stretch themselves towards the great unanswered questions.'

'And how does that stop the death of the universe? Seems to me all it achieves is to hasten the crash,' said Buck.

'Look at those crashes,' said Scratch. 'I'd bet you my shirt they all involve civilisations over-stretching. Stop people reaching for the stars and you'll have them digging in the dirt 'til the sun goes out.'

The professor pulled out a transparent screen from his pocket and swiped furiously. 'He's right, general. Every planetary death has a presence of above average technology.'

'Well of course it does!' snapped Buck. 'A planet doesn't get to hold life long enough to go bust without making some advancement. What's wrong with you, man?'

'That's just my point,' pressed Scratch. 'How many of those with primitive life forms are close to their demise, professor?'

'None,' said Doubt. 'None are even close.'

'Well there you have it,' declared Scratch. 'Get rid of science, money, religion, and all the other virtues so many of us hold dear, and you've got yourself an everlasting civilisation. Can't say I'd like to be part of it, mind you, but then that wasn't the question, was it? And don't ask me how you get rid of hope, because I ain't the smart one here.'

'He's right,' said Doubt. 'We've been looking at the wrong question.'

'Twenty-nine trillion Arcadian cubits says we haven't,' said Buck.

'That's rather the point,' said Scratch. 'You're thinking about money and the trappings of success, but you've taken your eye off the real question. You shouldn't be asking how we can save life in the universe, you should be asking how it can live in harmony with technological advancement. Old Lenny was right. I can't wait to see his face when I tell him. Speaking of which, are we done here? Only, I was in the middle of a rather lucrative project and Clobber will be wondering where I've got to.'

'There is one loose end,' said Archer.

'Just the one?' said Buck.

'The book. How did the author know about Scratch?'

'I'll field this one,' said the professor, trying to reclaim some ground. 'There's only us here who know of its significance. All we have to do is send one of us back in time with the book and have them be the author.'

'Very good of you to offer,' said Buck, tossing the tattered copy of *Lady Bumpkins And The Case Of The Knotted Artichoke* to the professor and pressing a button.

Professor Doubt twanged into the vortex and, a moment later, walked through the door.

'Well done, professor,' said Buck. 'And congratulations on becoming the best-selling author of the third millennium. You can tell me all about it later.'

General Buck slumped into his chair and rolled a small blue ball on his desk. Pantz entered a moment later carrying a teapot and a plate of biscuits.

'Yes sir?'

'See to it that our friends here find their way to wherever and whenever it is they want to get to.'

'Anywhere, sir?'

'Yes, anywhere. And anywhen. Oh, and see that the short one gets a porcelain jug and a newspaper. Ancient Chinese would be a fair price, I think.'

'I don't think they had newspapers then, sir.'

Buck turned to Scratch. 'You can explain it to him on the way.'

'On the way where?'

'The Zooming chambers.'

'Lovely. One quick question before I go,' said Scratch.

'Go on.'

'What about the other me? The one floating in that room.'

'Oh, I wouldn't worry about him,' said Buck. 'He's history.'

Pantz opened his body to indicate to Scratch that he should leave the general's office.

'One last thing,' said Scratch. 'Any chance you could drop me off exactly where you found me?

Only, Clobber will get all confused again like he did in the post office that time if I start appearing and disappearing at the drop of a hat.'

'Consider it done,' said Buck, dismissing them with a wave of an arm.

The diamond doors slinked shut again and an ominously contemplative look passed over Buck's face.

'We are at a critical point in our great crusade,' he began, standing up and leaning on the back of his chair. 'There is much to do.'

'I thought we'd finished, sir?'

'My dear sergeant,' said Buck with worrying friendliness, 'we've only just begun. We can't go around taking away people's hope. Great Gammadrons, no! We must find another way.'

'Excuse me, general, but may I be so bold as to ask a question?' said Archer.

'Go on.'

'Well, we brought the Earthman here to send him to other planets' End Days in the hope he would add some perspective to our research, but you've just sent him back home again before we've had a chance to really use him in the way we intended.'

'I thought you wanted to ask a question,' said Buck. 'Perhaps you forgot to put it in? I am a busy man, Archer, and I'm sure you wouldn't wish to delay me unnecessarily.'

'Why did you dismiss him?' asked Archer flatly.

General Buck turned to the professor. 'I thought you said she was a bright student?'

'It does seem rather odd, general,' said the professor bravely. 'We have not yet collected any data that could be considered reliable.'

'My, my, professor,' said Buck, standing now and pacing the floor behind his desk. 'We have not sent Scratch home at all. We have merely sent *a* Scratch home. There's another one hanging in the Training Room, is there not?'

'Well, yes,' conceded Doubt. 'But therein lies the problem, I'm afraid. Never had a draw before, you see? We're not sure we'll be able to restore him to an animated state, and even if we do there's no knowing how the suspension has affected his functions.'

'Spoken like a true scientist, professor. I, on the other hand, have been shaped by the military and politics. By finding ways to win, whatever the cost. I didn't get to where I am by giving up at the first signs of difficulty. No, no, laddie. We battle on through and we will be triumphant when it matters most.'

'All Archer and I are saying, general, is that we needn't have had this hurdle in front of us at all if you hadn't let him go. He was right here and now he's back home sipping tea and watching the racing when he could be here saving the universe. That's all we're saying.'

'It is rather fortunate that we have another Scratch to use then, wouldn't you say? Some might even go so far as to call it *fate*.'

'Ah!' said Bakewell. 'That's what he meant. *Use the other one*.'

'What who meant?' said Buck.

'Emirc. I thought he was spouting gibberish as we negotiated our way off his planet, but perhaps he was on to something.'

'Well don't just stand there like a frog in a freezer. What other information have you withheld from a superior officer at a time of planetary crisis?'

'Sorry, sir. I didn't think it was important.'

Buck pushed his nose up against Bakewell's. 'Do you think your arms are important, sergeant? Because I could arrange for them to be forgotten too if you don't tell us everything in the next thirty seconds.'

'Four, nine, delta, seven, eight, omega, omega. Use the other one,' said Bakewell hastily. 'That's all he said.'

'Use the other one, eh?' said Buck thoughtfully.

'It does appear that the Earthman was right on the money,' said Doubt, half to himself. 'We can find the data, identify those planets with too much hope and not enough time, and take away all unnecessary expectation.'

'Perhaps you did not hear me correctly, professor? I will not remove hope from the universe. Life ceases to be so when the very thing that drives us forward is removed. The Arcadian people will not be the ones to sacrifice life for the sake of existence.'

'We won't?' said Bakewell. 'I thought that was the whole point?'

'Why are you still here, Bakewell?' snapped Buck. 'Haven't you got paperwork to do?'

'Yessir!' said Bakewell gratefully. 'Permission to leave, sir!'

'Granted, now bugger off.'

Bakewell opened the diamond doors and scampered away. There was another satisfying click as they closed behind him.

'Here are your orders, Professor,' said Buck. 'Do whatever it takes to reanimate our other Scratch and continue with the mission as planned. You now have the added bonus of knowing where to send him too, so please don't balls it up.'

'Never had a draw before though, general. I'm not sure we'll be able…'

'Whatever it takes, professor,' interrupted Buck.

'What about the others?' asked Archer. 'Two of them are wandering around the Training Room for a start, and the other two are in suspended animation.'

'Which is why you two are paid so handsomely. It is a puzzle, Archer. A puzzle that needs sharp minds and innovative thinking. Now get to it and report back within the hour.'

Archer and the professor gave a shallow nod and backed out of the room.

CHAPTER TWENTY-FOUR
ENERGY DISPLACEMENT

*A*rcadian technology was so advanced that most had forgotten how things worked at all. They just did. How they came to that state was of no concern to anyone. If something went a bit squiffy they would just make a new one. Or, at least, they would find the person who knew how the blasted thing was made in the first place and ask them to do whatever it is people with that sort of knowledge do. That person would then consider the myriad variables involved in the construction of the thing and try to map out an equally complicated solution.

As a result, their approach to problem solving was a little over-whipped. A broken door, for example, would often be addressed through several committee meetings that involved more information slides than anyone should have to sit through, and a sixteen-point plan on how to fix the hinges.

Professor Doubt and Archer stared in silence at the whiteout. The suspended figures of Scratch and Mr Raisbeck hung stubbornly in the air as though the fate of the universe wasn't dependent on their reanimation.

'Never had a draw before,' muttered the professor from his seat at the command board. 'Look at them, just hanging around there while another version of themselves wander the galaxy sparking untold damage to the balance of... *everything.*'

'All we need to know is why they were split in two,' said Archer in an altogether more pragmatic tone. 'If we can identify the primary causation catalyst, we can reverse it and restore them to normality. Or at least this version of normality.'

'Yes, but we've never had a draw before, Archer. Never happened. Not once.'

'I think we can agree that it's unprecedented, professor. If we could focus on how to unravel things we might just be able to save all life in the universe for all eternity. I have an idea that I think might...'

'Of course, of course,' said the professor, wobbling his head a little. 'Must focus on the job at hand, eh Archer? Can't just go about dithering over the details, even if they're rarer than a rat in a bath, eh?'

'Indeed. Perhaps if we just…'

'Right!' announced Doubt as if seeing the puzzle for the first time. 'What we have here is a maiden Zoom of life forms from an uncontacted planet. The Zoom worked as it should, notwithstanding the three additional lifeforms, and they were delivered successfully to the Training Room without their insides becoming outsides. They were functioning well enough to maintain normal operating protocols; conversation, walking and so on, and seemed capable of rational thought, although one of them appeared to be disproportionately concerned about a sofa. Have I missed anything out, Archer?'

'No, professor,' said Archer patiently. She knew the professor well enough to understand that sometimes you had to let him go at his own pace, like a parent running slowly so their child could win a race to the other end of the garden.

'Then two of them pressed the large, red button at precisely the same time. *Precisely*, Archer. Never happened before, never. In all my years of…'

'And then …' coaxed Archer.

'Ah, yes. Then the two men are suspended four metres above the floor and their life forces are split into existential conundrums, while the women are frozen to the spot. Very unusual, Archer, very unusual indeed. Possibly even unique. I'm not sure there's ever…'

'So the primary causation was the depression of the button,' interrupted Archer.

'Well, of course it was,' said the professor. 'Doesn't help us much though, does it?'

'I was thinking that we could…'

'No, no help at all, that. Can't undo what's been done, can we, Archer?'

'We could Zoom to the moment before they pressed the button.'

'That wouldn't do any good, no, no. That would only make matters worse. We'd have two of each of us and two of each of them. We'd be asking for trouble.'

'I have one more suggestion, professor. What if we simply pressed the button again? It might toggle the action and bring them back down.'

'I don't remember making it a toggle button' said Professor Doubt. 'That feels like something I'd remember.'

'Alright, maybe toggle isn't the right word. If we press the button again, without a draw this time, it may kickstart the training programme to begin, as should have happened in the first place.'

'Not a bad idea that, Archer. Why didn't you pipe up sooner? Go on in there and give it a wellie.'

'In *there!?*' exclaimed Archer. 'I'm not going in there. I could be scattered halfway across the galaxy.'

'Well how else are we going to do it?'

'We could use a big stick,' offered Archer. 'We could slide it into one of the nitrogen vents and lever it down onto the button.'

'Worth a go, I suppose,' said the professor. 'Seems a little archaic to use *mechanics* with all this technology lying around, but then I was never an expert on that sort of thing. Perhaps it's just what's needed. You could sit on one end as a counter-weight while I manoeuvre it into place.'

'Perhaps we should just use a dead weight, professor. There's less chance of it moving about and hampering your aim.'

'Quite right, Archer. Good thinking, that. We'll make an engineer of you yet.'

'I hope not,' said Archer.

'You get the stick, I'll get the weight. Meet you in the vent room in ten minutes.'

'Are you sure that's the right kind of weight?' asked Archer as the professor lowered a dark red armchair to the floor. 'I thought we had decided on a stable dead-weight?'

'Had a change of heart,' said the professor. 'Plus, I couldn't find any chickens in the refrigerators. This will do fine, though. You just perch yourself on top there, I'll move the pole into place, and *bing, bang, bosh,* we'll have ourselves a restored reality. It's all rather exciting, actually. We're riding the waves on the edge of technological achievement here, Archer. *Pioneering*, that's what this is.'

'It's a real thrill' intoned Archer neutrally.

Doubt lifted the chair onto one end of the large, metal pole, tied it down with copper wiring, and slid the pole towards the vent opening. He then placed a ladder beside the chair and inched it upwards.

'Take the weight for a minute, would you? Need to get this pole further in.'

Archer gripped the metal and watched the professor climb down from the ladder and attempt to push the pole inwards. After several wheezy attempts, he gave up.

'Maybe I should take the weight?' he said. 'Wouldn't want you putting your back out.'

'Indeed,' said Archer, moving to the end of the pole and sliding it in until the counterbalance was enough to hold the weight of the chair.

'Now, up you go, Archer.'

'I'm not sure this is…'

'There's no time for messing about, Archer. We're *testing*. Come on, up you go.'

Archer closed her eyes patiently for a moment, then clambered up the ladder and onto the armchair.

'Right then, here we go!' announced the professor giddily.

He peered through a gap in the vent at the four humans. 'Left a bit!' he called back to Archer.

'What do you mean, left a bit? I can't do anything from up here.'

'Alright, we'll start with you on the floor then. Down you come. Right, left a bit.'

'Was that right or left?'

'Left.'

Archer pushed slightly to the left.

'Not your left, *its* left!'

'*Its* left?'

'Yes, *its* left. You just moved it further right.'

'Right.'

'No, left.'

'How's that?' asked Archer.

'Better. Now, right a bit. Bit more. Bit more. Stop! That's it, hold it. We're directly above the button.'

'Now what?' asked Archer.

'Now we press it.'

'But the chair is touching the ceiling here, professor. There's no more *down* for us to give.'

'What do you mean?' said Doubt turning around. 'Ah. Bugger.'

The dark red armchair was pressed against the ceiling of the vent room like an elephant in a fish tank. The professor climbed up the ladder and began unfastening the copper wire.

'Don't do that!' cried Archer. 'It'll fall!'

The armchair wobbled.

'Never been much of an engineer,' said the professor from the top rung. 'Far too many letters where numbers should be if you ask me. Not to worry though, Archer, I think I can manage a simple knot. Ah, here we are.'

The professor fiddled with the copper wire. He was extraordinarily talented when it came to matters of technology, and this, he surmised, was just a low brow version of the stuff. What he hadn't reckoned with, however, was the obstinacy of knots. He was not entirely unlike a kitten who, on spotting a ball of wool under a coffee table, sees nothing to stop it knitting a nice warm jumper for itself.

The armchair wobbled again.

'Maybe we should lower the chair first, professor?' offered Archer.

'Too late for that, I'm afraid,' said Doubt. 'I've nearly got it.'

There was a *twang* as the knot gave way, firing strands of copper wire to the floor. The armchair then did exactly what Archer, and any other observing life form of moderate intelligence, knew would happen. It fell to one side of the pole, landing with a splintering crunch. The professor swayed on the ladder before pushing against the ceiling for balance. The pole swung in a spiral of physics, stopping every so often as if hitting a barrier before slowly settling back at the ceiling.

'What was that?' said Archer, wide-eyed.

'I would think it was rather obvious,' said the professor. 'It was the chair being emancipated from its shackles.'

'Not that,' said Archer, as the sound of groaning came through the vent. '*That!*'

Archer grabbed the ladder, swung it over to the vent, climbed up, and peered through the gap. The whiteness had turned a sullen mustard colour and four groggy humans, each rubbing a body part, staggered haphazardly around the room.

'We did it, professor! They're back!'

Zoomers

CHAPTER TWENTY-FIVE

TRAINING

'Welcome, one and all, to the Promantory Nebula, to Arcadia, and to the greatest learning establishment this side of the Kiplian Gravity Mines,' said the professor from behind a classroom desk. 'May I begin by apologising for the unorthodox nature of your arrival.'

'I reckon instantaneous space travel is a little bit more than unorthodox,' said Scratch. 'I was in the middle of a job. The smallest sound can do all kinds of things to your nervous system in my line of work. You could have given me a heart attack!'

'I was referring to the bumps on your heads with a big stick,' said the professor, 'but it is useful to hear of your priorities, nonetheless. It can be rather tricky to know where to place the bar when it comes to Uncontacted Lifeforms. I can see we will have to begin at the beginning, as it were.'

After two hours of listening to Professor Doubt's version of Arcadian history and how it was instrumental in the creation of Zooming, Archer cleared her throat.

'Perhaps now would be a good time to go through the fundamental principles of Zooming, professor? Then we can get on with the selection.

'I ain't selecting myself for anything,' said Scratch. 'There's always trouble when you go *selecting* yourself. Stands to reason, doesn't it. If you haven't been involved in the decision to do the thing that needs a *selection*, but are being asked to get stuck in to the *selection process* for it, then there's probably a good reason why the people who decided whatever it was that had to be done haven't selected themselves, ain't there?'

'I'm sorry, you lost me at *ain't*,' said Doubt honestly. 'Did you follow that, Archer?'

'I believe he is trying to say that he would prefer to avoid any unnecessary entanglements with existential variables as possible, professor.'

'Oh, I see. Well, it's a good thing you don't have a choice then, isn't it? No, you'll be Zooming before you know it Mister Scratch, don't you worry about that. Oh, the adventures you will have. I'd go myself, of course, but at my age you have to watch the old bones. Brittle buggers these days, I'm afraid.'

The professor swiped across his desk and a hologram of the universe appeared in the centre of the room.

'Your own selection has already been made,' he continued. 'That is, the selection of *you*, Mister Scratch. The rest of you were something of an oversight, I'm afraid, but these things happen when you're working at the limits of knowledge. Something was bound to go slightly awry really. All that remains is for you to select the planet for your maiden Zoom. But first, allow me to illustrate *how* Zooming works, in extraordinarily basic terms, naturally. I assume you are all familiar with Zangrid's extended theory of matter absorption in an unrepagitated helix?'

Archer turned the palms of her hands to face the floor and made a lowering gesture.

'Really?' said the professor, swiping through his notes. 'Alright, we'll go back a step or two. As we all know, matter holds a latent ability to travel through contra-magnesium flexoidal spirograms. Well, so long as you don't mess about with the forial carbunculates, eh?'

He chuckled to himself and looked up from his notes. Four ignorant pairs of eyes stared at him blankly. 'No?'

Archer shook her head and made the lowering signal again.

'Any ideas, Archer? I'm not sure I can get any more basic than that. Was there something in The Observations you could use?'

Archer leaned on the armrests of her chair and stood up slowly. 'Albert Einstein.'

Four sets of eyebrows ascended four foreheads.

'Great. He showed that it is possible to travel in time so long as you travel faster than the speed of light. Are you all familiar with this concept?'

'Of course, who doesn't know that?' said Cantina.

'That's how I feel about Zangrid,' mumbled Professor Doubt bitterly.

'Well,' continued Archer, 'Zooming is, fundamentally, the flinging of matter so fast and so far through space that it arrives back at it's starting place slightly before it left.'

'Or so slowly that it arrives afterwards,' said the professor, doing his best to be helpful.

'With a little tweaking we can dictate the time at which the matter arrives back at the start. We can also apply the same logic to the destination. When certain adjustments are made, we can determine the location to which we send the matter.'

Scratch adjusted himself in his seat. 'So what you're saying, is that you can send people all over the universe to whatever time in history they like?'

'In very basic terms, yes,' said Archer.

'So you could send me to Rushmore Street on, say, the fourteenth of March, nineteen ninety four? Just for argument's sake, of course.'

'It would be possible, with a bit of preparation.'

'That'd be great, I'll choose that one. Harold the Budgie won't know what's hit him.'

'I'm afraid there are limited options available to you,' said the professor. 'We have done our best to identify six planets nearing their End Day. That is, close to the moment that all life on these planets ceased to be. It is our intention to send you to one of these planets and allow you to observe the life forms there. You are in a unique position, we believe, to see behavioural patterns where we only see data. You will then return here and share all you have learnt. It is hoped that the information you provide will allow us to prevent biological extinction across the universe.'

'And that's a good thing, is it?' asked Glorious.

'Of course it is!' said Doubt. 'Life would flourish where it once decayed. The universe would be teeming with it, with no limit to the advancements we could achieve.'

'That was my point,' said Glorious. 'Is it not better for the stronger species to outlive the weak? If the weak can survive as well as the strong, then it would stunt evolution.'

'You see? That's precisely the sort of perspective we hoped you would bring. Marvellous stuff!'

'We should get on with the selection,' prodded Archer. 'Before we get too sidetracked.'

'Of course, of course,' agreed the professor gratefully. 'Now, Earthians. Is that the correct term, *Earthians*? Doesn't sound quite right to me.'

'I think a better word might be Earthlings,' suggested Archer.

'Or guys,' offered Scratch.

'People?' said Mr Raisbeck.

'People. That'll do,' said Doubt. 'Now, *people*. Here are your choices.'

The hologram spun gently, then swooped in to focus on a collection of dots. A helpful arrow appeared, pointing at one of them.

'This,' continued the professor, 'is the planet Theradon. It has held life in one form or another for more than twelve million years. The latest, and possibly last, species is the Theradian Mining Shrew, a highly intelligent mammal with flexible, fingered pincers and a penchant for daring feats of bravery, usually involving leaps from high places. Due to the elevated levels of accidental deaths recorded here, we believe their evolutionary progress may have gone a little off track.'

'Once a species' genetics has moved away from a sustainable path, it is almost impossible to recalibrate it,' said Cantina.

'On the contrary, doctor,' said Doubt. 'Redirecting their genes would be quite simple. It is the prevalence of cliffs there that concerns us most. The ratio of fatally high outcrops to organisms is so skewed you need a team of statisticians working twelve hour shifts for a week just to write the number out.'

'Why did you choose that one then?' asked Mr Raisbeck. 'Seems to me it's already too late for them.'

'That is our opinion, too,' said Archer. 'But that is also the reason it has made the shortlist. It is vital that we have your perspective included in the final decision. There may have been something there that you could see but we could not.'

'Safe to say we're not going there,' said Scratch. 'I can't stand heights anyway, on account of that business with the fire escape in Lambourne Road.'

'Perhaps we will place Theradon into the *maybe* pile for the moment,' said Professor Doubt. 'This is no time for hasty eliminations.'

'Very good, professor,' said Scratch. '*Hasty eliminations*. Ha!'

'Quite,' said the professor, who had not, in fact, intended any such pun. 'The second planet we have identified is Capa; a very interesting and unique place.'

'Not that one,' said Cantina.

'You haven't even heard what it's like yet,' said Doubt with a dash of teenage petulance.

'That does not matter, professor. If it is unique then it will not help us to find a solution for the whole universe.'

'Well, maybe not, but it is very interesting. Can't I at least tell you the good bits?'

'Depends how much of a rush we're in, doesn't it?' said Scratch. 'I still don't know why you can't just take your time, since you're going to Zoom us to wherever we choose anyway.'

'One must minimize the variables, Mister Scratch. If we all went around Zooming willy-nilly we'd land ourselves in quite the existential pickle, as it were. No, we must try to find the answer in one Zoom if at all possible.' The professor swiped at his notes again. 'Fine, we will move on to planet number three; Prentonia'

The hologram shifted again, this time closing in on a cluster of three planets orbiting a lone star. The arrow pointed to a blue green planet in the middle.

'That one,' said Scratch. 'That's my choice.'

'You don't know anything about it yet,' said the professor. 'There could be a man-melting atmosphere, or a surface temperature that would freeze the centre of a white dwarf!'

'It wouldn't have made your shortlist then, though, would it? said Scratch. 'Does it have a carnivorous atmosphere?'

'Well, no, but that's not the point. You can't just go around picking your planet at random, it wouldn't be *scientific* then.'

'Why not? It looks pleasant enough to me. Has a nice familiar look about it too. I always prefer my planets to be a sort of bluey green. Makes me feel less like I'm millions of light years from my bed, see?'

'You can't just pick the destination based on colour, that would be preposterous!'

'Perhaps you could enlighten them with a little information, professor?' said Archer diplomatically.

'Fine,' said the professor. 'We scanned almost four-fifths of the accessible universe for planetary bodies as similar to your Earth as it was possible to find. This, people, is the result. The planet Prentonia in the Garnett Nebula.'

The hologram shifted again and was now solely a magnified image of Prentonia.

'Told you,' said Scratch.

'But *not* because of its colouring,' said Doubt, glaring slightly at Scratch. 'That was merely a coincidence. The important similarities concern the evolutionary trajectory of its dominant species. It can be mapped with a startling correlation. It is the difference, however, that makes this planet such an interesting possibility.'

The hologram of Prentonia shrunk slightly, allowing an unpopulated graph to appear beside it. Two lines, one red and one blue, appeared at the zero:zero point and meandered their way neatly towards the opposite corner of the graph.

'This is the evolutionary progress of Prentonia, the red line, and of Earth, the blue line. As you can see, they are remarkably similar.'

The lines stopped.

'This point is Earth's current evolutionary position, and that of Prentonia at the same point in its history. Here's the fun part. We have a further four million years of data we can add to Prentonia's line. Here's what happened.'

The red line began moving again. It pivoted sharply upwards and crashed through the ceiling of the graph, shattering the holographic image like a thin pane of stained glass.

'That bit was for show,' admitted the professor immediately, as if regretting the decision to include such flamboyance in something as important and serious as the fate of the universe. 'Nevertheless, it illustrates the destruction of their organic denizens rather well.'

'Why are you asking us to choose?' said Glorious. 'It seems to me you think this is the obvious candidate.'

'We do,' admitted Archer, 'but it must be your decision. It is your perspective we need to ensure the integrity of the mission.'

'If it's all the same to you,' said Mr Raisbeck, 'Can we not call it a *mission*? Makes it sound like we might not come back.'

'Ah,' admitted the professor.

'Of course,' said Archer. 'Your perspective will ensure the integrity of the safe journey to a relatively familiar planet.'

'Much better, thank you,' said Mr Raisbeck before clearing his throat. 'I do have one question, if I may?'

'Please,' said Archer. 'Ask as many as you need.'

'Will it be possible for me to be home before two o'clock? I'm expecting a delivery.'

'I'm sure we can arrange that, can't we professor?'

'Oh yes, quite sure,' said Doubt.

'Then I say we get this over with. That one,' said Mr Raisbeck, pointing to the image of Prentonia.

'I concur,' said Glorious.

'Why not,' agreed Scratch.

'I would prefer to see more data on the first two planets,' said Cantina. 'It is not possible to make an educated assessment of the variables involved without seeing more of them.'

Professor Doubt clasped his hands behind his back and began pacing up and down in front of his desk. He scrunched his lips in thought, then leant over his desk and brushed his finger across one corner of it. A hologram of four graphs appeared, each with the Earth's evolutionary progress mapped onto it in phosphorescent blue. A red line then appeared on each of the four graphs in turn. Three showed no obvious correlation with Earth.

'As you can see, Prentonia is considerably more Earth-like than the others. So much so, in fact, that we thought it was a data entry error by one of the abacus monkeys in the basement. The chances of one planet being this similar to another is so infinitesimally small as to be zero.'

'Are the other three planets the next closest to Earth, or have you eliminated some that fall between Prentonia and the others?' asked Cantina.

'A very astute question, doctor. It can be tricky to find reliable data, but we think we have the best available options for you. There was one planet that showed a waning population during our initial inspection, but when the short range readings came back their population was more than double our original estimations. They had terrible trouble with journalists, you see?'

'I'm not sure I do, no,' said Cantina. 'What have journalists got to do with it?'

'They were, how shall I put this? They were prone to exaggeration.'

'They lied a lot,' said Archer helpfully.

'Sounds like journalism to me,' said Scratch.

'You have monkeys in the basement?' said Mr Raisbeck.

'Their fabrication was delivered with such ferocity and frequency that they ended up just making the whole thing up as they went along, including stock values and sports results. Caused all kinds of problems with their economy. In the end they were ordered to draft a *Retraction and Clarification* document whenever they ran a story that wasn't true. Then they had to ensure that more people saw the apology than the original story. It led to the discovery of thirty-two previously uncontacted tribes in a remote hilly region of their eastern hemisphere.'

'Sounds like we could learn a thing or two from them,' said Scratch.

'So, to answer your question; yes, we did find a few others, but they were removed from consideration on account of their data being rather... explainable.'

'What do you mean by explainable?' pressed Cantina.

'Well, they were handed a cessation order from The Council.'

'*The Council?*'

'That is a very short question with a very long answer,' said the professor. 'I would be happy to fill you in on your return. Suffice to say, one was shrunk to the size of a small orange and was rather skillfully potted into a middle pocket of the Great Billiards Table of Irby Major.'

'And the other?' asked Cantina, despite herself.

'Accidentally blown up by a great big laser in the White War. Nothing especially poetic about that one I'm afraid.'

'Can we get on with it?' said Scratch. 'Only, I haven't eaten in a hundred light years and I could murder a bacon sarnie.'

'Ah, my apologies,' said the professor. 'I should have told you this when you first arrived. You have, in fact, travelled more than seventeen thousand light years from Earth.'

'No wonder I'm starving,' said Scratch. 'Is there a canteen here somewhere?'

'A light year is a unit of distance, mister Scratch, not…'

'What the professor is trying to say,' interrupted Archer, 'is that you have, as you say, travelled rather a long way to be here, and we will do our best to ensure you have a good meal this afternoon.'

'Will it be before two o'clock?' asked Mr Raisbeck.

The professor waved a delegatory arm to Archer.

'You will be home in time for your delivery, no matter how long you spend with us on Arcadia, Mr Raisbeck.'

'Not if I'm here all day, I won't.'

Archer gave a sigh. 'Trust me, you will be home in time.'

'I never trust anyone who says *trust me*,' said Mr Raisbeck. 'There'd be no point in saying it if there was no reason not to trust them now, would there?'

'I'm sorry, you lost me halfway through the triple negative,' said the professor impatiently. 'Now, if we could press on with matters. Show of hands, if you will. All those in favour of Zooming to Prentonia, raise your hand.'

'Wait, what are the co-ordinates of Prentonia?' asked Cantina.

'You do like to be thorough, don't you?' said Doubt. 'Let's see. Prentonia is at... it's here somewhere, hold on a minute. I could have sworn I saw... ah, here we go. Galactic Location Reference four, nine, delta, seven, eight, omega, omega. Sounds rather familiar.'

'Sounds like that Emirc character knew a thing or two about our mission,' said Archer.

'Then I believe we are all agreed, are we not? Show of hands, please. All in favour of Prentonia?'

The four Earthlings raised their arms with varying degrees of reluctance.

'Marvellous!' cried the professor. 'We can move on to your training.'

'You mean we haven't even started yet?' complained Mr Raisbeck.

'It won't take long, I assure you,' said Archer. 'Professor, perhaps you could go through the details?'

'Right you are,' said Doubt. He pulled out his chair, sat on the very edge of it, and leaned forward conspiratorially. 'Hold on tight,' he said quietly.

A confused silence wafted around the room.

'When you're ready, prof,' said Scratch.

'Oh, I'm sorry. I said *hold on tight*.'

'Yes, we got that bit. Any chance you could, you know, speed things up a bit? My stomach thinks my throat's been cut here.'

'That's all there is to it,' said Doubt, clapping his hands together gleefully. 'Ha! I bet you thought you'd be here for weeks learning about displacement trajectories and how to keep your stomach from climbing out of your mouth in the Zooming channel. No, no. Just hold on tight and hope to buggery you don't lose your grip before the wobbling stops.'

CHAPTER TWENTY-SIX

ONLY A DROP

'Welcome to Moon Shots,' said Cauliflower. 'The finest bar for a hundred miles.'

'*Only* bar,' corrected Bakewell.

'Either way, it's an experience you'll never forget. Or perhaps you will, actually. Depends what you choose from the menu, I suppose.'

'A menu!' exclaimed Scratch as if hearing his house had been saved from a terrible fire. 'At last! Where is it then? Come on, I've waited long enough, I'm starving.'

'Ah,' said Cauliflower. 'I was referring to the drinks menu. Food is downstairs on Level Four I'm afraid. We'll have a quick drink here first, just to whet your appetite you understand, then we'll go straight there. At least, as straight as anyone can go after their first Moon Shots experience.'

'If it's all the same to you,' said Mr Raisbeck, 'I'd rather not drink in a place that can be classed as an *experience*. Doesn't bode well for the repercussions.'

'Oh, the repercussions are what makes it such an experience,' said Cauliflower. 'Wait and see.'

'Yes, that's rather the problem.'

'This way please, people,' said Bakewell, doing his best to maintain an air of authority. 'A quick one here, then down to the canteen.'

Scratch, Mr Raisbeck, Cantina and Glorious followed the two Arcadians to the long, silvery bar at the far side of the room.

'Evening,' stated Drainer. 'Brought some guests along with you, I see.'

'Buck has asked us to give our guests a short tour. May I introduce our four Earth people' began Bakewell, a little too formally. 'This here is Scratch, Mr Raisbeck, Cantina and Glorious.'

'Pleasure to meet you,' lied Drainer. 'What'll it be?'

'Perhaps I should explain how things work here,' said Bakewell diplomatically. 'I'd say it's a little different to what you're used to.'

'You haven't seen The Nelson,' said Scratch. 'Once you've spent an evening in there, especially on darts night, there's no pub in the universe that could surprise you.'

'Even so, it would be prudent to give you a little pointer,' said Bakewell.

'There are probably a few more variables involved here,' said Cauliflower. 'Wouldn't want you to overdo it on your first night. Big day tomorrow, too.'

'Oh, you mean saving the universe? That thing?' said Scratch. 'I reckon that's all the more reason to have a few tonight, don't you?'

'Perhaps we'll take a look at the menu, Drainer,' said Bakewell.

'I'll have a...' began Cauliflower.

'Pomplefitzer with a dash of cheerfulness?' suggested Drainer.

'Hmmmmm,' considered Cauliflower, thoughtfully.

Drainer prepared the corporal's drink and slid it along the bar.

'Yes, I think that's what I'll... oh, thank you.'

'What's that?' asked Cantina.

'This, my good Earth person, is a Pomplefitzer. The greatest drink in the tri-galaxy area,' said Cauliflower. 'First mixed by Admiral Cheex in the Salt Wars, four hundred years ago. It was originally designed to be an anaesthetic for the...'

'It's bitter and refreshing,' interrupted Drainer. 'Tastes a bit like lemon.'

'Sounds a bit fancy to me,' said Scratch. 'Got anything a bit earthier?'

'I had never heard of your planet until a few days ago,' said Drainer defensively, 'so excuse me if I haven't rustled up a three page menu of Earth drinks especially for your arrival.'

'I meant *earthy* as in, you know, peat bogs, soil, full bodied, that sort of thing. Usually has a name like *The Sheep's Finger*, or *The Butcher's Laugh*.'

Drainer paused. 'I don't believe I have a drink that would be considered... *muddy*.'

Cauliflower picked up four menus and passed them to each member of the group. 'I suggest you start with a Pomplefitzer and add your own little *swoosh* to it. You can choose any of these,' he said, pointing to the diamond vials on the wall.

The four Earth people leaned forward, scanning the labels on the bottles.

'Pick your emotion,' said Drainer, sweeping an arm towards the shelves behind him. 'The higher the shelf, the more expensive the drink, and the more paperwork you'll need to fill out.'

'You mean we can just choose what mood we're in?' asked Glorious.

'Sounds like one of my old girlfriends,' said Scratch.

'Does that one really say bitterness?' asked Cantina. 'Why would anyone ever choose to be bitter?'

'Ignore that one, it's just water,' said Cauliflower.

'Is there one for organisation?' asked Mr Raisbeck.

'*Organisation?*' said Scratch. 'Really? You can choose any emotion you want and you opt for the equivalent of a paperclip and a plastic desk tidy?'

Mr Raisbeck took a patient breath. 'I was hoping there might be something to help make sense of arriving, rather suddenly I might add, on an alien planet with fresh orders to save all life in the universe. To *organise* my thoughts a little.'

'I think some bravado would do you good,' suggested Glorious. 'A bit of *oomph* to help you through.'

'That's actually not a bad idea,' said Mr Raisbeck. 'Erm, barman, do you have anything like that?'

'Let's see. I've got *audacity, boldness, intrepid.* Any of those take your fancy?'

'I'll have a pint of boldness,' said Mr Raisbeck decisively.

'You bloody well won't,' said Cauliflower. 'All you need is the tiniest of little drops. If you had a pint of that your eyeballs would be halfway to next week before you could blink, and that'd just be from seeing the bill.'

Cauliflower turned to Drainer. 'Maybe just a little taster shot for the Earth person here.'

'Couldn't agree more, corporal,' said Drainer, spiking a small yellow fruit with a cocktail stick and sliding the finished drink to Mr Raisbeck.

'Smells alright,' said the former human resources manager, before lifting the glass to his lips. He extended his little finger outwards as if drinking with royalty, took a gentile sip, and fell immediately to the floor without so much as a rolling eye.

'Come on son,' said Sergeant Bakewell, pulling Mr Raisbeck up by the armpits. 'It's just shock, that's all. The first one's always the worst.'

'Fbbmsmpfffph,' said Mr Raisbeck.

'Yes, it does, doesn't it?' agreed Cauliflower. 'I said the same thing when I had my first. Mind you, I was only a little boy then.'

'What does *disappointment* taste like?' asked Scratch, pointing to a glass on the lowest shelf.

'You should ask your mother,' said Mr Raisbeck.

'Oh good, you're back,' said Scratch. 'Can we get him something else?'

'I wouldn't recommend mixing your drinks in Moon Shots,' said Cauliflower. 'In much the same way as I wouldn't recommend skiing in the Azoic Nebula.'

The four Earth people reacted as distracted students do when asked to answer a question they hadn't known was coming.

'I see,' said Glorious non-committedly.

'The Azoic Nebula,' repeated Cauliflower unhelpfully.

'What the good corporal here seems to have forgotten,' said Bakewell, 'is that you are from a planet that has only recently experienced First Contact. So recently, in fact, that it is you who are to be the subjects of the story when your history books are written.'

'Right, sorry,' said Cauliflower, stirring his newly made drink like a scolded child. 'It's full of gaseous planets,' he mumbled sulkily.

'Get some of that down you and you'll feel better,' said Drainer. 'It's your usual.'

'Any questions?' said Bakewell.

'Who's picking up the tab?' said Scratch. 'Only, I've left my wallet at home, see?'

'I meant about tomorrow, your first proper Zoom. You must have lots of questions.'

'No point worrying about all that now, is there?' said Scratch. 'Que sera sera and all that.'

'A case of *what?*' said Cauliflower.

'Not case, *que sera*. It means don't bother trying to change anything because whatever's going to happen *is* going to happen whether you like it or not. It's Spanish I think. Gets sung a lot down at Roots Hall for some reason. Probably because it rhymes with Wembley.'

'French,' corrected Cantina.

'Wembley?' said Cauliflower.

'That doesn't rhyme at all,' said Glorious.

'Never mind all that,' said Bakewell, trying his best to contain the verbal chaos. 'Have any of you got a question about tomorrow. That is why General Buck sent us here for the evening after all.'

'Ah, so the bigwig's paying, is he?' said Scratch. 'Fantastic. Make mine a double.'

'The Zoom itself, perhaps?' said Bakewell desperately. He knew he would have to brief Buck on the conversation later and it would be much easier if he didn't have to make it all up himself. 'How to stop your brain from melting when it sees three suns and seven moons in one sky, maybe?'

'Will they have normal toilets there?' said Scratch. 'Or will they be those ones you get in some places where you have to crouch over a hole?'

'It may surprise you to learn I'm not entirely familiar with the mechanics of all bathroom facilities across the universe.'

'Right. What about food then? Will it be normal, honest grub or that fancy stuff that comes in tiny portions and looks prettier than a butterfly in a ball gown?'

'Perhaps it would be better if we focused on more… actually, bugger this. Drainer, I'll have my usual. A double I think.'

'That's more like it,' said Scratch. 'Make the most of it while it's free, that's what I say.'

'Cantina… Glorious,' said Bakewell, taking a swig between names. 'Any pressing question you'd like answered? Anything at all, please.'

'I'm sure we'll have plenty when the time comes,' said Glorious. 'It's hard to know what to ask when you're being sent to an alien planet to save all life in the universe.'

'Never done it before, see?' offered Scratch.

'Well, be sure to pipe up if you think of one, won't you,' said Bakewell, giving up. 'In the meantime, I'd better be going. Got a pile of paperwork taller than a startled tree-rat. Corporal, see them to their quarters when the time comes, there's a good man.'

'Right you are, sarge,' said Cauliflower, already calculating how many free drinks he could get through before his legs gave way. 'Ladies and gentlemen, follow me. I've got us a table.'

Zoomers

CHAPTER TWENTY-SEVEN
SALUTE TO SURVIVAL

'Your time has come, people,' announced Professor Doubt. 'Welcome to the Zooming station.'

The four humans stood in a neat line in front of two swirling purple and black vortices. Each wore a different coloured jumpsuit, all of which were too bright and made them look like contestants on a low budget adventure game show.

'You made the adjustments to the Zooming channel, Archer?'

'I have, but was only able to strengthen it enough for two life forms at a time, professor. Both channels should bring them all out at approximately the same place on the Prentonian surface.'

'Marvellous. Now, people, remember what I said. *Hold on tight!*'

'I have a question,' said Scratch. 'What are we supposed to do once we're there and how do we get back?'

'That's two questions, but I'll allow them,' said Doubt. 'As I have already explained during your training, you are to study the planet and its population and look for differences between their behaviour and that of your fellow Earth people, as I had hoped was obvious. It is the differences that hold the key to this whole caboodle.'

'Right, and we get back here by…?'

'Oh, I wouldn't worry about that, Mister Scratch. Archer and I will be watching things carefully from here. If you need a quick exit, or if you believe you have enough data, you can simply summon us to Zoom you home. Well, not *home* home, naturally, but you see what I mean.'

'And how do we summon you, exactly?'

'You simply need to use the nominated retrieval phrase. I have chosen one I believe is made up of words familiar to you, but are unlikely to be used in this sequence during normal conversation; *zen horseface*.'

'That is rather unlikely,' admitted Cantina.

'Now, if you would step forward please? Cantina and Scratch, you will be using this channel. Mr Raisbeck and Glorious, you'll be using this one. Stay one pace from the vortex please, we wouldn't want your feet to arrive before you do.'

They shuffled forward, each trying to move slower than the others like children lining up to kiss their granny, until they were a little more than arm's length from the swirl.

'Since you have more Zooming experience than the rest, you can go first Mr Scratch.'

'Do you think I've done this sort of thing before?'

'Ah, yes. That was the other you, sorry. You look so alike; I get confused.'

'Listen, I've got out of some tight spaces in my time alright, but I never quite got the hang of time travel at the speed of light.'

'Faster than light, remember?' said the professor.

'Either way, I'm not going first.'

'If you don't go first,' said Archer, 'then you will be Zooming in Cantina's channel and vice versa. You'd be shredded before you could blink.'

'Shredded, eh? Right, well I'd better get going then, hadn't I? See you on the other side, chaps.'

Scratch took a step towards the vortex, then paused and turned to the professor. 'Don't suppose there's anything to be said for doing this here, is there? You guys must have all kinds of whizzmajigs that could just show us the planet from here.'

'I'm afraid you need to be right there in the thick of it,' said the professor. 'It's the best way to get a real feel for the place.'

'Right, right,' conceded Scratch. 'Well, here goes! Best to get as much of me in there in one go, eh? Wouldn't want to arrive after my feet.'

He straightened his back and bunny-hopped into the vortex.

'Your turn, doctor,' said Archer.

'Can I bring a clipboard?' asked Cantina. 'For notes.'

'It's a little late for that, I'm afraid,' said Archer. 'The channel has been calibrated for your exact specifications. Now, in you go. Good luck.'

Cantina followed Scratch into the vortex and disappeared.

'Now you,' said Archer, gesturing to Glorious.

The plumber placed her arms firmly at her side and bounced into the vortex without a word.

'Now, listen here,' said Mr Raisbeck, summoning his suburban belligerence at last. 'You can't just make me go in there. I'm not comfortable with the level of health and safety precautions. What if I lose my grip as I'm hurtling through the universe? I could end up in the wrong galaxy with no way to get back. There'd be no chance of me getting a refund from Shufflebottom and Sons then. It's hard enough to get them on the phone as it is.'

'Let me help,' said the professor, moving to stand behind him. 'The safest way to do this is to…'

He pushed Mr Raisbeck in the centre of his back and into the vortex. Archer raised a single eyebrow. 'I didn't know you had it in you, professor.'

'He would have been dithering all day if we let him. Now, let's see how they're getting on.'

Scratch plopped out of the vortex and onto the grassy surface of Prentonia with remarkable smoothness. A moment later, Cantina landed next to him.

'Lovely day for it,' said Scratch, getting to his feet. He strolled around Cantina, exploring the immediate vicinity, then stopped dead. 'Don't move,' he said, holding out an arm.

About three paces from where they landed, the ground fell away in an almost sheer drop. Trees dotted the side of the ravine, sticking out like toothbrushes in a blancmange. At the bottom was a lake of such blueness as to demand that all other shades of blue be called something else.

The second vortex began forming beside Cantina. Unfortunately for Glorious and Mr Raisbeck it was about four paces away, and in the wrong direction. The two figures plopped out, opened their eyes wide at the vision of the alien planet, then a little wider as they realised they were suspended, albeit briefly, above an enormous drop.

They landed, then rolled. Their limbs flailed like excitable starfish as they tumbled towards the lake.

Scratch leaned gingerly over the edge and winced as Mr Raisbeck connected with a tree. To his surprise, and presumably that of Mr Raisbeck, the tree bent like a rubber sausage and twanged, sending Mr Raisbeck some way back up the ravine before allowing him to continue on his downward trajectory. Scratch looked around for Glorious and spotted her a little further down the slope. She floated upwards for a moment, then descended again. The two of them bounced their way down like pinballs until they were so far away as to be lost to sight.

'I reckon it's fair to say that wasn't supposed to happen,' said Scratch.

Cantina crawled along the grass and peered over the edge. 'Now what?'

'The way I see it,' said Scratch in the tone of a street-corner philosopher, 'is that we can't do anything about them, and they can't do anything about us, so we should just carry on about our business and get back home as quickly as we can. If they're in trouble they'll just say… well, they'll just use that phrase and be safe in Arcadia before the trees have stopped waving.'

'That all sounds very simple,' said Cantina. 'But what is it we are supposed to be doing? There's just a lot of field here and no sign of life anywhere. Listen, it's perfectly quiet. Don't you think that's a bit strange?'

They stood still for a moment, Scratch turning his head slightly to help him hear better.

'That's odder than Bingo Bill in a library,' admitted Scratch.

'What are we supposed to do if there is no evidence to collect?' said the doctor.

'We'll just have to go and find some. Come on!' said Scratch, heading off and away from the ravine. 'This way, I reckon.'

'We're just going to leave them down there?'

'Nothing else we can do, is there? Listen, in my line of work it pays to make decisions quickly. I've got a wotsits about it. A sixth sense.'

'I'm not comfortable leaving them without even *trying* to help. What if we were in their situation?'

'We're not though, are we?' said Scratch.

Cantina gave him a look that wouldn't have been out of place on a grandmother after watching their grandson slip a chocolate bar into their pocket in the local newsagents.

'Alright, fine,' said Scratch, leaning back over the precipice. 'Mr Raisbeck? Glorious? Are you there, can we help?'

Nothing.

'Well, can't say we didn't try. Let's go. There's a hedge over there, maybe all of Prentonia's civilization is hiding on the other side.'

He stood up and headed away from the slope. Cantina sighed and followed him to the hedge. It was about five feet tall and just as wide. Scratch found a break in the branches, turned himself sideways, crouched a little, and shimmied through with relative briskness. Once through to the other side he raised himself to his inadequate height, stretched his arms, and turned slowly around to take in the new scenery. He had expected more grassy hills, of which there were, in fact, many. He also expected more hedgerows on either side, of which there were two. What he did not expect, however, was a hundred soldiers in ceremonial military dress and feathers pointing from their helmets forming a guard of honour in front of a free-standing door that seemed to lead only to the continuation of the field.

'Teeeeeen hut!' roared a voice.

A hundred pairs of boots made a single thudding noise on the turf.

'Abooooooouuuut face!'

The soldiers turned as one to face each other.

'Steady!'

The door opened and a tall, bespectacled human stepped out onto the field and marched stiffly towards Scratch. He was dressed all over in dull, grey cloth. The kind of unremarkable, anonymous grey you could miss if you weren't looking directly at it surrounded by heavily armed soldiers and an extra-terrestrial landscape.

'You're late,' he said without preamble.

'I am?' managed Scratch. 'Erm, *sorry?*'

'Do you realise what time it is?'

'Shortly after you thought I'd be here, I'd say.'

'It is half past two in the afternoon. I'm sure you don't need me to tell you the significance of that.'

'Oh, you must be a dentist,' said Scratch, grinning slightly.

'I most certainly am not a dentist! I am Notlob, Commander of The Tasks and Guardian of the Sacred Sand.'

'Good for you,' said Scratch, a man for whom intimidation came with handcuffs and a truncheon, or not at all. 'How do you command these tasks exactly? Do you shout at them until they offer clear and concise instructions?'

Cantina chose this moment to pop her bedraggled head out from the hedge. 'Next time I'm finding a gate,' she said before looking up at the scene and freezing.

'Looks like we found your data,' said Scratch.

'Come,' ordered Notlob. 'There is lots for you to do and little time with which to do it.'

The Prentonian Commander of The Tasks and Guardian of the Sacred Sand opened the door again. The far side of the threshold no longer showed the green grass of the field, but rather an absolute blackness. It was as though this version of black had been practising since the beginning of time and had gone beyond a mere absence of light. It was pure and uncompromised, as physical as the centre of a mountain, only darker.

Scratch and Cantina followed Notlob to the door.

'After you,' he said, opening an arm.

'Ladies first,' said Scratch, hopefully.

'Not a chance,' said Cantina. 'You got us into this mess.'

'How is it *my* fault? All I've done is to get involuntarily kidnapped by aliens and be told to redirect the fate of the universe.'

'Exactly, now get in.'

'Alright, but you're doing the next dubious leap of faith, right?'

He approached the door and stopped at the threshold, turning to Notlob.

'And I just walk in, do I? Nothing I should know before I, you know, pass through to the other side?'

'Oh, that won't be happening for some time, Mister Scratch. There is much to be done before then.'

'Comforting to know, thank you.'

Scratch backed up a little, then a little more.

'Don't be playing silly beggars now,' said Notlob. 'There is no escape. You are surrounded by the best guards the universe has to offer. They have been *specially selected* for this moment.'

'Ah, but you haven't heard about that misunderstanding with a display cabinet in the Prince Albert museum, have you? My extrication is the stuff of legend back in Southend.

'Your use of one of those red queueing ropes was rather ingenious, I will admit. I hadn't realised they could be so… *distracting*.'

'Ah.'

Scratch sagged his shoulders in defeat. He walked steadily to the doorway, stepped through, and disappeared into the void.

To the great surprise of Cantina, the guard of honour slowly deflated, followed by Notlob and the doorway. They sagged to the ground, which was turning an unexpected shade of orange, and melted into the surface. To her greater surprise, she began to dissipate in a fresh breeze that had sprung up. Bits of her floated away into the sky like helium confetti until all that was left were hedgerows and fields once more.

Mr Raisbeck rubbed his head pointlessly as he sat against what was undoubtedly the most flexible forest he had ever encountered. After several minutes of human bagatelle, he had finally come to a stop in the small centre of an emphatically steep crater. Glorious was nowhere to be seen, partly because she was still bouncing from tree to tree several metres above and to the left of Mr Raisbeck, but mostly because he hadn't yet felt brave enough to open his eyes.

She landed with a thump and a groan, picked herself off the ground and headed straight for Mr Raisbeck.

'Let's go,' she announced, as if she hadn't just been subjected to one of the strangest experiences in human history. 'The quicker we get back up there, the quicker we can get this over with.'

'Steady on,' said Mr Raisbeck, peeling one eyelid open. 'Can't be too careful when you're on an alien planet. There might be all kinds of dangers we don't know about.'

A popping noise pierced the air, as though someone had broken the paper seal of the largest coffee jar in the universe with a spoon, only less satisfying.

'Like being stuck at the bottom of a crater as the ground opens up?' suggested Glorious, pointing at the fissure that had appeared in front of them.

'Yes, precisely!' said Mr Raisbeck, unaware of the literal nature of Glorious' remarks.

Glorious rolled her eyes, grabbed Mr Raisbeck by the arm, and began climbing up the slope. A rumbling noise sounded as she planted her right foot on the ground, followed by a slight increase in the gradient of the hill. She scrabbled around with her left foot, found a grip, and tried to heave herself upwards. She slipped as the rumbling sound came again, changing the gradient once more and tumbling them back to their starting point. The slope was vertical now and the chasm in the centre was edging closer and closer.

'May I make a suggestion?' asked Mr Raisbeck with inappropriate politeness. 'I believe now would be a good time to say *zen horseface*.'

CHAPTER TWENTY-EIGHT
END OF THE BEGINNING

*I*n my experience, which is as close to infinity as makes no difference, one of the main drivers of species extinction is not a flaming ball of cosmological rock, nor a planet's ill-advised proximity to a black hole that had skipped breakfast in the hopes of really enjoying lunch. When you boil it all down, the blame can often be placed at the feet of over-thinking. Or, worse still, an over-thinking committee.

On Earth, for example, almost all of the wars in its history began because of something simple: An assassinated figurehead, a narcissistic leader, or, as in the case of the one Neanderthal tribe on the southern coast of Europe, a rather heated debate on the merits or otherwise of cooking, or ruining, their meat with a bit of fire.

It is surprising, therefore, how infrequently simple solutions are offered for problems that began that way. If the Gauls had focused all their efforts on popping one in the eye of Julius Caesar as he rampaged across their lands, instead of trying to kill every last one of the thousands of Roman soldiers he brought with him, they wouldn't have gotten into the mess they did.

Equally, when the Dargonians of Metrilia Major discovered the key to making a perfect bowl of their immortalising Hagrovian soup, they would have been better off scratching the recipe into a rock for future generations instead of burning it onto the surface of a nearby star in quadravexical code.

When the fate of all life in the universe is at stake, in particular, it pays to keep things simple.

'Welcome to Prentonia, Scratch. May I call you Scratch? So sorry about all that pomp outside. I don't enjoy being all high and mighty like that, but one has to keep up appearances, doesn't one?'

Scratch was in a lobby of sorts; a large square room with dozens of doors lining each of the four walls. Mahogany panelling covered every vertical surface and paintings of men with frills around their necks hung precariously from the ceiling. He had an unsettling sense of having been here before, but no notion of how that might have happened. It wasn't that he couldn't quite put his finger on it, it was more as though his finger was buried in a Jurassic lava flow on Easter Island while his brain was sunning itself on Southend pier with a bag of chips and a bovril.

'This is the medulla of Prentonia,' continued Notlob. 'The practical epicentre of our jurisdiction.'

'…' said Scratch.

'Yes, it can be rather a lot to take in, so I'm told. Still, you're here now and that's the main thing. We have been waiting for you for rather a long time.'

'Two thirty,' managed Scratch.

'Oh no, dear chap, not that,' said Notlob, chuckling gently. 'I mean, you *were* late today, that's true. No, the wait I was referring to was the time we have spent preparing for your arrival.'

'I suppose it must take a while to get all those feathers to stay in the helmets,' said Scratch, gathering his wits a little.

'Almost fourteen billion years, give or take,' said Notlob.

'Of course you have,' said Scratch. 'Stands to reason, doesn't it? If you're going to send someone to save all life in the universe, you may as well start planning from the moment it pops into existence.'

'Very astute of you, if I may say so?'

'I was joking. I'm only thirty-seven for a start.'

'You may be thirty-seven, Mister Scratch, but the idea of you is as old as the universe itself. We are at the Grand Convergence. All that's left now is for you to choose the right door to begin your journey.'

'*Begin* my journey? Bloody hell, what just happened if this is only the beginning?'

'That was all, erm, *positioning*,' said Notlob. 'It is rather a complicated affair, I'm afraid. Mixing existential conundrums with time-travel tends to add one or two layers to the organisation of the bally thing. Suffice to say, you are now where we had hoped you would be.'

'What about Cantina? And the others?'

'Yes, they were a bit tricky to neutralise, but we managed it in the end.'

'You mean you've bumped them off!?'

'In a way, yes.'

'What sort of a way? In a dead way? Or in a *sent them home with a fancy new sports car and more cash than the Bank of England* sort of way?'

'It was the former, I'm afraid, but we can always make a few changes if it would help you focus on saving the universe?'

'Sounds a bit late for a spot of tweaking if you ask me.'

'Quite the contrary, we have all the time in the world. I will make arrangements at once.'

'Maybe don't give Mr Raisbeck a Lamborghini though. He's more of a Volvo man; far more reliable.'

'Right ho!'

Notlob swished a hand haphazardly through the air like a conductor with hiccups. 'There, done.'

'Come off it, you don't expect me to believe that do you?'

'Of course, why wouldn't I?'

'There ain't no evidence, that's why not. All you've done is wave an arm about.'

'Ah, my apologies. It is hard to remember your limitations. Your friends are quite well, I can assure you. Nevertheless, I will *wave my arm* again.'

He motioned in the air once more, briefly this time, and stopped just as a pocket watch appeared in front of them before dropping to the granite floor with a clink.

'I believe you will recognise this particular timepiece.'

'Buggering Mondays, that's impressive. Can you do that for things I haven't nick... borrowed?'

'We have become rather adept at certain *functions*, Scratch. What may seem impossible to you is but a trifle to us.'

'Well, you've had billions of years to practise, haven't you? I'd be pretty good at plenty of things if I had all that time to fill.'

'I was not being boastful, merely stating a truth. Please, allow me to make it up to you.'

Notlob waved his arm again and a newspaper appeared and fluttered to the floor.

'That's all I get, is it? The others get a hypercar and a sack full of cash and I get a tattered copy of the Daily Mirror?'

'I believe this is more your sort of thing.'

Scratch scooped up the paper and turned it over to the headline on the front page.

SOUTHEND MAN WINS RECORD LOTTERY – BUYS HIS OWN POLICE FORCE

'And you can do that, can you?'

'Of course, a lottery win is less than a moment's work.'

'I meant the *buying a police force* bit. That's a thing, is it?'

'Well, it is a little trickier, but do bear in mind we have recently arrived at the culmination of almost fourteen billion years of data with precisely the scenario we predicted. The variables alone are enough to melt the legs from your hips. Yet here we are, right where we said we would be. Do not underestimate the abilities of those with a singular focus and an eternity to kill.'

'Throw in a lingerie-model wife who doesn't care for money and you've got yourself a deal.'

'Done,' said Notlob, handing Scratch a tightly wound length of leather with a small loop at one end. 'You will need this.'

'Why?'

'There will be many perils on your journey,' said Notlob with exaggerated gravity. 'Who knows when such an item will prove invaluable?'

'You lot, presumably? You seem to know everything there is to know. Plus, you wouldn't give it to me if there wasn't a use for it, would you? Stands to reason.'

'We can't just go about giving the whole game away, can we? There'd be no drama to it! Could you imagine if we just gave you a key and said *here, you 'll need this when you get to the room with the hungry tiger and a trap door.*'

'So what's this for then, lassoing a mouse?'

'All in good time, Scratch, all in good time. Now, you must choose a door. Please, come with me and I will show you around.'

Notlob guided Scratch around the lobby, pointing to the inscriptions nailed to each door and translating them aloud.

'Foul,' he announced.

'Is that *fowl* as in chickens, or *foul* as in a dirty sliding tackle by a Tottenham midfielder?'

'Neither, actually.'

'Listen, if you knew it would be me arriving at precisely this time and place, why didn't you just write them all in English so you didn't have to call them out and I didn't have to wonder what you were talking about?'

'Drama, my dear boy, *drama!*'

'Bugger drama for a lark,' said Scratch. 'If I'm going to choose for myself then I want to be able to read them with my own eyes. Wave your arm about again and turn them all to English, or you can shove your deal up your…'

'Ahem!' interrupted Notlob loudly, as if there were children in the room. 'We can arrange that if it means so much to you.'

He flicked a finger and the writing sparkled. The grooves of the letters shifted and formed nice, neat and, most importantly, English words.

'That's more like it,' said Scratch. 'Alright, let's see. *Pathway To Pain*, eh? Might give that one a miss. *Chasm Of Inescapable Doom*? Nope. *Hallway Of Indeterminable Risk*. Well, that's the best one so far.'

He peered at the words on the next few doors, shook his head at each of them, and moved on. He had made it almost halfway around the room when he stopped and pointed.

'This one,' he said with conviction. 'This is the one I'll choose.'

'But that says *Status Quo*,' said Notlob.

'Exactly! Can't beat a bit of Status Quo on the old karaoke. I used to do *Rocking All Over The World* in The Nelson. No key changes, see?'

'We do not believe it is referring to the rock band in this particular instance,' said Notlob. 'It is Latin. *Maintenance of current conditions*, that sort of thing.'

'Even better,' said Scratch. 'That one please.'

'It is up to you, in the end. You may choose any of these doors as you see fit. Perhaps this one here; *Unremarkable Corridor*. Or this one; *Safe Passage To Your Destination*?'

'No, this is it, if it's all the same to you.'

'Alright then, *Status Quo* it is,' said Notlob, fishing a key from his pocket.

'I never thought I'd have to ask this question so many times in one day,' said Scratch, 'but what is it I'm supposed to do when I get in there? Only, if I'm going to do something that'll save all life in the universe I reckon I need more than a gentle push through a doorway and a friendly wave goodbye.'

'We believe it will become apparent as you make your way through the rooms. And you have your leather, of course.'

'Oh yes, couldn't forget that, could I? Where would I be without my precious strip of cow skin?'

'Precisely! Now, chop chop my dear fellow, mustn't keep everyone waiting.'

'Hang on, keep who waiting? And come to think of it, why do you keep saying *we* when you seem to be the only bloke about?'

'Why the Games Keepers, of course. Who else could it be?'

'You never said anything about games.'

'Didn't I?'

'No, you bloody well didn't. Are we talking Scrabble and Ludo here, or *Avoid The Man-Eating Wombat*?'

'Somewhere between the two, I suppose,' said Notlob honestly. 'I don't recall there being any that included aggressive marsupials though.'

'Well, that's just spiffy, ain't it? What happens if I say no?'

Notlob clasped his hands together and chuckled. 'Bravo, Mister Scratch. Very amusing. Now, if you would be so good as to step aside so I can unlock the door.'

'I wasn't joking!'

'I'm sure you weren't. Now, the door if you please?'

'What if one of the rooms has spiders in it? I bloody hate spiders. And don't give me the *they're more afraid of you than you are of them* speech because it's nonsense. They don't have the imagination I have, do they? Creepy little devils.'

'Just stand on one if you see it.'

'What if it's ten feet tall?'

Notlob rubbed the bridge of his nose patiently. 'I'm told you were selected because of your ability to use your wits in tricky situations. Just keep them about you and I'm sure everything will turn out for the best in the end.'

He leaned across Scratch and tried several times to push the key into the lock.

'Here, give it to me,' said Scratch. 'You should have just used one of those fancy doors with the black stuff in the middle instead of something as old fashioned as a barrel lock.'

'Drama, dear boy, drama!'

'Well it ain't that dramatic now, is it? You've got the game show contestant showing the host how his set works. Bloody amateurish if you ask me.' The key gave way and Scratch pushed down on the handle. 'So I just, you know, walk in, do I?'

'Yes, that would be the thrust of it,' said Notlob. 'Best of luck. The universe will be watching your progress with interest.'

'No pressure, then?' said Scratch, and stepped through the doorway.

CHAPTER TWENTY-NINE
EITHER OR

Professor Doubt inched sheepishly into General Buck's office.

'This had better be good news, professor,' said the general without looking up. 'Private Pantz just broke one of my favourite teapots, so I'm not in the best of moods as I'm sure you can appreciate. It was the yellow one with the baby turtles on, too. Can't get them anymore since that messy business with the eggs. No, it's gone for good and I'm just going to have to get over it.'

Doubt was never sure how to deal with his commanding officer at the best of times, and nothing the general had said thus far had done anything to ease the sense of impending anger displacement.

'Time to focus on something else,' continued Buck. 'Distraction always helps to get over the hardest of times, eh professor? Any news on saving life across the universe? How's our little Earth man doing?'

'Well, sir, we've had a few minor hiccups, but nothing we couldn't work around. We Zoomed all four of the Earth people to Prentonia, as planned. Unfortunately, there was an unexpected change in the topography of the place, I'm afraid, and two of them had to be extracted rather hastily.'

'And the others?'

'One of them was vapourised, but we don't think that's going to be a problem. Should have them back to their old self shortly.'

'Did they happen to notice any teapot shops while they were there?'

'Erm, no sir, not that any of them have mentioned. I'll double check when I get back.'

'Yes, do that. Could be the perfect place to find something unusual.'

'Indeed, general.'

Doubt studied the daydreaming face of General Buck and wondered, not for the first time, whether he was quite right in the head. 'The final Earth man, Scratch, has been successfully placed inside the lobby and has selected the correct door. Notlob is overseeing matters on Prentonia, of course.'

'Is there a gift shop there? You can sometimes get a teapot in a gift shop if you know where to look.'

'Not that I am aware of, sir, no.'

'Right, right. So definitely no teapot shops at all, then?'

'That's my understanding, sir.'

'Shame,' said Buck, staring blankly at a wall.

'If that's all, sir, I'll get back to the mission,' said Doubt hopefully.

'Yes, yes,' said Buck, waving an arm half-heartedly. 'As you were, professor. Oh, and be sure to report back the moment you have news.'

'Of course, sir.'

'And if anything happens with the mission, too.'

'Ah, right. Yes, that too, sir.'

There were very few characteristics that Scratch had expected of the Status Quo room, as is often the case when having the sort of day he was, but he had at least expected it to be a room. He adjusted his expectations and stepped out onto the smooth, grey surface of wherever it was he had been sent. A gust of icy wind swept his face and he pulled his tweed cap down tighter, huddled his arms around himself, and began walking.

A tinny female voice called out from the sky. 'Welcome to Status Quo, Level One: Two Choices. Please make use of the facilities and we hope you enjoy your stay.'

Scratch spun around looking for the source of the voice and noticed two things, equally disconcerting. Firstly, there was no sign of anyone, and secondly the door had disappeared. The landscape was as unvaried as it is possible to be. The ground was perfectly smooth and perfectly grey. The sky, assuming there was one up there, was of an identical shade and uniformity. It was like being trapped inside a pencil. He carried on walking, muttering to himself.

'Two choices, indeed? Seems like there's only one to me. Keep bloody walking until I can see something that doesn't make my eyes melt with boredom.'

He walked for ten minutes without seeing anything to tell him he was making any forward progress at all.

'I'm probably going round in circles like one of those people who get lost in the desert,' he grumbled. 'I could have my own documentary at this rate.'

Just then, he noticed a dot in the distance. A tiny speck that could only be seen from such a distance because it existed in a vista of uninterrupted greyness. He picked up his pace and marched towards it. As it grew, it formed the shape of a door, much like the one with the guard of honour when he first arrived on Prentonia.

A black Volvo drove past with a large neon sign above it that read: *Thirty Miles Per Hour*.

'That's odd. This looks more like a seventy zone.'

His brain wobbled a little.

'They should never have bought a black one, neither. Hardest colour to keep clean, black.'

He gave his head a brisk shake. His thoughts felt unfamiliar, as if someone had shoehorned an alternate set of rules into his brain.

A clock flew past, overtook the Volvo and disappeared into the distance, followed by a tan sofa lumbering along like an overfed walrus. A few moments later they were gone. Only the door remained to break the monotony of the landscape.

'Better see what that's all about then.'

It was an unremarkable door, painted a very practical white and with a solid, round door knob. There was a small, half-moon, glass panel about two thirds of the way up and a Yale lock about halfway up one side. The letterbox was chrome and looked like the type that has stiff brushes inside whose only purpose is to crumple envelopes and annoy the postman.

Scratch peered around the side and found a similar door facing in the opposite direction. He studied it, leaned back to see the first side, then back again. The only discernible differences were the doorknob and the lock. The side facing away from where he had come was a simple lever handle, rather than a round one, and the lock was a more secure mortice. That was it. The letterbox looked equally unfriendly to postmen on either side.

'A Volvo, a sofa, and an unremarkable suburban door,' he mumbled. 'All admirably practical things. Must be something to do with Mr Raisbeck. Two choices.'

He oscillated between the doors to be sure he hadn't missed anything, planted himself in front of the one that had the handle you could open with a bag of shopping in each hand, nodded absent-mindedly to the more secure lock, and pushed down on the handle. The door opened, revealing an absolute absence of everything that wasn't black.

'Congratulations,' said the tinny voice. 'You have passed Level One, Part One. Please prepare for Level One, Part Two.'

'How many bleeding parts are there?' asked Scratch.

There was no reply. He took a deep breath and stepped over the threshold.

'Buggering Mondays!' cried Scratch as his forehead connected with something hard and cold.

He scrunched his eyes tight as he massaged his head vigorously. When he opened them again he was in a room no bigger than a coffin for a morbidly obese mafia boss. A light came on ahead of him and he could now see he was facing the circular opening of a copper tube, just large enough for a short human from Southend to crawl through with a frustrating amount of inefficiency.

'Welcome to Status Quo, Level One, Part Two: Pipe Dreams. Please make use of the facilities and we hope you enjoy your stay.'

'No choices this time?' said Scratch to the metallic voice. 'Pipe dreams, eh? Perhaps I just have to have a quick kip and Bob's your uncle, on to level two.'

He clambered into the pipe and steadied himself on his hands and knees. A light appeared above him, illuminating about three feet in either direction. As he inched slowly along the tunnel the light clicked off and another came on just above him. After about thirty seconds the pipe forked left and right.

'Is it going to be like this every time? Choose wisely, or the universe gets it? How am I to know which one I'm supposed to be picking?'

A whirring sound rumbled beneath him, followed by an ominous *click*. His knees gave way as the floor of the metal pipe split in two and sent him falling into a dark void.

He reappeared a moment later inside the mafias boss' coffin.

'Fail,' announced the voice. 'A further error will not result in a reset and will force a permanent cessation of The Games. It will also remove your life from this universe.'

'Just this one? That's a relief,' said Scratch. 'Are you sure we can't just play rock, paper scissors? This all seems a little unnecessary if you ask me.'

The pipe opening lit up and he crawled in once more. He slowed down as he neared the fork and pressed his hands and knees as far up the sides as he could manage. The whirring sound rumbled again, followed by the *click*. He braced himself a little more and waited. Just ahead of him, the floor parted and a draft of warm air wafted up. A moment later it closed again. He edged forwards, staying as high up the side as he could, and stopped as he reached the fork. He peered into the left-hand pipe and could just make out a faint brightness at the end. It grew as he watched, the copper falling away to reveal a wide vista of beaches and cocktail bars. He startled a little as a head popped into view directly in front of him.

'Tahiti welcomes you,' said the beautiful, scantily clad woman. 'Your team of masseuses have warmed their tables for your comfort. Please, come with me and experience all that paradise has to offer.'

Scratch gave a long, bewildered blink and shuffled backwards up the pipe. 'Just give me a minute,' he said. 'Have to check the other one before I do anything too hasty.'

He leaned towards the right-hand pipe and smelled it before he saw it. His eyes began watering and his head spun from the fumes.

'Oh, come on!' he pleaded with the universe in general. 'Really? Hairspray?'

He looked back at the lithe Tahitian, then at the empty pipe to his right.

'Sorry,' he said, a little pathetically. 'I think I may have an appointment with the president of Kenya. Perhaps another time?'

'I'm afraid not,' said the Tahitian. 'We are ready for you now.'

'Lennie Pillarbox will never believe this.' He turned away from paradise and towards the altogether less alluring intoxication to his right.

His nose twitched as he crawled into the fume filled pipe, his elbows and knees pressing hard against the sides as he inched his way along. The light followed him for a short while, then blinked off.

'Bugger,' he said, with experience.

A pin-prick of light appeared in the distance and a droning, mechanical noise echoed off the copper. He vibrated slightly and slipped to the floor, just as the pipe began to tilt downwards.

'Congratulations,' said the voice, more cheerily than before. 'You have passed Level One. Please prepare for Level Two.'

The change in the voice's tone did nothing to ease his well-honed sense of imminent justice. The pipe tilted more quickly now and he slid uncontrollably towards the growing light. To his brief alarm, the pipe spat him out considerably further from the ground than he would have liked. He landed with a graceless thud, then sank to his waist in the strange surface.

Glorious and Mr Raisbeck sprang out of the vortex and landed in a graceless heap in front of Archer and the professor.

'Aha! Welcome back,' said Doubt cheerily. 'Bit of a close one, that, eh? Small problem with the old landing coordinates, I'm afraid. Turns out we didn't allow for the changeable nature of the topography. There is usually a century or so's warning for that sort of thing, but it seems the Prentonian surface changes a little more rapidly than your average planetary tectonics. Well, not to worry, you're here in one piece.'

'All's well that ends well,' said Glorious with more grace than she felt.

'Great Gammadrons, that's not the end my dear fellow. We still have to save the universe, remember? No, no. We will be sending you *back in*, as it were. Just one of you this time, though. Don't want to overload the zooming channel.'

He held out a plate to the shell-shocked figure of Mr Raisbeck. 'Custard cream before you go?'

Zoomers

CHAPTER THIRTY

TABLETS

Scratch was surrounded by small, white tablets. He picked one up and turned it over in his fingers. Each was embossed with the letter 'S' and they made up the entirety of the seemingly infinite landscape. There were no walls that he could make out and no undulations in the pharmaceutical monotony.

'Welcome to Level Two, Part One,' came the metallic voice. 'Find The Green Tablet.'

'Oh come off it,' said Scratch. 'I can't help but notice there doesn't appear to be any edges. How am I supposed to find a single bloody pill? It's impossible. Give us a clue, eh?'

'Correct,' said the voice. 'There does not appear to be an edge.'

'And that's a clue, is it? Buggering Mondays!'

'Use your brain,' said the voice.

'You know the fate of the universe is up the swanny if I don't get out of here in one piece, right? You could at least point me in the right direction.'

'There will be no more assistance.'

A humming sound that Scratch had not realised was there before abruptly disappeared and he suddenly felt utterly alone. He took a handful of pills and threw them at the silence. One hit him on the back of the head. He grabbed some more and threw them again, this time doing his best to follow them in the whiteness. They disappeared about eight feet away from where he stood.

He lifted himself up and started walking. The only object that could be used as a reference point was the opening of the copper pipe high up to his left and he stared at it as he walked. It slid slowly out of view behind him as he moved away from it, then reappeared ahead of him with equal speed.

'Gotcha!' he announced. 'Right then, can't be that hard to find now, can it?'

He burrowed into the mass of tablets, shovelling them aside with his arm. He expected to see a fleck of green somewhere, but instead was surprised to hear a deafening klaxon sound and a woodpecker appear beside his shoulder. It pecked at him once, then flew up and into the pipe.

'Negative,' said the tinny voice.

'Alright, Scratch my old mucker, time to get your thinking cap on and save the universe. The bloody universe! Ha! Who'd have thought it, eh? The poor lad from Southend who wouldn't amount to nothing. Well, I hope you're watching this Mr Bromsgrove, with your posh bow tie and your thermos of Ovaltine, 'cos it looks like you were wrong about how important ox-bow lake formation was. Knowing what all the different parts of a glacier are called doesn't seem so vital now either, does it? No, quick wits and an eye for danger, that's what's needed.'

He slapped his hand down onto the surface of tablets in triumph, then cried out in pain as he realised how much he had misjudged the surface tension of compressed powder.

A man appeared, rather unexpectedly, in front of him. He was almost entirely submerged in pills, but Scratch could still see his bow tie and disapproving scowl.

'Geography teachers are the cornerstones of a rounded education,' stated the man.

'Mr Bromsgrove?'

'Don't you use that tone with me, boy! Show some respect.'

The klaxon roared and the woodpecker appeared again, pecked his shoulder, and flew off into the pipe.

Mr Bromsgrove popped out of existence.

'Pull yourself together, son. It's just a little puzzle, like jimmying a lock. Think, think. We've had Mr Raisbeck and we've had Glorious, so this has to be Cantina and her drug problem. A farmer-something.'

He stared into the endless distance for a moment, moving his lips silently as he thought through the possibilities.

A vacuum cleaner came into being. He picked it up and switched it on.

The klaxon roared.

The woodpecker appeared.

'Not hoovering, then,' said Scratch. He considered the technology that was, he presumed, now available to him. 'What about…?'

Something not entirely unlike an airport baggage scanner, complete with conveyor belt and topped with a red and green light, manifested itself and sat there, dormant. A cheeky smile grew on Scratch's face.

'Can't test the colour if you can't get the pills through, can you?'

He willed a loading operator into existence.

'Hello again,' he said to the Tahitian masseuse. 'Do you mind giving me a hand putting these pills through? Got to find a green one, see? It'll take me ages if I do it on my own, you know how it is.'

'I would be delighted to help in any way I can,' said the Tahitian. To Scratch's squirming horror it spoke with the grating voice of Mr Bromsgrove.

'Buggering Mondays. Forget it, I'll do it myself.'

The Tahitian Mr Bromsgrove disappeared.

Scratch clambered out of the ground and stepped over to the conveyor belt. He scooped up an armful of pills, dropped them onto the belt and watched them bump their way into the scanner.

The red light spun and flashed. The klaxon sounded. The woodpecker plopped into existence again and pecked his shoulder.

Scratch slumped to what constituted the floor and wracked his brain.

'Aha!' he cried. 'Bloody simple when you think about it.'

He closed his eyes and pictured a green pill, identical in all but colour to those in which he was currently bathing.

The tinny voice buzzed into life. 'No cheating.'

'How is that cheating? You haven't even told me what the rules are! Can't call it cheating if I don't know what…'

He paused.

'What's the opposite of cheating?'

'Ignorance of the rules is no defence,' said the voice.

'You sound like Constable Pickles down at the station,' said Scratch, collapsing onto the floor again. 'Don't suppose you could give me any clues as to the nature of these rules, could you? What if I'm only allowed to use my left hand to wipe my nose, but only while I'm balancing on an antique cigar box?'

He picked up a handful of pills and let them fall between his fingers. His lips began to move silently again.

'Billy the Accountant!' he cried. 'That's it! Cantina does stuff to do with how your geneti-wotsits help you handle your drink.'

An old lady appeared.

'Hallo!' she said.

'Oh, hello,' said Scratch. 'Are you a drug farmer?'

'Was meinst du? Ich bin nur eine einfache alte Dame aus der Schweiz.'

'I see' said Scratch, emphatically unaware that he had, in fact, translated flawlessly from German. 'And would you happen to be related to someone called Cantina? Only, I need to find a green pill, you see, on account of me being on a bit of a crusade to save all life in the universe.'

'Natürlich sie ist meine Enkelin.'

'Great!' said Scratch. 'Now what?'

'Das ist dein Problem, nicht meins,' said the old lady.

'Yes, I suppose it is. You weren't fond of a little opium back in the day, were you? No, of course not, sorry. Buggering Mondays, what do I do now?'

'Find a green pill. You could die,' said the old lady in perfect English.

'Brilliant,' said Scratch flatly. 'It's a good job you're here to... wait, what did you say?'

'I said, find a green pill. You could die.'

Cantina's grandmother popped out of existence at precisely the same moment as the klaxon failed to blare. The woodpecker remained unmanifested.

'Haha!' cried Scratch. 'That's it!'

He closed his eyes, as much for needless effect as anything else, and waited for the tinkle of glass on the tablets.

Tinkle.

He scooped up the small glass bottle and read the label.

Ma Baker's Famous Food Colouring - Emerald

He gave it a shake and unscrewed the cap. He then picked a tablet from the ground and allowed a single, green drop to land on it.

There was no klaxon, which was a good start, nor a woodpecker. There was, however, a distinct absence of fanfare. He closed his eyes, concentrated, then opened them again when he heard the *plink*. A flashing neon sign with an oversized arrow had appeared, displaying the rather helpful message *Place Green Pill Here*.

He put the green pill in a small dish below the arrow and took a step back.

'Congratulations,' said the tinny voice with unsustainable giddiness. 'You have completed Level Two, Part One. Please, follow me.'

'Where to?' said Scratch. 'You're a disembodied voice, not a tour guide with a sign on a pole.'

'This way please,' said the voice.

Before Scratch could reiterate his point he plopped into existence in the hollow of a deep sand dune.

'Oh great,' he muttered.

He scrabbled up the dune with frustrating inefficiency, finally reaching the summit with a wheezing slump. He levered his neck to take in the scenery which, to his sighing resignation, was made entirely of golden sand and blue sky.

'What is it with you guys and vast, barren landscapes? You wouldn't have tied a camel to a post for me, no?'

He stood up and trudged down the gentle slope towards more sand. When he reached the nadir of the dune he began to traipse up the next one. Then down. Then up. Then down again, like an ant clambering over a bowl of puffed rice.

He imagined a glass of water. A moment later one plopped into existence in front of him and fell to the floor.

'Oh, come on!'

He thought about a glass of water again, this time in his outstretched hand. It appeared, nestling perfectly in his grip. He drank it in one go and threw the glass to the floor, landing on the first and shattering.

'Sounds like The Nelson at last orders' said Scratch to the disembodied voice, whose silence seemed to indicate a lack of appreciation of the humour.

He began another climb. *One more up and down*, he thought. *Then I'll change direction.*

As he reached the next hollow, his musings were interrupted by a break in the monotony of the landscape. A pin-prick of black had appeared in front of him, growing into the familiar swirling purple and black of an Arcadian vortex.

Nothing happened for a short while, then a figure was spat out ungracefully looking rather confused and slightly irritated.

'Alex! What a nice surprise,' said Scratch with remarkable composure.

'It's Mr Raisbeck,' said Mr Raisbeck, his policy on salutation being admirably unscathed from the day's unusual activity. 'And it isn't a nice surprise for me, I can assure you.'

'Oh, knew you were coming, did you?'

'Of course I didn't! I was referring, of course, to the *nice* nature of my arrival. If I'm not back before two o'clock there'll be hell to pay. Pardon my language.'

'Right, so we're still on that one, are we? Good to know where your focus is. Now, if you don't mind, I have a universe to save.'

'Just the one,' said Mr Raisbeck. 'Should be done by about half twelve then, shouldn't you. Come on, hop to it.'

'Have you set aside a space in your living room for this sofa?' asked Scratch.

'I'm not a lunatic,' said Mr Raisbeck, offended at the very suggestion he may not have used a measuring tape and a spirit level as part of the purchasing process. 'I have it all planned out, naturally. We're moving the sideboard to the opposite wall, underneath Oliver's graduation picture where the old sofa is, and the new one will fit precisely where the sideboard is now, next to my display cabinet of toby jugs.'

'You have toby jugs' stated Scratch, rubbing the bridge of his nose. 'Of course you do. Mahogany cabinet, too, no doubt? Well, your lovely display of jugs, the sideboard, and the picture of Oliver looking like a depressed wizard with a heavy weight on his head will all be gone in a puff of existentialism if I don't find… if *we* don't find a way to pass Level Two and save all life in the universe.'

'What do you mean, *Level Two*?'

'I'll explain later, there are more pressing matters to attend to.'

'Never trust someone who says they'll explain later, that's what I always say.'

'Do you know what I say, Mr Raisbeck? I say shut up and start walking.'

'Fine, but don't think I'll forget you owe me an explana... ooooooow!'

Mr Raisbeck yanked his foot upward and began hopping in a circle.

'What are you doing?' asked Scratch. 'It's sand, mate, not a scorpion nest.'

'Whatever that was, it wasn't sand,' said Mr Raisbeck, now sitting down and trying to bend his stubbornly inflexible legs in a vain attempt to see the sole of his foot.

Scratch crouched down beside him and held his ankle. 'The bloody glass.'

'It is now, yes.'

'How'd that get there?'

'Wait. What glass?'

'I'll explain later,' said Scratch. He stood up and scanned the horizon. 'We need to get to the next dip, come on.'

He put out a hand to help Mr Raisbeck up. The retired human resources manager grabbed

Scratch's hand with both of his and began to lift himself up.

'Wait!' cried scratch, letting go of Mr Raisbeck's hand and sending him unceremoniously back to the floor with a dull thump. 'Wait here. Don't move!'

'You'd better not leave me here on my own, Mr Scratch. I'll be something's dinner before too long with this foot.'

'What are you expecting will show up? An annoyed camel? An unusually violent iguana?'

'Well I don't know what kind of a desert we're on, do I? There could be vicious aliens with big teeth and a family to feed just roaming the dunes.'

'I'll be back before you know it,' called Scratch as he sprinted up the dune and out of sight.

'See, what did I tell you?'

Mr Raisbeck spun around on his backside and stared agog at Scratch. 'How did you…? You were just… and now you're…'

'Precisely, my old mucker. It's just like Part One. Bit lazy of them if you ask me, but I ain't complaining. Here, watch.'

He took off his tweed cap and threw it to their left. It disappeared, before reappearing to their right and landing on Mr Raisbeck's leg.

'Not a bad shot, either. That's the arm of the captain of the Nelson Nuggets darts team, that is.'

'Marvellous, but leaving your sporting prowess to one side for the moment, can you explain how this great discovery has helped us save the universe?'

'We're not saving the universe, Mr Raisbeck.'

'But I thought we were…'

'We're saving all *life* in the universe. It's a very different thing altogether.'

'It is?'

'Oh yes. How are we expected to save something as big as the universe? Doesn't make any sense. What would I do, put Jupiter in my pocket and hope some universe destroyer doesn't notice?'

'And saving all known life forms in the entire bloody place is more your size of crusade, is it? Pardon my French.'

'Exactly! If you want to save life you just have to find the reason it's going belly up for everyone. Stands to reason. Once you've worked that out the rest just sort of falls into place, doesn't it?'

'No, I don't think it does,' said Mr Raisbeck, not unreasonably.

'Alright, it may be a little trickier than that, but these Arcadians seem like a bright bunch. I'm sure they'll be able to crunch the numbers and come up with some clever way of fixing the problem. All we have to do is give them the question.'

'Great. Now explain to me again how a never ending loop of desert is going to help us in that regard. If anything it seems as though it's made our jobs more impossible than they already were.'

'Notlob says he's the Guardian of the Sacred Sand, see?' said Scratch, as if that was all the explanation required.

'Ah, well that clears it all up. Should be home in time for supper now. Hang on, my bloody sofa!'

'That's two curse words in the last two minutes, Mr Raisbeck. Perhaps you should have a lie down and leave the thinking to me for a while, eh?'

'I'll have you know I've done the Times crossword every day since I retired. The *cryptic* one, too.'

'Buggering Mondays, why are you bringing up your crossword ability at a time like this? We're trying to be universal heroes, not work out what fourteen down is.'

'*Over-rated Lancashire football team, running backwards* is what I would say,' said Mr Raisbeck.

'Would you, indeed? Well that's bloody marvellous, that is. Solved the whole buggering shooting match with that one, haven't you? Now, if you wouldn't mind either helping out or shutting up, I'm sure everyone in the universe would be bloody delighted.'

'Notlob,' said Mr Raisbeck. 'Shall I spell it out for you?'

Scratch let out a patient sigh. 'Fine, spell it out, then leave me to work out what the hell it is we're supposed to be doing here.'

'N-o-t-l-o-b,' said Mr Raisbeck unhelpfully.

'So you said.'

'It's backwards!'

'Ah, just like your priorities. Great, now can I bugger off please?'

'Bolton! It's Bolton backwards.'

'Oh, so it is,' said Scratch with faux surprise. 'Doesn't help us much though, does it? Unless the answer involves me spouting on about a football team I can't bloody well stand. Do you know, they came to Roots Hall a few years ago and all they did was roll about on the floor whenever a Southend player got within three feet of them. Bloody cheats, that lot. And their manager is a total... well, let's just say I wouldn't invite him round for dinner at my grandmother's on account of me being likely to kick him where no man wants to be kicked.'

'I think you're missing the point,' said Mr Raisbeck. '*Bolton Wanderers Football Club.*'

'I'm not stupid,' said Scratch defensively. 'I could tell you the nicknames of all ninety two league clubs, and their grounds and what colour their away kits are. I know it's Bolton bloody Wanderers, I've cursed the buggers often enough.'

'So, *Bolton* backwards is *Notlob*.'

Scratch screwed his face in concentration. 'sre-red-naw,' he managed at last.

'I suspect that isn't where the solution lies,' said the Times crossword completer. 'Try wandering around the desert, but backwards.'

'If you think for one minute that I'm going to try and save all life in the universe by walking backwards around an alien desert because some extra-terrestrial gamekeeper's name happens to be a backward spelling of an obscure, and bloody horrible, lower league football club from the north of England, then you're out of your buggering mind!'

'I thought you might say something like that. Well, if you don't mind, I'm going to get on with it.'

Mr Raisbeck stood up, tested his foot on the ground, and set off to the crest of the dune, backwards. Scratch shook his head, not for the first time today, and began scrabbling around in the sand for something that wasn't sandy.

After several minutes of backwards walking, and often falling, Mr Raisbeck returned to the hollow where Scratch was furiously digging with his hands. It appeared to Mr Raisbeck that he had made no progress at all, and each time Scratch shovelled sand away, more poured down to take its place.

'I wouldn't bother if I were you,' said Mr Raisbeck. 'It's too dry. All you're doing is changing which bits of sand are there.'

'Yes, thank you *Mr Stating-The-Bleeding-Obvious*, but it's a damned sight more productive than your backwards walking.'

'Perhaps we should rethink our strategy.'

'Perhaps you should shut up,' snapped Scratch.

'It's alright for you, you were *supposed* to be here. You were *selected*. I was just minding my own business waiting for Shufflebottom and Sons and before I knew what was happening I was on an alien planet with no obvious complaints procedure.'

'Oh yeah, I'm laughing handcarts here, ain't I? Listen, it's not as if I was waiting at an intergalactic bus stop for the Arcadian Day Trip Special to arrive, was it? I'm just as put out by this whole mullarkey as you are.'

'I'm a little more than put out, Mr Scratch. I'm furious! Three months I've had to wait for a slot. Three months!'

Scratch tilted his head curiously. 'You do realise there are more important things going on than your sofa, don't you? I appreciate it's an important issue for you, but when you put it up against the fate of the universe, not to mention our chances of ever getting home again, then it rather pales into insignificance, don't you think?'

'We got it specially made for our living room, too,' grumbled Mr Raisbeck. 'Margaret will be so disappointed.'

'About the sofa, or about life being snuffed out?'

'Both, I suppose. I'll be given a list of jobs to do around the house longer than my arm, mark my words. She always gets that way when she's disappointed.'

'Well, there's only one way to make sure you don't spend the next three months painting and hammering, ain't there?'

'You're right, we should just give it up as a bad job.'

'*Give it up as a bad job!?* What the bloody hell is wrong with you? I meant we should get thinking and find a way out of here.'

'I wouldn't even be here if it wasn't for that red button.'

A ponderous look came over Scratch.

'Maybe it's just like Lenny Pillarbox and that time he got caught shoplifting.'

'I should have just used Patterson's.'

'He said he was just re-enacting the crime,' continued Scratch. 'You know, to help him get into the mind of the culprit so he could work out which way he scarpered. Ended up working for the police for six months, poor bugger.'

'Won't be making that mistake again,' said Mr Raisbeck to nobody but himself. 'We're due to change the armchair next year and I can tell you one thing, Shufflebottom and Sons won't be getting our business then, I can assure you of that.'

'I reckon the plan was for me to be here on my own, but that was kiboshed when we hit the button at the same time. Now you're here with me, and if this place is as advanced as it appears to be, then they've probably changed whatever it is I have to do.'

'You get what you pay for, I suppose. My own fault, really.'

Scratch stood up and stepped to the side, waving his arms around until his hands disappeared. He craned his neck to look behind him and saw them waving back at him.

'Get up, Mr Raisbeck. I have an idea.'

Zoomers

CHAPTER THIRTY-ONE
HANDY SOLUTION

'I still don't see how this will help,' said Mr Raisbeck as he stood at one edge of the unending desert.

'I accept it's a long shot, but it's still a damned sight more likely to work than your walking backwards idea,' said Scratch from the opposite side. 'If we touch at precisely where the boundary is, at exactly the same moment, it might trigger something like it did in the Training Room.'

'Alright, but if this doesn't work we're trying mine again.'

'If this doesn't work, Mr Raisbeck, you can dance a jig to the sound of church bells for all I care. Now, on the count of... what are you doing?'

Mr Raisbeck appeared beside Scratch with a hopeful look in his eye. 'Did it work?'

'Of course it didn't. I hadn't even started counting.'

'You said *now*.'

'I have to count back from three first. How else can we get our timing right? It has to be perfect, son.'

'Fine,' said Mr Raisbeck, trudging back to his spot.

'Alright, ready?' said Scratch.

'Ready.'

'Three… two…'

'Hold on a minute,' said Mr Raisbeck. 'Are we going *on* one, or *after* one?'

'After,' said Scratch patiently.

'Right, after. Got it.'

'Three… two… one… now.'

The two men stepped across the boundary. Scratch headbutted Mr Raisbeck's chin and they each bent over rubbing their respective body parts.

'That was your fault,' said Mr Raisbeck.

'How was that my fault?'

'You never mentioned *now*. You just said to go after one.'

'Bloody Nora, you must be a delight at parties. Right, I'll count back from three and we go when I say *now*. Is that pedantic enough for you?'

'Perfectly clear, thank you.'

'Great. Now, let's try it again.'

After eight attempts, Scratch sat down on the sand. 'There has to be a better way,' he muttered.

'We could start by having a better idea than just running into each other,' said Mr Raisbeck, rubbing his shoulder. 'A man of my age shouldn't be engaging in such violent activities.'

'That ain't violent, Mr Raisbeck. If you want to see violence you should watch Harry the Butcher when his team loses. It'd strip the skin from your potatoes.'

'I don't want anything to do with a man whose nickname is *The Butcher*, thank you very much. I didn't make it all the way to retirement to get caught up in organised crime, Mr Scratch. I have a rose garden to maintain, and you can't do that from a prison cell, can you? I've seen documentaries on what they do to snitches in that line of work too and it isn't for me, I can tell you that much.'

'He's a butcher,' said Scratch. 'An *actual* butcher down the market. Legs of lamb, pork cutlets, that sort of thing. He just happens to be six foot six and a... *passionate* Southend United fan. I saw him push a vending machine over once when we got beat four nil by Tranmere. Bloody Tranmere! Mind you, we'd have done better with a bunch of schoolgirls that season. Had no muscle in the middle of the park, see?'

'I think we may be getting a little off track,' said Mr Raisbeck. 'I believe we were trying to save the universe, perhaps we should get back to that?'

'It's all about timing,' mumbled Scratch half to himself. 'Timing, timing, timing…'

'If you're looking for an enlightened conversation on the tactics of association football then I'm afraid I'm not the best man for the job,' said Mr Raisbeck.

'Now isn't the time to talk about football,' said Scratch, waving a hand to indicate it would be best if he was left to his thoughts for a while.

'Do let me know when you're ready,' said Mr Raisbeck, meandering away to kick up puffs of sand and stare at his feet absent-mindedly.

'Schoolgirls!' announced Scratch. 'Mr Raisbeck, take your position. I have an idea.'

'Another one? Marvellous. What are we going to do this time, burrow into the sand and hibernate for a few years until all this blows over?'

'You know that game that girls play at school?'

'Assume, for the moment, that I am not au fait with such things,' said Mr Raisbeck.

'What's it called? Pat-a-cake or something. You know, the one where they stand in front of each other and clap their hands to a rhythm.'

'Oh,' said Mr Raisbeck with surprise. 'I do know that one, actually.'

'Good, we're doing that.'

'I'm a little afraid to ask this, but why, precisely, are we resorting to schoolyard games when the fate of the universe is in our hands?'

'Because all we need to do is get the timing right. Doesn't matter what it takes, does it?'

'Assuming that your idea is correct. Otherwise, we're just two men playing pat-a-cake on an alien planet.'

'There is that,' conceded Scratch. 'It still ranks as our best idea so far, though, so get over there and start clapping.'

Mr Raisbeck took up his position and the two fully grown adults began clapping their hands, then each other's, in turn.

'Shouldn't we be saying the rhyme?' said Mr Raisbeck weakly. 'I mean, I'd rather not, but it would probably help.'

'I suppose so,' said Scratch. 'Clobber would have a field day with this.'

Mr Raisbeck and Scratch exchanged nervous looks, then began.

Pat-a-cake, pat-a-cake, baker's man, make me a bread as fast as you can.

It said a lot about what's wrong with old-fashioned masculinity that they found this to be one of the most disconcerting parts of their day.

'What's the next line?' asked Mr Raisbeck.

'No idea,' said Scratch. 'That's the only bit I know. We'll have to just repeat it until it works.'

Pat-a-cake, pat-a-cake, baker's man, make me a bread as fast as you can.

Pat-a-cake, pat-a-cake, baker's man, make me a bread as fast as you can.

Pat-a-cake, pat-a-cake, baker's man, make me a bread as fast as you can.

A crackle of energy ripped through the space, followed by a soft *poof* as the two men disappeared.

CHAPTER THIRTY-TWO

IF THE LASSO FITS

Scratch and Mr Raisbeck plopped into being on a cube of red glass in a small, circular chamber. The floor appeared to be missing, for the most part, and the walls were lined with a dark green velvet.

On the far side of the room was a cube similar to their own but blue, and on it was a lever pointing directly up to the ceiling. Two signs hovered above it; one behind it and one on the side nearest the would-be lifesavers.

'We did it, Mr Raisbeck, look!' cried Scratch as he read the words. '*Push this way to end all life in the universe. Pull this way to save all life in the universe.*'

'I'm not an expert in these things,' said Mr Raisbeck with emphatic accuracy, 'but I would have thought it would be slightly less... *instructive.*'

'I couldn't give a monkey's uncle,' said Scratch. 'We did it. It's time to go and see my old mate Clobber and his pocket watch, and you'll get to go home and position your sofa.'

'There is one small matter before you get excitable, Mr Scratch. How, do you suppose, are we to get to this lever to move it to the less Armageddon-focused outcome? The floor is rather sparse.'

'There is that, yes' conceded Scratch. 'Maybe it's one of those *leap of faith* things where we just take a step forward and it turns out the ground is solid all the way along. Like in that film Indy-wotsits. The one with Han Solo in it, only he's a teacher.'

'I'm not familiar with the reference, but suffice to say I will not be stepping anywhere until someone tells me it isn't going to send me plummeting into an abyss without so much as an umbrella to slow me down.'

'We'll throw a coin down or something, like you're supposed to do on the top of the Eiffel Tower. That way we'll know how far the drop is. Might be one of those optical illusion wotsits. You know, like those stairs that don't go anywhere. Could be just a small step, couldn't it?'

'I'm not sure you're supposed to do anything of the sort,' said Mr Raisbeck. 'You could kill someone doing that.'

'We're going to kill everyone in the universe if we don't do *something*,' said Scratch, rummaging through his pockets for a suitable object to drop. 'Buggering Mondays! We've got this!'

He pulled out the long, leather strap and held it aloft dramatically. 'This'll do the trick.'

'Don't use that, it looks like top quality leather.'

'Please keep up, Mr Raisbeck. I'm not going to drop it, I'm going to lasso the lever.'

'So now you're the Lone Ranger, are you? It must be thirty feet away.'

'Ah, but I'm the captain of the Nelson Nuggets, ain't I? I can hit a treble twenty from all the way back at the jukebox. Famous for it, I am.'

'Famous, indeed? The length and breadth of Southend, I shouldn't wonder.'

'Right, stand back and give me some room.'

'You want some room? On four square feet of glass that's the only thing between us and oblivion? You'll have to make do with what you have. Now come on, I haven't got all day.'

Scratch unravelled the leather and swished it back and forth, testing the motion.

'Indiana Jones! That was it.'

'That was what?'

'The film, with Han Solo as a teacher. Indian Jones and the... something something. Bloody brilliant, it was.'

'So good you can't remember the title. I must look it up.'

'Right, here we go,' said Scratch. 'Time to save all life in the universe.'

He swung it over his shoulder, then forwards in a great arc.

It missed the lever by about four feet.

'That was just a practise shot,' he said, defensively. He flung the leather again, missing by two feet this time. 'See, getting closer.'

'Just like our demise if you don't hurry up. Look, the cube is shrinking.'

'Buggering Mondays, and I thought today couldn't get any worse.'

'We can reflect on it in our old age, if we get one. Now stop dithering and lasso that bloody lever!'

Scratch could tell Mr Raisbeck was agitated. To a certain extent this was because he hadn't excused himself for using a profanity, but mostly it was because an anthropomorphic personification of death had appeared between them and the lever and was, presumably, about to clasp them rather fatally on their shoulders.

'Come on Scratch, old boy,' said Scratch. 'Time to show the universe what it means to be captain of the Nelson Nuggets.'

He threw the strap once more. It hit the top of the lever and ricocheted into the air slightly. It came down again in slow motion, quite literally. The possibility of it landing true teetered on a knife edge.

'Bloody typical,' said Scratch. 'The one time death is gliding towards me, everything starts happening slower than a builder before Christmas.'

The lasso finally made contact with the lever, or, more precisely, the edge of it. It fell down into the abyss and swung back towards the two almost-dead humans, dangling limply below Scratch's clenched fist.

'Buggering Mondays,' said Mr Raisbeck.

'That's the spirit,' said Scratch. 'Nice to see you lightening up a bit with the old curse words. You'll find it does wonders for your stress levels.'

'Give it to me,' said Mr Raisbeck. 'I've got an idea.'

'What are you going to do, complain about it until it withers into submission?'

'Better than that, I'm going to fulfil a dream.'

Mr Raisbeck puffed out his chest and shouted. '*Zen horseface.*' He seemed to flinch, as if caught unawares by a sneeze. The positioning of his shoulders changed to something a little more athletic. More *prepared*.

'Was your dream to stall for time while the grim reaper inches closer? Because if it was, it was a bloody terrible idea.'

'What was happening exactly when I left? I'm afraid it's been rather a long time.'

'Have you gone completely mad? Can't say I'd blame you after the day we've had, but your timing could've been better.'

'Ah, that was it. You were trying to lasso that lever, weren't you? The fate of all life in the universe depended on it if I remember correctly.'

'*If you remember correctly?* Yes, all the bloody life, and we'll be the first to get it if that thing gets any closer,' said Scratch, pointing to the seven foot skeleton in a graduation outfit. Now, give me the lasso. I've got my eye in now, next one's the money shot.'

'Bother! I knew I'd forgotten something. Wait there a minute, would you?'

Scratch looked around the room with bewildered incredulity.

'Zen horseface.'

Mr Raisbeck flinched again and the lasso appeared in his hand.

'Did that just…' said Scratch, struggling to describe the sudden appearance of something he hadn't noticed had gone.

Mr Raisbeck raised his right arm, swung it around his head a few times, and launched the leather strap towards the lever. It landed neatly over the top and wriggled down to the bottom of the metal pole.

'That should do it,' he said, as if he had just tightened a screw on a shelf. 'Now, if you wouldn't mind helping me pull?'

They hefted back on the leather, releasing a great squeal of long-stationary metal that bounced off the curved walls in a symphony of discord. The grim reaper lifted his skull slightly, as if rolling unseen eyes in a show of teenage hurrumphery, and disappeared with an uncharacteristic *plink*.

The red and blue cubes began to grow until they met in the middle to create a complete floor with no obvious abyss at the edges. Scratch and Mr Raisbeck took an instinctive step away from each other and sagged in relief.

Notlob appeared suddenly, accompanied by a blaring fanfare of music that wouldn't have been out of place after a grand-prize winning performance on a cheap gameshow. This scared the last remaining willies out of the two Earthmen and they fell to the floor in a heap.

Notlob leaned over Mr Raisbeck cautiously, then gave his chest a gentle nudge with his foot.

'Well that just takes the biscuit,' he said to the prone figures. 'Fourteen billion years I've waited to give this speech, and now the time has finally come, my audience chooses *this precise moment* to slump into an inconsiderate unconsciousness. Just about sums up my day, that.'

A purple vortex appeared between Scratch and Mr Raisbeck and Cantina stepped out. She took hold of each of their hands, muttered *zen horseface*, and the three figures stretched into the vortex and away from Prentonia for the last time.

CHAPTER THIRTY-THREE
SOMEWHERE OR SOMEWHEN

'Well done everybody,' said Buck, as if they had just successfully completed a parking permit application form. 'Good job all round.'

'Yes, it all went rather well in the end,' agreed the professor. 'A few bumps in the road, but that's to be expected when you're working at the very edge of technology.'

'Don't worry, I'm sure I'll find a replacement,' said Buck. 'Now that we've saved the universe there'll be all kinds of opportunities to add to my collection.'

Scratch, Mr Raisbeck and Cantina hadn't moved, so long as you didn't count lolling tongues or swaying heads. Their dishevelled look gave them an appearance not entirely unlike a group of inexperienced humans who had just made multiple Zooms with the future of life hanging on their shoulders.

'How are you feeling?' asked Glorious. 'Would you like a glass of water?'

'What about my sofa,' said Mr Raisbeck groggily. 'I was assured I would be home in time.'

'Give it a rest, would you?' said Scratch, coming round. 'What was all that wobbly business with you and the leather hoop?'

'Your friend here was rather resourceful,' said the professor. 'Not to mention the great personal effort involved.'

'Who, him?' said Scratch, pointing at Mr Raisbeck.

'Indeed. He is now a champion javelin thrower… I believe the tournament he competed in was called *The Olympics.*'

'Now listen, I'll be the first to admit that I've experienced some events from the far end of the probability spectrum recently, but I'm not buying that Mr Raisbeck here is a gold medal-winning Olympian.'

'It's true, I'm not,' said Mr Raisbeck a little gloomily.

'There, see? Now what really happened?'

'I only managed to get the silver. That damn Bulgarian.'

Professor Doubt cleared his throat. 'Your friend here spent fourteen years training to be sure he could lasso the life-saving lever when he returned to you. The Olympic thing was a childhood dream, so I believe.'

Scratch turned to Mr Raisbeck. '*You* had dreams of javelin gold?' he said incredulously.

'And what's wrong with that?' said Mr Raisbeck defensively. 'A boy can dream, can't he?'

'Yes, but you're not exactly the sporty type, are you?'

'I am now,' said Mr Raisbeck, flexing a bicep.

Cantina came round with a look of utter confusion in her eyes. She made a vague grunting noise at Glorious.

'Glass of water?' said Glorious.

'Water, yes,' managed Cantina.

'I'll have one of those green drinks from last night,' said Scratch. 'With some of that weird stuff from the crystal bottles. Do they have one called *put the mushy pieces of your brain back together after saving the universe*?'

'I'm afraid not,' said Archer. 'That's a little too specific, I'm afraid. I think there may be one called *recover*.'

'There is,' confirmed Doubt with experience. 'Doesn't work as well as you'd like though, especially if you've been on the Pomplefitzers past midnight.'

'They're not crystal, man, they're diamond,' said Buck. 'We're not made of money.'

'Di…' said Scratch, before a brief catatonia took hold of him as his brain tried to make sense of the opportunity.

'Crystal indeed! Ha!' said Buck. 'You're a strange lot, I'll give you that. Now, there are a few things we need to get straight before we send most of you home again.'

'*Most* of us?' said Cantina.

'I *have* to go home,' said Mr Raisbeck desperately.

'Diamond?' mumbled Scratch.

'The thing is...' began the general. 'The thing is...'

Diplomacy was never a strong suit for General Buck. It was one of the reasons he had chosen a career in politics. Delegation, however, was a skill for which he could captain a *Rest of the Universe Select XI* team in the Galactic Delegation Games without getting up from his bed.

'Professor, I think you're best placed to fill the chaps in on the details, wouldn't you say? A man of your knowledge and all that.'

'It would be an honour,' lied the professor.

He adjusted the pens in his breast pocket, clasped his hands behind his back, cleared his throat, and began to pace up and down the room in a vain attempt to come up with a subtle way to break the news.

'The thing is,' he began. 'Time travel can be a little tricky. There are all kinds of variables involved, you see, and sometimes the...

sometimes… what can happen is… you see, there can be a problem with the, erm… Archer, perhaps you could break the news? I mean, explain. Explain, yes.'

Archer sighed and turned to face Scratch and Mr Raisbeck. 'When you both pressed the button in the Training Room simultaneously, it created duplicate versions of you. One set remained suspended in the Training Room until the professor and I were able to reanimate you with a big stick. That's you now. The other versions were sent Zooming around the universe until they found a way back. They were returned home to Earth in the end with no memory of what they went through. It would probably turn their brains to blancmange, you see? There's a little more to it than that, of course, but that's the gist of it.'

'So what happens to us?' asked Mr Raisbeck.

'Well, that's the thing,' said Archer. 'You can't go back home because there'd be all kinds of existential contradictions going on. I wouldn't worry too much about that though. You can do something for the good of Arcadia or, if you prefer, retire to a life of your choosing - interplanetary travel perhaps, or embroidery.'

'Wouldn't worry!?' cried Mr Raisbeck. 'I'm sure I don't need to remind you that I have a delivery I need to take.'

'You are already there,' said Archer. 'It's hard to explain, but you are now existing in two planes.'

'Did I take any of the diamond bottles home?' asked Scratch, mostly to himself.

'What have planes got to do with it? I have a lovely three bed semi in Woking, thank you very much.'

'Planes of existence,' said Archer. 'A version of you is at home now waiting patiently for the sofa. Another version of you is here, experiencing all that Arcadia has to offer.'

'Like diamonds,' said Scratch.

Archer approached Cantina and Glorious. 'Neither of you were duplicated, so it is safe for you to go whenever you wish. The Zooming channels are ready.'

'When will we be returned?' asked Cantina.

'Whenever you like,' said Archer.

'I meant what will be the time and date we arrive home.'

'So did I. You are the only version of yourself, so there are fewer variables involved. It's still tricky, of course, but if you have somewhere or somewhen you'd like to go, we can arrange it.'

'I'll need some time to think. How long do I have?'

'Forever,' said Archer honestly. 'Glorious? How about you?'

'I'd like to go back to where I was. Better the devil you know, I say.'

'Then you may leave now. Thank you for everything you have done.'

'And for not buggering up the space time continuum,' added Doubt.

'Private Pantz will escort you to the Zooming station.'

'Pantz!' roared Buck unnecessarily.

'I think I'll go home, too,' said Cantina. 'Glorious is right.'

'Then it's settled,' said Buck.

Private Pantz entered the room and looked at General Buck for an order.

'Take these two Earth people to the Zooming station, Pantz. See to it they have everything they need.'

Glorious and Cantina nodded to Scratch and Mr Raisbeck.

'Good luck,' said Glorious. 'I'll look you up if I ever visit England.'

'That's that, then,' said Buck, clapping his hands together and removing any chance of an emotional farewell. 'Marvellous stuff.'

The diamond doors clicked shut and an awkward silence filled the room.

'What now?' said Scratch at last.

'Now, my dear fellow, we get you behaving like an Arcadian,' said Buck. 'If you're going to be staying here a while you'll have to learn to fit in.'

'Moon Shots, then?'

'Pantz!' shouted Buck. 'Bring Bakewell and Cauliflower in here.'

'I believe Pantz is on his way to the Zooming station, general,' said Doubt diplomatically, as if the private hadn't just left the room.

'You'll have to do then professor. Take these men to Moon Shots and begin their assimilation. Can't have them experiencing the highs of Arcadian life before they've really seen the lows, eh?'

'Indeed, sir. I'll be sure to get them roasting drunk before dinner time.'

Scratch and Mr Raisbeck followed Professor Doubt out of the room and into the maze of corridors. A cleaning robot whizzed towards them, beeping furiously as it zigzagged past them.

'Are they really diamond?' asked Scratch.

'The cleaners? No, they're your standard Darmstadtium alloy. Nothing fancy.'

'Not them, the bottles in the bar. Are they all solid diamond?'

'Ah, those. Yes, just diamond. There's no point using anything too fancy in there. A bottle's life expectancy in Moon Shots is shorter than a biscuit in Buck's office.'

'*Just* diamond, you say?'

Scratch fell into a brief, thoughtful daze.

'What do they do with all the broken bits?' he said at last.

Doubt gave Scratch an incredulous look. 'They put them in the bin, naturally. What else would they do with them?'

'One more question. Is it possible to send an object through a Zooming channel without a life form being in there with it? Just curious, you know?'

'It is possible, I suppose,' said Doubt.

'Mr Raisbeck,' said Scratch. 'How would you like to give your other self more sofas than he'd know what to do with?'

'Whuh?' mumbled Mr Raisbeck, who had been deep in thought.

'Any functionality you like. Buggering Mondays, it could be solid gold if that tickled your fancy!'

'That would be terrible for your posture,' said Mr Raisbeck pragmatically. 'You're better with a hard-wearing fabric. Lasts longer, you see? I remember old Jimmy Carpenter bought something like that from…'

'What I'm saying,' interrupted Scratch, 'is that you - the other you - could choose whichever sofa he wants, and as many as he likes. He could even have a whole room dedicated to them in a big, detached mansion.'

'I think you may finally have tipped over the edge, Mr Scratch.'

Scratch nudged Professor Doubt with his elbow. 'I've decided what I'd like to do *for the good of Arcadia*, prof.'

'Excellent. What is it? Zooming consultant? Earth Liaison Officer? Something like that?'

'Nothing of the sort,' said Scratch. 'I'm going to be a bin man.'

EPILOGUE

*L*ife is complicated, it turns out. I have at my disposal all the time in the universe and an infinite power with which to play. I have shaped galaxies and created life, but in doing so also created free will and more variables than a gathering of drunken teenagers at a cliff top trampoline party.

What I lack, however, is perspective. Immortality is useful for many things, like mastering the art of shadow puppetry for example, or testing probabilities to fourteen decimal places, but there are downsides too. It drags on a bit after a while, in much the same way a great uncle's eightieth birthday party can once the cake has been eaten and the singing starts. The finite nature of life gives rise to several unexpected results, particularly when the life in question is shown how they may not be quite so alive for much longer if they don't learn how to run very fast in the opposite direction.

There is never an end to learning, though. Even for an immortal entity like me. I will leave life to its own devices for the moment and focus my efforts on a new passion – knitting. So far, I have created a lovely tank top for one of the smaller moons of

*the planet Nacius and a rather fetching scarf for
the ice planet Griplar.*

*I tried to play a game, and it entertained me for
a while, but now I am bored again. Perhaps once I
have mastered knitting, and possibly crochet too, I
will come back to life, but for the moment I will
leave it to its own devices.*

Now, was I dropping one or knitting one?

Newbury,
England

The driver from Shufflebottom and Sons was on
time. He prided himself on always arriving within
the specified six hour window, and was doubly
pleased with himself today. Not only had he found
his own diversion around the roadworks on
Enborne Road, he had also adjusted his route to
deliver a pair of Windsor chairs to Mr Turnpike and
a three piece set to Mrs Cribbins on Greenham
Road. He rarely changed the prescribed schedule,
but after thirty years in the job he knew when to
take risks.

He rang the simple, practical doorbell of number thirty-one, Sowerby Crescent and waited.

'Margaret!' came a voice from inside. 'Would you get that? It'll be Shufflebottom and Sons. I just have to change out of my slippers.'

The door opened and Mrs Raisbeck smiled at the driver. It was the sort of smile that said *I only answer the door here, my husband will look after the details.*

'Can I get you a cup of tea?' asked Mrs Raisbeck. 'I've got a kettle on.'

'No, thank you,' said the driver. 'I've got to get up to Highwood Close before two o'clock.'

'Well, if you change your mind.'

Mr Raisbeck arrived at the door, hopping as he adjusted the heel of his shoe. 'Shufflebottom and Sons?' he asked, despite the overwhelming evidence parked in front of his driveway.

'That's right,' said the driver patiently. 'Three seater Belgian roll arm sofa in beige.'

'Oatmeal beige' corrected Mr Raisbeck.

'Right you are, sir. Oatmeal beige,' said the driver, offering a clipboard and pen to Mr Raisbeck. 'Sign here please.'

'Not until I've seen it first, if you don't mind. Can't be too careful these days.'

'*These days*, sir? Are there reports of unscrupulous sofa delivery drivers doing the rounds?'

'Well, not as such, no. But, you know?'

'I'm not sure I do, sir, no. This way please.'

The driver walked back to the lorry and rolled up the shutters. He stepped up into the space and slid a three seater Belgian roll arm sofa, in oatmeal beige, out to the edge.

'Happy, sir?' he asked.

'So far,' said Mr Raisbeck. 'Of course, I'll have to see it in situ before I finalise the arrangements.'

The delivery driver took a deep breath, hopped out of the lorry, and tapped on the passenger side window. A teenager appeared and loped around to the back of the truck. In a few minutes, they had placed the sofa next to the mahogany display cabinet of toby jugs.

'Sign here, please,' said the driver, handing Mr Raisbeck the clipboard and pen.

'I have to say, I've found this whole process to be thoroughly efficient. Can I get your name please? I'd like to write a rather complimentary letter to your head office.'

'Certainly, sir. The name's Bakewell.'

Peacock Apartments,
Southend-on-Sea,
England,
Present Day,
Well, one of them.

'What was that, mate?'

'I said, it's like a pair of silk ferret's knickers in here,' said Clobber.

'Bloody expensive and totally pointless?' offered Scratch.

'How did you know I was going to say that?'

'I've no idea. Must've been luck.'

'Well, I can tell you we've got lucky here, my old mucker. Wait 'til you see what I've found.'

'A pocket watch, next week's newspaper and a nice porcelain jug,' said a part of Scratch's vocal cords he hadn't realised were outside his control.

'How did you…? Wait, *next week's*?'

Clobber placed the jug on the floor, unfolded the newspaper, dropped it onto the floor as he saw the date, and followed it to the ground with a dull thud.

'Come on, Clobber, you're usually more polite than that.'

Clobber didn't move, which wasn't altogether unsurprising. Or, at least, it wasn't if you didn't consider the burglar alarm that had started screeching at an impossibly high pitch from a box in the hallway.

'Don't be playing silly buggers with me now, we've got to get out of here. The coppers will be here in a minute and I'm not climbing down another drainpipe after last time.'

Scratch picked up the jug and ran to the kitchen, filled it with ice cold water, and decanted the contents unceremoniously onto Clobber's face.

'Whufushufug,' said Clobber.

'Exactly mate. Now come on, we've got to get out of here.'

Scratch lifted Clobber by the armpits, slapping his cheeks a little to coax him to a state of self-balance. Clobber's eyes began to refocus, just as a door slammed shut in the main corridor.

'Buggering Mondays,' said Scratch. 'Any bright ideas? Only, if we don't think of something soon we'll be spending a few years at the pleasure of the old lady in the palace.'

'We could jump out of that window,' said Clobber, pointing. 'Easy.'

'Oh yeah, you're right there, son. Jumping *would* be easy. It's the landing I'd worry about, though, with us being three floors up. We'd be better taking our chances with PC Plod.'

A swirl of colour whooshed into existence behind the two thieves and deposited a sack of something tinkly onto the floor.

Nothing happened for a moment. Then a head popped out from the colour and cocked itself as if listening intently to a distant whisper. 'Buggering Mondays,' said the head.

Two arms appeared from within the purple and black eddy. They reached out towards Scratch and Clobber, grabbed them by the collars, and pulled them backwards into the vortex.

THE END

About the Author:

John Drake is originally from Liverpool, England but is now an adopted Dubliner. He specializes in the criminally under-represented genre of satirical historical fiction and wrote his first 'serious' line of writing at the grand old age of forty. He is the author of both Making Man – a comedy centred around a Neanderthal with itchy feet and the mind of an engineer – and Cheating Death – another comedy set during the famously jovial Black Death of 14th century Europe. He can usually be found sandwiched somewhere in between a good pun and a thesaurus.

Lightning Source UK Ltd.
Milton Keynes UK
UKHW021911210621
385931UK00009B/810/J